THE CAT, THE COLLECTOR AND THE KILLER

A CATS IN TROUBLE MYSTERY

LEANN SWEENEY

AN OBSIDIAN MYSTERY

OBSIDIAN
Published by New American Library,
an imprint of Penguin Random House LLC
375 Hudson Street, New York, New York 10014

This book is an original publication of New American Library.

First Printing, August 2016

For more information about Penguin Random House, visit penguin.com.

ISBN 9780451477408

Printed in the United States of America
10 9 8 7 6 5 4 3 2 1

Penguin
Random
House

Other Novels by Leann Sweeney

The Cats in Trouble Mysteries

The Cat, the Sneak and the Secret
The Cat, the Vagabond and the Victim
The Cat, the Mill and the Murder
The Cat, the Wife and the Weapon
The Cat, the Lady and the Liar
The Cat, the Professor and the Poison
The Cat, the Quilt and the Corpse

The Yellow Rose Mysteries

Pushing Up Bluebonnets
Shoot from the Lip
Dead Giveaway
A Wedding to Die For
Pick Your Poison

This book is for you, readers.
Your kind words, the faithful way you follow
this series and your friendship over ten years
have kept me writing and, most of all,
brought me much happiness.
Thank you.

"You can't help that. We're all mad here."

—The Cheshire Cat
from *Alice's Adventures in Wonderland*
by Lewis Carroll

One

The sound of the shower running made me close my eyes and smile as I lay beneath the double wedding ring quilt I'd finished last week. My husband of six months, Tom Stewart, was getting ready for work as acting police chief for Mercy, South Carolina. Though not ready to admit it, this job suited him to a tee. Previously he'd been doing PI work—mostly following cheating husbands or wives—and it had worn him down. These days, he smiled more and enjoyed the camaraderie of our small-town police force.

I couldn't believe half a year had passed since we'd exchanged vows. I'd enjoyed the holidays more than I had in years and rediscovered that winter cuddling was something special indeed. Having someone to hold me close at night topped the marital benefits list. Having a partner to play with our feline family while I was busy in my craft room finishing quilt orders—I make little quilts for cats—made me far more productive. They seemed quite happy to stay in the living room with Tom.

The town council kept begging him to take the police chief job permanently, but he still wouldn't commit. I'd not given him advice on the subject because he needed time to mull it over—and over—and over. He'd ask for my opinion when he was ready.

I pulled the quilt tighter around me. All the cats liked the rust, green and taupe fabric as much as Tom and I did. Our kitties surrounded me, waiting and watching. They wanted to make sure I didn't fall back to sleep. If I failed to get up soon and provide breakfast, there would be face pawing and maybe even a few nose bumps—and not gentle ones, either.

Chablis, our seal point Himalayan, nestled the closest to me. Syrah, the sorrel Abyssinian, sat at the end of the bed, his stare unwavering. Merlot, the big red Maine coon, and Dashiell, our gray tabby, huddled together on Tom's still-warm side of the bed. Dashiell moved into this lake home with Tom, and these four cats took up almost as much space in the king-size bed as we did. We'd signed up for this, and the felines and humans here on Mercy Lake seemed quite happy with the arrangement.

Chablis started in for that nose bump just as Tom's phone rang. I picked my girl up and set her to one side and quickly crawled to the other side of the bed. Grabbing Tom's mobile off his nightstand, I squinted at the screen and recognized the Mercy Animal Sanctuary number. Shawn Cuddahee, the owner, usually called *me* when he needed help, so this seemed strange.

I answered with, "Hey there, Shawn. What's up?"

He didn't bother saying hello. "Oh. It's you, Jillian. This is Tom's number, right? Is he there?" Shawn sounded a tad confused, probably surprised that I'd been the one to answer.

"He's in the shower. Can I have him call you back? Or maybe I can help?"

Shawn blurted, "I'm gonna kill Chester. I swear I will, Jillian."

Chester was Chester Winston, the county animal control officer.

I said, "Do you need Tom to intervene because of the restraining order?"

Chester did have an order of protection against Shawn. Those two had seen their share of conflict. With Shawn being in the animal rescue business, and Chester being in the round-'em-up-and-send-off-to-somewhere-else business, they definitely didn't care for each other. Shawn was louder and bigger than Chester, and I suppose that was the reason for the restraining order. But Shawn would never hurt Chester, despite what he'd just said. He'd never hurt anyone.

"I guess if I don't want to end up in jail," Shawn said, "I better let Tom get hold of that good-for-nothing man. I've left messages and he's not calling me back."

According to what I understood, Chester and Shawn could communicate only by phone, about animals in trouble, a step he'd tried to take. "Why do you need him?" I asked.

"Kind of a long story. There's this sweet lady with a bunch of cats over on Mill Creek Road. I've known her for a long time. Anyway, the neighbors say that they couldn't reach Chester, either. Seems she's letting her cats outside, and she's never done that before. They're worried about her. Her mental health's not exactly what it was a year ago."

"Are we talking about a hoarding situation, Shawn?"

"I don't call seven or eight cats a hoarding situation. I'd call her a collector. I'm sure Chester would beg to differ, and in a way, maybe I should be glad he's not returned calls from me or anyone else. Still, I can't go over there and risk Chester showing up at the same time. You and me both know he'll have me tossed in jail for violating the protection order. Long story short, I was hoping Tom could help me out."

Sitting cross-legged, I rested my back against the deep red padded headboard. Chablis immediately crawled inside the triangle my legs made. "You sure you need the police? Because I'd be glad to help—that is, if you're being absolutely straight with me about her not being a hoarder. I couldn't bear to walk into her house if that's the true situation." Hoarding bothered me because, though I had sympathy for folks suffering in those situations, the cats were usually wallowing in filth and neglect, something I couldn't bear to see.

"I *swear* she's not a hoarder. Her house was always neat as a pin, with all sorts of space for her babies, as she called them. When she applied to get this tuxedo kitten from me late last year, I brought up how many cats she already had. I told her I'd have to check the premises before I'd let her have a new one."

"Everything was fine?"

"She's a great kitty momma, Jillian. She's devoted to those animals. Never lets them outside, neither. So when this neighbor called me—"

"A nice neighbor?" I understood some people became very upset when stray cats took up residence on their doorstep.

"Super nice. Mrs. Applebee. You know her?"

"Sorry, no."

"Anyways, when she said she'd left a message for Chester, I figured I could get in some real trouble if I decided to round up those cats myself. The young lady at the county shelter where Chester takes strays was no help whatsoever. She said she didn't have time to walk out to the animal prison they got over there and check up on Chester. I can't be snooping around because of that stupid restraining order. It's not my fault if no one cares about this but me."

"You know I care. Sounds like you have a dilemma. I could go to the county shelter and talk to Chester if you want."

"Waste of your time and mine. Can we maybe drive by Minnie's house? That's her name—Minnie Schultz. This could be a big to-do about nothing."

"Are you sure we shouldn't go to the county facility? I've donated cat quilts several times to that place and—"

"You won't get anywhere. Their funding's been slashed. They're so understaffed and overworked it's made the people who kept their jobs wary and tight-lipped. Okay, maybe we also shouldn't go there because I've been kind of judgmental and made a few suggestions they didn't appreciate."

I sighed. Shawn's passion for animals who needed help could often come across as anger. I understood this all too well. "Okay. But if no one's home at Mrs. Schultz's house or I don't see a problem, we can go to the county shelter and ask for Chester—or at least *I* can ask to talk to him."

Shawn reluctantly agreed and we made the arrangements. I'd made the decision to drive because Chester would recognize Shawn's truck if he happened to show up at the same time we did. I hung up just as Tom walked into the bedroom. His dark hair was wet and he had a towel wrapped around his waist. Four cats made a beeline for him. After all, this human was actually upright and moving. That meant he might get them their breakfast.

"Hey, Jilly. You're tempting me to be late for work, sitting there, looking so gorgeous." He tilted his head and squinted at me. "But something else is going on. What's up?"

I held up his phone. "I answered your phone. Seems Shawn needs a little help."

Tom pushed hangers around in the closet as he looked for a shirt. "Am I supposed to call him back?"

"I can take care of it. He's worried about violating the restraining order, but I don't think he needs police assistance with this one."

"Chester's involved, then. That's never good. What's the problem?" Tom chose a pale green shirt and removed a pair of trousers from a dry cleaner's bag.

I explained about the *collector*, Minnie Schultz, while Tom dressed. I enjoyed the scenery and had a hard time staying on track. He agreed this was more my territory than his. Once he had his trousers on, I jumped out of bed to lead the cats to the kitchen before he found himself covered in cat hair. Dashiell needed his insulin shot, too. I'd gotten quite good at giving the diabetic boy his medicine.

The new programmable coffee machine we'd gotten as a wedding gift offered up its magical aroma as three cats raced ahead of me down the hall and into the open-concept living, dining and kitchen area. Merlot, my big boy, never joined any races he couldn't win. He ambled alongside me.

By the time insulin had been administered and four cats were served breakfast, Tom joined me, his police shield dangling from a lanyard around his neck. As I stood at the coffeepot, he leaned in close from behind and wrapped his arms around my waist. I poured us each a mug of coffee. This brand had been specially roasted in New York City and was sent to us by a professor we'd met a while back when he'd come to visit his mother in Mercy. When the man's visit was over and he left for his home in New York, he took with him a special cat I'd fostered. I received frequent updates about Clyde, that big orange tabby, along with a bag or two of this amazing coffee.

Tom kissed my neck before he let me go and headed for the small mosaic-topped table that offered a wonderful view of Mercy Lake. Morning sun spread its promise of a beautiful day in shimmers of color. "You're sure you can handle Shawn and this woman? Mrs. Schultz, you said?"

"I'm happy to do it. I asked Shawn to let me check up on these cats and the owner by myself, but he insisted on riding along to her house."

"When Shawn is determined, there's no dissuading him. I could send Candace to help you out."

Candace was the newly promoted Detective Candace Carson, and also my best friend. She was originally supposed to go by *sergeant*, but she pleaded for *detective*, mostly because in her mind, detectives could wear street clothes. Yes, she wanted to give up that uniform and Tom and the town council approved her request.

I said, "You mean Candace should be there in case Chester shows up and he and Shawn come to blows? That won't happen."

"If you're comfortable—oh, wait. There might be cats in trouble that need rescuing." He grinned, his blue eyes smiling, too. "You'll be more than comfortable."

I laid my hand over his. "Glad you understand."

Two

I pulled up to the office entrance of the Mercy Animal Sanctuary after driving on the gravel road through heavily wooded property. Maybe once Shawn's wife, Allison, hung up her "vet" shingle this summer, they'd have enough money to actually pave the road. The shelter itself could use a makeover, too. For now, Allison remained in North Carolina, finishing her veterinary internship.

I stayed in my air-conditioned van watching Shawn's animated gestures as he gave last-minute instructions to the two volunteers who would tend to the shelter in his absence. It might have been spring but the temperature would probably rise to at least eighty degrees if the weather person was right.

Once we took off, Shawn gave me a little more of Minnie's story. I learned she'd brought many strays and litters of kittens to Shawn's shelter in the last decade. He called her *eccentric* and said as far as he knew, she had few family members in the area and had been widowed several years. She loved to garden, but her greatest passion was her cats. She doted on them, and for any one of them to be outside, well, there had to be something amiss. He'd noticed she'd been more forgetful than usual the last time he'd visited her a few months back. Perhaps she'd taken ill.

"Is she a senior?" I asked as we parked at the curb in a quiet middle-class neighborhood where all the residents seemed to be in competition for a "prettiest landscaping" award.

"I'm not a great judge of a woman's age, but not really. I'd guess she was in her late fifties, maybe?"

"A little early for dementia, then. Though I hear there's early-onset Alzheimer's disease." I touched Shawn's arm as he reached for the passenger door handle. "What do you think you're doing?"

"I don't see Chester's prisoner wagon, so—"

"His *what*?" I asked.

"The vehicle he uses to cart animals off to critter jail. I hate that truck."

"He may not be here right now, but you said you'd wait in the van. I am perfectly capable of making friends with cats—and even people, sometimes."

Shawn grinned. "You're sure better with people than me. But—"

I gripped his arm a little tighter. "No buts. Wait here and if no one answers the door, I'll check the backyard."

I noted the grass needed cutting and the front shrubs could use pruning. Drawn shades and curtains shrouded the front windows and I felt a tickle as the hairs on the back of my neck raised. This place seemed almost *too* quiet. What was that book Tom told me about? *The Gift of Fear.* My instincts definitely warned me something wasn't right here.

I rapped on the front door, and when no one answered, I knocked again. A minute later, I followed a stone path leading to a fenced backyard. Though tall, even this fence wouldn't contain a cat if it wanted to escape. But a fence didn't matter since the gate stood wide-open. Had the neighbors been here to check things out? Should we talk to them first? I glanced back toward my van and decided I couldn't offer Shawn any excuse to join me—and he would if I came into his sightline.

A pitiful meow erased my thoughts and I continued on. More kitty cries came from a holly bush beneath a large window. Holly is a mean plant to tangle with, and I hoped the cat wasn't stuck or too afraid to come out. I could use a pair of long leather gloves about now.

I sensed a presence behind me and my heart sped up. I whirled.

Releasing the breath I'd withheld, I said, "Shawn Cuddahee, you gave me the fright of my life. You shouldn't be back here."

"Couldn't stand it, Jillian." He glanced beyond me at the holly bush. "Great. I knew I shouldn't have left my gloves in the van. Too late now."

He marched past me and knelt in front of the holly. In a soft, gentle voice he said, "Come on, baby. It's gonna be fine."

While Shawn was coaxing that kitty, more cats began to appear from beneath bushes and from behind the tall pampas grass lining the fence at the back property line. There had to be a dozen cats—tabbies, tuxedoes, gingers, long-haired, short-haired and even a few purebreds. I spotted a fluffy orange Persian, and right behind that one, a Siamese slinked between daisies and mums. More than the seven or eight Shawn had mentioned—that's for sure.

I knelt and extended one hand. "Um, Shawn. Take a look."

"Holy crap. You've got to be kidding me. She didn't adopt these from me." He then returned to his task. The cat behind the holly wasn't cooperating and he'd pulled out his pocket knife to cut away a few leaves.

A long-haired gray tabby reached me and rubbed his cheek on my knee. I stroked his head and he began to purr. Soon I was surrounded by felines. I sat in grass still moist from dew and allowed the cats to rub on my legs and climb in my lap. They were probably hungry. Could there be empty dishes on that screened porch?

I glanced in that direction. Through the haze created by the screens, I thought the door leading into the house was ajar—and the door from the porch to this little backyard haven was wide-open. No wonder the neighbors were concerned.

"Gotcha, baby," Shawn muttered.

I glanced his way and he held a fat gray shorthair with green eyes in his arms.

"I see the problem, Shawn." I nodded toward the porch.

"Maybe Minnie needs medical help—or was injured during a break-in." Clutching the cat, a worried Shawn headed for the open porch door.

I marched behind him after picking up the tabby. Other cats followed us. "Sure, Shawn. Jump to worst possible scenarios." But that feeling of dread hadn't left me.

Empty cat dishes and saucers lay on the brick floor

and had been licked clean. Though I hesitated to enter the house, Shawn plowed right in, calling Minnie's name.

I was not prepared for what I saw as I followed him inside. Though the kitchen did not smell of spoiled food or dirty kitty litter as I'd feared, the crowded room was almost claustrophobic. Unopened shipping boxes and cases of cat food were stacked almost to the ceiling. More boxes sat on a maple kitchen table. A hallway leading from the kitchen into the rest of the house seemed almost impassable due to even more boxes.

"Since there's plenty of food, can you feed these cats, Jillian? Meanwhile, I'll find Minnie. She'd never let her cats outside if she was okay." He meandered through the maze of cardboard, mumbling, "She's got to be okay, right, baby?" to the gray cat he still held in his arms.

Probably not okay, I thought as I set down the sweet tabby and pulled a case of cat food from the lowest stack of boxes in the corner. I gathered the dishes on the porch, making sure no cats followed me out there. The large farmhouse sink in the kitchen held no dirty dishes. I quickly washed the bowls I'd brought inside. Soon, all the cats were gobbling up their meals as fast as they could. Poor things probably hadn't eaten in a while.

"Jillian, you better get in here," Shawn called.

His tone was tense, even ominous. No . . . downright scary. The spooky, quiet aura in this house seemed magnified by his command. Then I reminded myself Shawn leaned toward the dramatic.

I started down the hall, bypassing the dining and living room combination—boxes in there, too—and had to sidestep in the hall most of the way as went toward where Shawn was. I'd just reached another room—office maybe?—also crammed full of boxes, when my cell rang.

It was Tom's ring. I answered while trying to figure out exactly which room Shawn had called me from.

Tom's sounded sad. "Jilly, we just found Minnie Schultz wandering downtown in her nightclothes. Are you at her house yet?"

I sighed with relief. "That explains some of what we found—but why is she in her nightclothes?"

Shawn appeared in a doorway to my left. "This isn't good, Jillian. Not good at all."

I put my phone on speaker and held it out with one hand. "But Tom says they found Minnie downtown and—"

"Tom," Shawn called, "you need to get down here pronto. There's a body in Minnie's bedroom."

I gulped down the bile that rose in my throat and nearly dropped my phone. No matter how passionate Shawn was about cats, he'd never call the police for a feline death. No, this body was most certainly a human being.

Three

After I disconnected, Shawn held out the cat he'd been holding. "Come get this girl. I recognize her as one of Minnie's cats that she adopted from me. I don't want her messing with this dead person. Cats will do that, you know. I won't go into details."

I didn't want to be anywhere near that room, so I was relieved Shawn felt the need to stand guard. Though I tried not to look beyond the door while I retrieved the cat, it was difficult to keep my eyes averted. Thank goodness all I saw was a pair of work books sticking out between twin beds. Big boots. A man's boots. He was obviously lying facedown.

"Do you know who that is?" I asked.

"Nope. I felt his ankle and he's cold as an iceberg."

I shuddered. "This is *awful*."

Gray kitty purred and snuggled close, perhaps to distract or comfort me. She wore a collar with tags. I checked them once she was in my arms. A pink one read Minous. Remembering the four years of French I'd taken in high school, I believed that was a word for *kitty*.

"I'm gonna close this door now, Jillian. I'll wait right here in the hall until Tom shows up. The cavalry will come soon after, I expect."

By "the cavalry," he'd meant not only the police but every fireman and paramedic in town. "Is it bad? I mean, has he been there a long time?"

"I'm not speculating. You shouldn't, either."

"I thought you said Minnie was a widow. Did she have a companion who might have had a heart attack or—"

"Jillian, it's none of our business. That sweet kitty there must be hungry." Shawn was right, of course. The cats were our business and the dead man wasn't. Besides, why would I want to know more about what Shawn had seen in there? I didn't.

I carried Minous to the kitchen. She hadn't gotten this chubby by accident. As soon as I put her on the floor in the kitchen, she bulldozed between two other cats and chowed down.

Since it only took about five minutes to drive from one side of Mercy to the other, I could hear sirens closing in already. Not wanting to think about Shawn or what he'd found, I awaited Tom's arrival by taking a few calming breaths and trying to think about something else.

I knelt and stroked the Siamese, who preferred kibble to the wet food I'd provided. The cat purred and kept on eating. I glanced around again. This place reminded me more of a warehouse than a home, considering the unopened boxes everywhere. Yet, the place seemed so tidy at the same time.

Shawn labeled Minnie Schultz as a *collector* rather than a *hoarder* and I decided he must have known she wasn't disorganized or mentally ill, just loved cats enough to care for them well and not be obsessed. The amount of cat food on cardboard pallets was necessary. But what about the rest of these boxes? They bore big-box-store logos. Cat toys? Litter? Treats?

I blinked myself back to the terrible reality of a body in the other room. My stomach started to churn as I heard the sirens sounding so close that a patrol car was probably already in the driveway. There was no avoiding the reality of the situation. Fearing I would let cats escape if I tried to go out the back door to greet Tom or whoever responded first, I stayed put and considered how to keep all these felines contained.

My cell phone jangled and I stood as I pulled it out of my pocket. It was Tom.

"Are you still inside the residence?" he asked.

He sounded so formal, his voice tension-filled. "Yes. The back porch leads into the house and we found it open. I doubt you'll be able to enter through the front. You'll understand why when you get in here."

"Thanks. I'm headed your way."

Detective Candace Carson entered first with her gun drawn.

I breathed in sharply. "Please put that thing away. There's no one here but Shawn, me, these cats . . . and a *dead person*."

"Can't be too careful." She holstered her gun at her side. Her utility belt was as loaded down as in the past, when she'd worn a uniform. Today, however, her olive khakis and pale blue shirt made her look like a female cop on TV. She was truly a beautiful young woman, twenty years my junior, and these days, sans uniform, she could show it off.

"What happened to the victim, Jillian?" she asked.

"Bless his heart, I have no idea. Got a glimpse of boots in the guest room. Shawn found him, not me."

Tom, thank goodness, was *not* holding his weapon when he entered the kitchen. Sidestepping a few cats who decided to greet him by rubbing against his legs, he came to my side and put an arm around my shoulder. "Trouble seems to find you, Jilly. You okay?"

"I'm fine. The dead man needs you two right now. Meanwhile, I'll take care of the half-starved cats."

Candace, her hands on her hips, took in the felines and gazed at all the boxes through narrowed, curious eyes. "Actually, they all look pretty healthy. The cats, that is. What's with the boxes?"

"I don't know. The cat food was in open pallets and I didn't think I should mess with anything else. I feel like a trespasser as it is."

Tom said, "I'd say it's a good thing you two came inside."

"What about Minnie Schultz?" I asked.

"She's at the hospital for a mental health check," Tom said. "We didn't bother with questions, just called for an ambulance immediately. Walking around Main Street in your nightclothes while carrying your suitcase-size tote bag means you're not all there."

Candace remained fixated on the boxes. "Maybe she was packing?"

"These are purchases, as far as I can tell," I replied. "I was wondering if maybe Mrs. Schultz was doing business or liked to collect more than cats."

Tom nodded. "Ah, obsessive-compulsive. Could be. As for the dead man, we can't let these cats roam the house while we check out the situation. Did you see any other animals beyond the kitchen?"

I shook my head. "But that doesn't mean scaredy-cats aren't hiding all over the place. That's their MO. You might need help with them, if that's the case. If they're as hungry as these guys were, they could be skittish at best and aggressive at worst."

"We'll leave them to you and Shawn," Candace said. "I saw a few cats in the backyard."

"Really?" I said. "I thought they'd all come inside. Maybe I can lure them with food."

"We'll need your help first, Jilly. If you could guard the entrance to the hallway, I'll barricade you and these cats in the kitchen with some boxes. Candace and I will let folks in through the front door. We called the paramedics, so they should be here soon."

Candace said, "If this person is actually dead—"

"Shawn told me he's cold . . . ice-cold," I said.

"Well, that's certainly a sign of being dead, so they can't move that body to the morgue until I've taken all my pictures. We also have to call Lydia." She raised her eyebrows and her expression said, *And won't that be fun?*

Tom drew an exasperated breath. "Why did you have to remind me?"

"She'll have your hide if we *forget* to call her," Candace replied.

Lydia Monk was the coroner's investigator. Mercy had an elected coroner—the man wasn't even a doctor—and he sent Lydia out on all unexplained deaths. After she observed the body and asked her questions, she would deal with death certificates, make an official case file and report to the coroner. If an autopsy was needed, she'd assist families in navigating the sad territory known as death in America. Unfortunately, Lydia was quite the character, and even more unfortunately for me, she was obsessed with Tom almost to a stalking level. She believed one day he would see the light, divorce me and marry her.

As for the need for an autopsy on this dead man, I'd learned a few months ago that in South Carolina, autopsies are required only if a "living person" caused the death. If it was an accident or even a suicide, the coroner could rule no autopsy was required. As of right now, none of us had any idea what caused the man's death and I wasn't sure I wanted to know.

Candace left Tom to deal with barricading me and the cats in the kitchen while she went to relieve Shawn of corpse duty. Goose bumps rose on my arms. *Corpse duty. That's a terrible way to put it, Jillian.*

Soon, with boxes in place to the ceiling at the kitchen entry, the mission was accomplished. I wasn't sure I should touch any more dishes or even run water again to rinse the ones the cats had eaten off. Candace was a stickler for anything that might be evidence—and I could have already destroyed some. But a few kitties still seemed hungry—if wrapping themselves around my ankles, crawling up my pant legs and meowing pleadingly was any clue. The ones still outside had to be famished as well. They'd have to eat off dirty dishes for now.

Getting the cats who were outside—all six of them—to come in and eat was easy. Soon Shawn came through the back gate and joined me, being careful not to let any of them escape. The slumped shoulders and troubled frown spoke of a deep sadness.

The Siamese leapt onto his shoulder and rubbed its cheek against his. He stroked the cat, but his mind was definitely on other things.

"Are you all right?" I asked. "Seeing a dead person can cause shock or—"

"No, I'm not all right," he practically barked. "It's Chester dead in that room. After Candace pulled a wallet out of his pocket, she told me. Now I know why he never called me back."

"Oh my gosh." I raised a hand to my mouth.

Shawn swiped a freckled hand over his face. "This is a lifetime of bad karma, Jillian. I shouldn't have been such an ass. I should have made peace with the man." Shawn met my gaze, his hazel eyes glistening.

I'd never seen him like this. He was always so . . . *tough* when it came to people. Animals were a different story, and obviously how he treated them was the true measure of Shawn Cuddahee. Now his soft heart extended even to a man he'd professed to despise.

"Don't punish yourself. Deep down you didn't hate Chester. You simply didn't appreciate the way he treated animals."

"You're right. I never hated him. Not really." Shawn's expression changed from remorse to concern. He lifted the cat off his shoulder and held it up so he could examine it. "This one looks healthy enough. Spayed not too long ago. In fact, all these cats, aside from being hungry, seem in fine shape."

Shawn had changed the subject to avoid dealing with his emotions, no doubt. I went along, hoping to ease his discomfort. "I was thinking the same thing. Mrs. Schultz, from the state of her home and the condition of these cats, doesn't seem like a hoarder. I mean, hoarders become so overwhelmed they can't properly care for animals, right?"

"Usually over time that's what happens." He glanced around the kitchen. "Hoarding is definitely an illness.

That's why I called this lady more of a collector. Up until lately, she seemed perfectly normal. She took wonderful care of her cats. Last time I was here, she may have been a little *off*, even a bit confused, but she still only had seven or eight cats." He glanced around the kitchen. "All these boxes sure as heck weren't here. What *is* all this stuff?"

"I have no idea. My question is, what happened to Chester? Heart attack? Stroke? He *was* getting older."

"I have no idea." He set the purring Siamese on the floor and stroked her.

Why did I get the distinct feeling he *did* have an idea? That thought gave me a chill. Whatever happened deeply affected Shawn—that much was certain.

The cat sniffed at one of the few dishes with its remnants of food, and the kitties who'd most recently been outside began to beg for refills. Shawn and I busied ourselves in silence, opening more cans and topping off the kibble bowl. Since I saw a clean stainless kitty fountain on the floor in working order, I broke the tension that seemed to have filled the kitchen by warning Shawn not to run water.

I said, "Touch as few things as possible until we know exactly what happened to Chester. This house could be a crime scene. Candace and Tom have taught me that anything might be evidence—even a houseful of cats."

Four

Thirty minutes later, at Candace's request, I drove Shawn back to the shelter so we could pick up enough carriers to remove the cats from the house. We put equal numbers in my van and Shawn's truck, then drove in our separate vehicles back to Minnie Schultz's house. An ambulance sat in the driveway but what seemed more ominous was the crime scene tape Deputy Lois Jewel currently wrapped around trees and shrubs to keep folks at a distance. I took a deep breath and exhaled slowly as I parked my van. This was not good.

Lois waved to me as I unloaded the pet carriers. I wondered if the county had been notified that their animal control officer was . . . *gone*. My thoughts were then interrupted by a neighbor standing in his yard across the street calling to us. He was maybe midthirties, with that scruffy-beard-and-messy-hair look his generation had adopted. "Would someone tell me what the heck's going on? I live here. I should be kept informed."

I glanced at Lois and she gave a tiny shake of the head indicating I shouldn't say anything—not that I would.

The man definitely didn't sound like he was originally from South Carolina. The other folks in the neighborhood were apparently content to let him stand in his yard and demand answers, because no one else was being disruptive, though a few folks *were* outside observing. I'm sure more watchers were peering out their windows, too.

Shawn pulled to the curb behind my van. When the man yelled at him, too, Shawn shot him a look that said far more than words. The neighbor threw up his arms in disgust, turned on his heel and walked back inside his house.

"How do you do that without saying a thing?" I asked as we loaded carriers on the flat dolly Shawn had brought along.

"My charm is far-reaching and effective." He offered a small grin. But his smile faded quickly. "Crime scene tape means trouble. Lots of trouble. If I were Minnie's neighbor, I'd be worried. But what's sticking with me is the kitty-litter thing. Strange."

"What are you talking about?" I said.

"Let's just focus on the cats." Shawn rolled the dolly up the driveway, leaving me a tad confused.

Lois pulled a notebook from the pants pocket of her forest green uniform. Beads of sweat dotted her forehead, and her expression was grim. "Give me a minute to write down your names and what you got there."

"We have a total of twenty pet carriers," Shawn said.

"You'll need that many. I'm just glad I didn't run into any mean cats inside." Lois stared at her notebook and scribbled away. I understood she had to keep track of who went in and out of the house. "You're good to go around back now."

We walked up the driveway toward the back entrance. "How's that new puppy?" I said over my shoulder.

"I'm lucky I have a pair of wearable shoes left." She was tying off the last strip of crime scene tape on the gutter spout. "One day he'll be the best police officer on the planet."

Lois, who'd come to us from Detroit, had opened up her home to what would be the one-dog K-9 unit in Mercy. This change had been pushed by Tom, our best temporary police chief. Drug problems plagued Mercy—as it did so many rural towns in the South. A canine officer would be a tremendous help. The dog and the trainer came from donated funds, so it had been an easy call. Unlike most police dogs who stayed with their trainer, Lois was being instructed along with the Belgian Malinois puppy by a specialist from Atlanta who'd agreed to relocate temporarily and help our police force out. He'd then be returning to his home. The trainer must have been caring for the dog right now. The animal was never left alone.

Shawn slipped in through the screened porch door to make sure no cats escaped. He herded the few who'd somehow gotten out to the porch back into the house. That was another small mystery to be solved. The door to the house had been closed when we left.

It took us several minutes to place all the carriers inside the porch. The next step would be far trickier. Getting cats inside carriers was never fun. They were not fans of unwilling containment.

A window over the kitchen sink proved to be the kitty escape route. Using a paper towel to prevent leaving my fingerprints, I closed it carefully—and then berated myself immediately afterward. Candace would have taken a picture first, though I doubted any human had gained access to this house through a window only cats and creatures smaller than they were could have breached. I'd have to confess when I saw her. As for now, we remained sequestered in the kitchen.

The more cats we captured and put into crates, the more meowing filled the porch and kitchen. I wondered if the irritated neighbor could hear this cacophony. With all the noise, Tom made it into the kitchen without me hearing him. Shawn was already carrying cats out to his truck. I was kneeling, hoping to coax a scaredy-cat from under the table rather than crawl under there and grab the poor baby.

I felt a hand on my back and nearly hit my head on the table, I was so startled.

"You scared the bejesus out of me." I cocked my head and stared up at him. His eyes seemed troubled. I said, "You okay?"

"Someone was pretty angry at Chester." He offered his hand and helped me up.

"It's bad?"

"Yup. I need your help with a couple of things."

What was wrong with Tom? He seemed more ill at ease than I'd ever seen him. "You know I'll do anything. Well, almost anything, as long as I don't have to go in that room with Chester."

"Nothing like that. I got a call and apparently Minnie Schultz had an unexpected something in her tote bag. A kitten. Can you head out to the hospital and pick it up?"

I smiled. Kittens I could handle. "Sure. You want me to take it to Shawn's place?"

"Um, no. I want you to stay away from there and wait for my call. See, I'll be following Shawn back to the sanctuary so he can drop off the cats and then I need to question him. If he won't cooperate, I'll need to take him to the station. If that's the case, someone needs to phone Allison—someone who happens to be the kindest person I know and who I happen to live with. Do you know precisely where Allison is in North Carolina?"

I blinked several times trying to process what he'd just said. There was a kitten. And . . . he suspected Shawn might have done something to Chester? *Really?* Yet his suspicion was strong enough that he wanted *me* to call Shawn's wife. "Tom, surely you know Shawn would never hurt Chester, much less kill him."

He grasped both my upper arms and stared down at me, his expression grave. "Anyone is capable of murder given the right circumstances. Shawn had a restraining order against him—taken out by Chester. If you were in my shoes, who would be a person of interest right off the bat?"

I looked away, shook my head. "No. No, Tom."

He put a finger under my chin and gently guided my face so he could look into my eyes. "I need your help. Do you know where Allison is? Can you reach her?"

"Y-yes, but—"

"Thank you. It might not be necessary, so wait for me to give the okay on that, but if Shawn ends up in jail, she'll want to be here. I understand how hard this is, how much you care about Shawn, but I have to do my job and this is the right place to start."

Tears welled and Tom pulled me to him. "I am so sorry. The last thing I want to do is upset you. I need to rule Shawn out, and if he hates my guts forever, so be it."

"Um, what the heck is going on here?" came a familiar voice from the direction of the porch.

Tom and I pulled away from each other when we heard Lydia Monk's voice. The bad news just kept coming, this time in human form.

"Glad you got here so quickly, Lydia." Tom gestured for her to follow him as he headed for the back door. "Watch out for cats. Don't know if we found them all."

Lydia did not budge. She stood there in her denim leggings, fuchsia tunic and wedge sandals, glaring at me. "First I want to know what *she's* doing here. Is it bring-your-wife-to-work day?"

Tom, who had made it to the back porch, returned to the kitchen. Meanwhile I was hoping this irrational person hadn't seen my tears. I wanted to speak, but I'd just had my second serious shock of the day and I *had* no words.

"Lydia, please follow me and do your job. Now." Tom's edgy tone was not lost on her.

"Oh, or you'll tell my boss? How about I tell the town council about you making out with your wife at the scene of a suspicious death?" She hadn't taken her eyes off me as she spoke.

I'd never done anything to her except fall in love with someone she was obsessed with. I often laughed off her delusional shenanigans, but this time I only felt hurt and confused.

Tom must have recognized this. He walked in and stood between her and me. "You are wasting time, Lydia. Move it. *Please*."

How I wished the last of the cats hadn't been crated. I needed one in my arms about now.

"Ah. Finally some manners. Where's the body?"

They left then and I let out the breath I'd been holding. I blinked away the remnants of my tears and went outside to help Shawn finish up and tell him where I was headed. I spoke quickly, told him I was rushed and had to get to that kitten as soon as possible. We had to transfer all the crates to his truck and it was a tight squeeze, but he had an extended cab and fit all the smaller carriers in the backseat.

Once we were finished and half the cats were pleading loudly to be released, Shawn broke the tense silence that we'd maintained while working. "I'm a suspect, right?"

Again, I had no words and found myself blinking back tears. He'd be cleared after questioning. So why did all this bother me so much? "It will be fine, Shawn. I need to get going."

"You don't think I killed that man, do you?"

"Absolutely not. This situation is simply overwhelming. Where will all these cats end up?" But the real question haunting me now was *Where will you end up, Shawn?*

"I'll keep them with me for as long as possible," he said.

I hugged him good-bye. I had to leave, had to get into my van and think this through without the plaintive symphony of cats without homes as accompaniment.

Five

I stopped for a berry smoothie at a drive-thru restaurant before heading to the county hospital. Though I felt recharged after finishing half the drink, I wasn't sure what to expect when I reached my destination. *Where would you store a kitten in this place?* After a conversation with a stern-looking older man wearing a suit, I claimed a padded chair I'd been told to sit in. I was at the spot where you wait while the hospital powers that be decide whether you have the right ticket to get in. I didn't like hospitals much, but then, who did?

Swinging double doors led into the emergency room not too far from where I sat. The smell of disinfectant hit me each time those doors opened. Chemicals like that were necessary, I knew, but certainly weren't conducive to making humans or cats comfortable. The poor kitty was probably as freaked-out as Minnie Schultz. I didn't know the woman, but from what I had seen of her home, she cared about felines. A lot.

Turned out, picking up this kitten was more of an issue than Tom had let on. The little one wasn't being contained in a box or in the arms of a caring hospital worker. It was, I had learned from the suited gentleman, being clutched tightly by Minnie Schultz in the emergency room. From what I understood, she wasn't letting go.

About fifteen minutes later my name was called and soon I took a seat in a cubicle. A desk separated me from the young woman who had summoned me. This was a spot where a patient or family member usually answered questions about health insurance or discovered if you were even in the right place.

"Do you know this woman, Minnie Schultz?" the receptionist asked. She'd apparently been given the task of dealing with an unusual situation and seemed less than thrilled.

"Not exactly," I answered. Perhaps I'd made this trip for nothing, from the look on the freckled face of the obviously stressed-out lady. She was maybe mid-forties, like me, with hazel eyes similar in color to Shawn's. The thought of him suddenly distracted me. Was he in jail this very minute?

"But you *are* Jillian Hart, correct? Sent here by the Mercy police chief?" She referred to what looked like a fax printout in front of her.

I blinked and refocused on the task at hand. "Yes."

"Could I see some ID, please?"

After she was satisfied I was who I claimed to be, she leaned back and her face relaxed. "Sorry, but it's been a rather strange day. We're told you can help, that our patient will give you this kitten."

I felt a wave of doubt wash over me. I handled cats just fine, but a human being who was clinging to a cat? Probably for comfort? I wasn't sure I was the right person for the job. But I found myself nodding and saying, "I can help. I'll do my best."

Soon I found myself being led through the double doors by a nurse's aide wearing purple scrubs. I must have gotten used to the antiseptic odor because it didn't seem as strong as before.

Still, an emergency room is a frightening place. The sounds that came from behind the many curtains on either side of me, sounds of pain and groans of protest, filled me with dismay. But rather than taking me behind one of those curtains, the nurse's assistant led me to a closed door. A locked door.

I swallowed the wad of fear threatening to close off my throat. Was the poor woman violent? Disruptive? I had no idea what to expect. Once I was inside, it seemed like any other hospital room, and I breathed a sigh of relief. I noted a bed with railings, a blood pressure cuff on the wall, gloves and hand sanitizer nearby. A muscular woman, her broad shoulders straining the fabric of her scrubs, sat beside the bed. I latched my gaze onto hers, not wanting to look at the thin figure in the bed.

The woman beside the bed stood, unsmiling, and I saw her name tag read NANCY, and below that, ORDERLY.

The nurse's assistant introduced me to Nancy and then to Minnie before leaving us. The door had a lock on this side, too, but Nancy told the aide she could leave it unlocked. I forced myself to look at Minnie and was shocked. This frail fiftysomething's gunmetal gray hair was braided and hung over one shoulder, and she bore a haunted expression. She wore a pale blue nightgown and filthy slippers. The fabric on both items of clothing bore printed-on paw prints. Then there was the tote bag—also bearing evidence of the woman's love of felines. It was had a large black cat on the side facing me.

Nancy was twice her size and hadn't managed to get that bag from Minnie's grip. Why not?

As if she'd read my mind, Nancy spoke. "We can't force her to do anything until we get the, um . . . *paperwork* completed. It's complicated. We can't even force her to give up the cat."

Minnie's high-pitched, tremulous voice matched her fragile appearance. "He's a *kitten*, Nancy. We've had this conversation already. Big difference."

I believed the "paperwork" Nancy referred to was probably commitment papers.

"I know we have, Minnie. I'd sure wish you'd let me hold him." Nancy's appearance didn't match how gentle and kind she sounded.

"Nope. Not happening." Minnie shook her head vehemently and glared at me. "You can't hold him, either. I don't trust you."

How was I supposed to change her mind?

Nancy stepped aside and offered me her chair, the one very close to where Minnie sat in bed. The patient's mouth was now a stubborn, tight line.

I decided conversing about felines might be the best approach. "I am a cat lover, and I know you are, too. I have four cats at my house and one of them is diabetic."

Minnie didn't look at me, but she did respond. "I've had several diabetic cats in the past. Do you keep Karo syrup in case your baby's blood sugar drops?"

"We do. But Dashiell is pretty stable and we haven't had to use it in a while."

Minnie addressed Nancy. "Diabetic cats pass out when their blood sugar drops too low. You rub Karo syrup on their gums after you check their blood sugar to be sure that's the problem."

"Ah. Good idea," Nancy replied.

"See, you don't know a thing about cats, Nancy. Apparently this lady does." Minnie looked at me for the first time. "What's your name again?"

"Jillian. And what's that kitty's name?" I nodded at the tote bag in her lap. The kitten had probably been asleep, but the conversation must have woken it, because the bag began to move.

"This is Otto. That's my husband's name, too. He thinks it's funny to name a cat after him." She stroked the bag, smiling as if remembering.

"Where is the *human* Otto?" I'd been told Minnie was a widow.

"Why, he's at work, I suppose. He'll be by around six to pick me up."

I glanced at Nancy and she gave a frowning, almost imperceptible shake of her head.

I took my smartphone from my pocket. "Can I show you my fur babies? We can see what they're up to right this minute." I activated the app for my cat cam. I scrolled on the screen until I found all four cats in the living room.

I held the phone in front of Minnie. "The one on the couch is Chablis. She loves to cuddle."

Minnie's eyes widened. "Pretty Himalayan. You took movies of them?"

Nancy leaned over to take a look.

"No, this is real time. It's what they're doing right now." I pointed to the three boys all looking out the window to the lake beyond. "There's Syrah, Merlot and Dashiell."

Minnie pulled the phone closer. "Is this yours? I've never seen anything like it."

"This is my phone. Where's yours?"

She pushed it away and shook her head. "At the house, of course. If you take me there I'll show you. *He* had one of those, one like yours."

"He?" I said. "You mean Otto?"

"No, that other man. I can't remember his name." She looked at me and I saw that her brown eyes had filled. "Why can't I remember so many things?"

I decided without a further thought this woman needed comfort. I placed a hand on her shoulder. "This all must be so difficult."

"What's *your* name?" she asked.

This would be the third reminder. I felt so sorry for Minnie. "Jillian. Jillian Hart."

"That's so pretty. You showed me your kitties, so let mé show you mine." With that, she reached in the bag and pulled out a sleepy tuxedo kitten. He looked to be about six to nine months old.

"Otto is beautiful." And he was. He had a smudge of black on his nose, sleek black hair and white feet. I made no move to touch him. We'd made progress and I didn't want to upset Minnie or the kitten any more than they probably both were already.

Minnie cocked her head. "Otto. That name sounds so familiar."

I felt an ache in my chest, like my heart had just broken. This must be the Alzheimer's—the disease she might have—revealing itself completely. Yet she couldn't be more than ten years older than me. What a terrible illness. What a vicious thief.

"No matter what, Otto seems like the perfect name for this guy." I smiled at her and then at the kitten.

The tuxedo boy looked at me, opened his mouth and let out a series of plaintive meows.

Minnie held him out to me. "You take him. He's hungry and there's nothing in this place for him to eat."

I was surprised at how abruptly this had happened. "Okay. Can I take him to my house and feed him there?"

"He still needs kitten food, you know. He's growing. I have plenty at my place." She hesitated, looking confused. "But I can't remember how to get there or where I left my keys." This time tears spilled down her cheeks.

I took the kitty, who was suddenly pretty squirmy and tired of what he probably considered nonsense. I pointed to the tote bag. "May I?"

"Yes. Take it." She was rubbing tears away with the heel of her hand.

Nancy, who had gone quite still in the last minute, handed her a tissue. After Minnie blew her nose, she held out her hands to Nancy, palms down and touching. "You can put the cuffs on now."

I blinked several times, speechless.

Nancy said, "What are you talking about, Minnie?"

"I killed him, right? The man in my house. I killed him."

Six

With Otto tucked in the tote and the bag cradled in my arms, I resisted the urge to get on the phone and call Tom immediately. Thank goodness Otto was a mellow boy now that he was back in the bag. He was purring so loud I could hear him through the fabric, so he was pretty darn content as I carried him out of the emergency room as fast as I could. I felt like a thief escaping from a house I'd just burgled. I needed to get this baby safely in my van before I made a call—because a phone call might distract me and lead to disaster. If Otto ran off, I'd never forgive myself.

I'd prepared a crate with one of the kitty quilts I'd made and the small carrier sat on the passenger seat. I petted and soothed Otto before putting him inside. He sniffed the quilt and curled up in a back corner. I poured a little bottled water into a dish I always kept in the van. He wasn't interested. I'd be a little freaked-out myself. No. I *was* freaked-out. I'd just heard a woman confess to murder.

My hand trembled as I punched Tom's speed dial.

Thank goodness he answered right away, saying, "How did it go?"

"She said she killed a man in her house, Tom. She confessed to murder."

"Really?" He sounded so calm that it unnerved me even more.

"How do you do that?" My voice sounded strained. I was having a hard time maintaining my composure, but the poor kitty had been through a lot and I needed to be careful not to upset him. Cats are quick to pick up on human emotion.

"Do what?" Now he seemed distracted and I could tell he was moving around. I heard voices in the background.

"Stay so calm."

"I shouldn't have made you go there, Jilly. I'm sorry."

"Don't be. I got the kitten away from her and now they can go about the business of helping that poor woman. But what about this confession? The problem for you, I'm guessing, is that because she's not all there, her statement is unreliable. She might be committed to some sort of psychiatric facility, and then what kind of case can you make?"

"How tall is she, would you guess?"

How tall is she? What an odd question. "She was in bed, so I can't be sure, but she's a small person. At the most, she's about five foot four." I tried to blink away my confusion. "What does her height have to do with anything?"

"The killer was at least five foot six, according to Candace's estimation. Remember, she took that CSI course last month about blood spatter, wound analysis, touch DNA and more? Anyway, she did a few quick calculations and a small person like Minnie Schultz would have had to be standing on a chair to deliver the blow to the head that killed the man."

I swallowed. I was hearing things I didn't want to know. But I'd learned that Tom often needed to talk through situations to make sense of them, and his cases were no different.

I said, "He was hit on the head so hard it killed him? That's terrible."

"Actually," Tom replied, "he might not have died if he hadn't bled so much—but that's a guess. We have to wait on the autopsy."

"Definitely not a suicide or an accident?"

"No chance. This was an assault that resulted in death. It's manslaughter at the very least. Mrs. Schultz may know something, but from what I'm hearing from you and the night shift officer who picked her up wandering around town this morning, she's an unreliable witness at best."

"That's what I said. Unreliable. I do have her adorable kitten—his name is Otto, after her husband. Shawn said she's a widow, but from what I heard her say, she might not remember her husband is dead. It's so sad to see a person so confused, especially at her age. She's relatively young—maybe midfifties."

"I was wrong, Jilly. I'm so sorry I asked you to go there. I didn't realize she was that bad off."

"No, it wasn't wrong at all. She needs help. It's just sad, that's all."

"I can assure you that her husband is dead, by the way. That was public record. He died in a car wreck about five years ago. We found the death certificate and insurance documents. The lady may be mixed-up, but at some point in time she was well organized."

"Except for the house that could pass for a mini-Costco." I put the keys in the ignition. "I'm taking Otto straight to Doc Jensen's for a checkup. Hopefully he's fine and can stay with us until this mess is sorted out."

"Drive safely. Love you, Jilly."

Once I disconnected and hooked up to Bluetooth for any future calls, I went on my way to visit the vet. The kitten, Doc Jensen told me, was in perfect health, already neutered and most likely about nine months old. In no time, he was chowing down in my basement cat room—the one where I first put any foster cats before introducing them to my own crew. As I watched him eat, I wondered how Dashiell would do with a visitor. I hadn't fostered any cats since he came to live here.

Our newest friend seemed tuckered out from all he'd been through today. He liked the little quilt I'd wrapped around him to carry him inside. By the time I shut the door, he was already curled up on it. I went upstairs to properly greet my kitties. I petted the three who rubbed against me, but Chablis sat by the pantry door, waiting for me to dole out treats.

"Okay, I get the message," I said.

I gave Dashiell freeze-dried pieces of chicken to limit his carb intake. Merlot and Chablis received their favorite tuna crunchies. Syrah, however, wanted nothing to do with treats. He crouched at the top of the basement stairs, and I imagined he'd soon make his way down, hoping to get a good sniff of Otto. Nothing got past Syrah, not for a second.

I ate yogurt, slices of cheese and an apple after my

stomach growled loud enough for Merlot to turn his attention away from the basement entrance. He was curious about the latest visitor, too. It was almost three o'clock and had been such a crazy day. Since I was already getting quilt orders for kitty Christmas gifts despite its still being spring, I was about ready to hunker down in my sewing room. The appliqué quilts would take the longest because those were always hand done. Today, I needed the hum of a sewing machine to drown out thoughts of a murdered Chester and a muddled Minnie.

I got in a good hour of work before my phone rang. The caller ID confused me. Mercy PD. Tom or Candace always called me on their cells. I couldn't remember either of them ever using the landlines in the police department.

I mumbled, "Must be someone there wanting to give me a message from Tom. Even B.J. would call me on his mobile if he was charged with delivering a message." But B.J., the young man who'd been the dispatcher for several years, had now joined Mercy PD as a deputy.

After I said hello, I was more than surprised to hear Shawn's voice. "Jillian, I need a lawyer. I don't know any. And maybe call Allison. I can't bear to talk to her right now." He spoke so fast I barely understood him.

"Slow down, Shawn. What's happening?" I wasn't sure if calling Allison was necessary quite yet—especially since Tom had asked me to wait.

"I'm in custody."

"You've been arrested for Chester's murder?" I was shocked to my sandals. Shawn would never hurt anyone.

"No good deed," he said. "You can finish the rest. I'm pretty sure I need a lawyer."

"Shawn, have you really been *arrested*?" I spoke

calmly and slowly. He was so agitated, I was hoping I could calm him down.

"They put cuffs on me, so you tell me. And by 'they,' I mean Tom."

Tom spoke in the background. "Okay, Shawn. That's enough."

"Whatever." Shawn sounded so hostile, I felt panic constrict my throat. *What the heck is going on?*

Tom came on the line, and I could tell he was exasperated. "He wants a lawyer. Can you help him out?"

Tom's voice calmed me almost instantly. "Sure, but did you actually arrest him?"

He sighed heavily. "No. He came back to the Schultz house after dropping off the cats at the sanctuary. He said he needed to make sure there were no more cats hiding in the house. I told him it was not the time for that because we were still processing the scene. He got agitated, said the cats came first. He marched into the house and began moving boxes. That's when I cuffed him and brought him to the station. I told him he needs to cool off so he can understand that we have a job today that takes precedence right now. He's not getting it, and who am I to deny a man the right to a lawyer?"

Tom's exasperation had turned to anger.

I heard Shawn shout, "You think I killed him. I know you do."

"I get it." I lowered my voice. "I know Shawn well enough to tell you that this is about the cats—because he probably thought you'd scare any lurkers with your search. Can I offer a suggestion?"

"Anything." His tone was soft and stoic. Calmer, thank goodness.

"Put him in an interview room, give him a Coke and

leave him alone for about thirty minutes. He'll settle down. Meanwhile, I know just the lawyer to call."

I told Tom I loved him and said calling Allison might not be needed and disconnected. My stepdaughter Kara's boyfriend was Liam Brennan. He'd been an assistant district attorney—they call them *solicitors* in South Carolina—but made the decision only a few months ago to leave and start his own practice. He wanted to be with Kara seven days a week. Not only did they live together in her big house now, they worked in the same building. Kara was the owner and editor in chief of the town newspaper—the *Mercy Messenger.* Their relationship was definitely serious and I was happy for them both.

Soon I was off to see Liam, blowing kisses to my cats before I left. The *Messenger* offices were located in a hundred-year-old renovated building on Main Street. The newspaper was on the ground floor and Liam's new office was on the second level. I'd called ahead and Liam's assistant stood up when I entered the reception area. This was no fancy law office. A ceiling fan squeaked in protest against the poorly air-conditioned space. Old paneling, recently painted off-white, and mismatched chairs for waiting clients filled the narrow space.

Sue Ann, Liam's legal assistant, whose sweet Southern charm sometimes fooled people into believing she might be an airhead, greeted me with a smile. Nothing could be further from the truth. She had a quick, sarcastic wit that took some getting used to, but I'd learned to appreciate how smart she was.

She'd dressed for the heat in the building, wearing a cotton tunic over linen pants. Her platinum hair, streaked with deep purple, framed her face. I'd met her several times in Kara's office downstairs—mostly because she had little work to do yet. That would change. Liam was a brilliant lawyer and word of mouth would bring him business.

Sue Ann said, "The AC guy is on his way—or so he told me about two hours ago. I told him it was hot as high school love in this place. But they got enough work they don't need to rush anywhere. Course you're here because we have a client. Best news I've had in a week. I'm bored as hell, so tell me all about him."

I explained Shawn's situation as she wrote the details on a legal pad in shorthand.

When I was finished, I nodded at the pad. "You still use shorthand, huh?"

"No one can read it but me. Isn't that great?" She grinned and her nose wrinkled in this adorable way. It was the first time I'd wondered how old she was. She could have been anywhere from twenty to forty.

I glanced toward the door that led to Liam's office. "Is he here?"

"He is. He promised me he wouldn't come out until I phoned in to him. I need to practice doing things in a *professional manner*. Business is so bad I'm thinking of offering free boiled peanuts to anyone who'll walk up those old stairs with a legal problem. I could put one of those placards for peanuts right outside the building."

Liam's office door opened. It squealed worse than the ceiling fan. "That's good enough, Sue Ann." He looked at me. "Hey there, Jillian. How are you?"

"I'm fine. But Shawn? Not so good." I considered what a fine-looking man Liam was with his Irish eyes and tall, lean physique. But a sheen of sweat on his forehead and his rolled-up dress shirt sleeves told me he was hoping the AC guy arrived soon, too.

He addressed Sue Ann. "Go through your spiel and tell me what Jillian said. Practice what I've taught you about office etiquette. Then I need to get down to the police station and speak with my new client."

She related to Liam everything I'd told her. He offered mock applause. "You don't need any more practice. When folks call, you do exactly as you did with Jillian."

She saluted. "Yes, sir. Now get out of here, you two. You're burning daylight."

Seven

The Mercy Police Department, located in a side wing of the town square's courthouse, seemed busier than usual. The murder of a county employee probably had a lot to do with it. Liam and I had driven in our separate vehicles after he assured me he wanted me to go with him to greet Shawn. Though Liam had met him before, had even visited the sanctuary with Kara once, knowing Shawn and *really* knowing him were two different things. His passion for helping animals ruled his life, and I believed that was how he'd ended up here at the police station.

B.J. Henderson looked quite different from the last time I'd seen him here. He was wearing one of the Mercy PD uniforms—forest green pants and the khaki short-sleeved shirt with green trim reserved for the warmer months. Apparently he was still doing some of the dispatch work until they found someone to replace him permanently. I remembered then that Tom had mentioned the part-timer they'd hired just wasn't catching on and they were still searching for a permanent hire.

B.J. had stood when we walked through the old scratched-up door into the small waiting area. Plastic molded chairs lined three walls opposite him and all sat empty. "Hey there, Jillian. And Mr. Brennan." He smiled stiffly and adjusted the heavy police utility belt.

"You're looking fine, B.J." I smiled. "That uniform suits you."

He blushed. "Thank you, ma'am. Let me call Tom and tell him you're here."

Soon Tom joined us and swung open the gate that separated the waiting room from the long hallway leading to interview rooms and offices.

He greeted me with a quick kiss and shook Liam's hand before inviting us back to his office. All of the former chief's personal effects were gone. They had been replaced by a smaller desk, bookshelves and a computer station. Tom had even replaced the upholstery on the chairs. Chief Mike Baca, who had been Tom's good friend, was gone and Tom wanted no daily reminders. He said it was too distracting.

Tom closed the door. "I want to bring you up to speed on Shawn. He is not under arrest, like I told you before, but he was so obsessed with getting the cats out of the house, then making sure he had the food they'd been eating go to the shelter, too—well, it was one thing after another. We couldn't have him contaminating the scene, but he wouldn't leave."

"Did you have to handcuff him?" I asked.

Liam spoke for the first time since greeting Tom. "The highest court ruled individuals can be handcuffed if they are interfering with a police investigation. It doesn't mean they are necessarily under arrest. Was that your thinking, Tom?"

Tom nodded. "Yup. I don't really want him here. He's a wreck. But I would like to ask him a few questions because he did have issues with the victim—as in the fact that Chester Winston had a restraining order against Shawn. Can you two help me calm him down so we can talk?"

"Of course," I said as Liam nodded his agreement.

Soon we all sat in the interview room, the one with a battered old table where they did the more informal interrogations. Shawn wasn't wearing handcuffs anymore and he was chewing on a thumbnail. His anxious eyes made him seem almost scary. He wouldn't look at Tom and barely acknowledged me.

Liam sat next to Shawn.

Shawn seemed surprised to see him. "Don't you *prosecute* people? Are you here to take me to jail?"

"I am no longer a solicitor for the county." Liam drew out the words in a slow drawl. "I opened my own practice. You are one of my first clients."

"Okay, here's the damn truth. I didn't kill that jerk." Shawn glance darted toward Tom, no doubt realizing that wasn't the best word to call a murder victim. "Sorry. The man's dead. I shouldn't have said that."

"Do you want everyone but me to leave?" Liam asked.

Shawn offered me a distraught look. "You don't think I killed Chester, right?"

I stood from the chair I'd taken across from Shawn, walked over and gave him a hug. "I *know* you didn't. Thing is, you need to stay away from that house. That's all Tom wants."

"Did you call Allison already? 'Cause she is going to be *so* pissed at me. She's busy, you know, and . . ."

I took Shawn's face in my hands and made him look at me. "I *didn't* call her. She doesn't know a thing."

His shoulders slumped with relief.

Liam said, "You're scared. It's written all over your face. The fact is, I'm not only here as a lawyer, I'm here as a friend. Everything will work out. You are not under arrest. You never were."

Shawn turned to Tom, who stood leaning against the door. "Is that true?"

"Shawn, you've never been under arrest. I kept telling you that, but I'm glad you've heard it from your lawyer."

Liam rested a hand on Shawn's clenched fist. "Do you believe Tom now?"

While I sat back down, Shawn closed his eyes and heaved a sigh of relief. "Good. Now I have to get back to the shelter. Candace drove my truck there with a few cats and they need to be examined and—"

"Shawn," I said, louder than was probably necessary. "Talk to Tom first and then I'll take you home."

Shawn rubbed his forehead with three thick fingers, his head down. "Okay, sure. But I can't be away too much longer." He began to rub one wrist, perhaps still feeling the metal of handcuffs against his skin. He looked up at Tom. "What do you want to know?"

Having seen Shawn agitated before, I was grateful he had calmed down. Getting so stressed-out couldn't be good for his health.

Tom grabbed a chair from against the far wall and sat at the head of the table.

Liam said, "This is an informal interview, correct?"

"That's right." Tom looked at Shawn. "How well do you know Minnie Schultz?"

"She's adopted cats from me before. Nice lady. But she came to the sanctuary a couple months ago. She wandered around looking at the rescues and then chose this tuxie kitten I'd just put up for adoption. Something didn't seem right with her. She kept losing her train of thought. Since I knew she had more than a few cats already, I wanted to make certain she wasn't turning into a hoarder. I don't let hoarders have my rescues. I told her I needed to make a home visit."

Liam looked confused. "What's a *tuxie*?"

"Short for *tuxedo cat*," Shawn replied. "You know— black and white, looks like the cat's wearing a tuxedo?"

Liam nodded and muttered an "Ah."

"How was she when you visited her?" Tom asked.

"More together than she was at the shelter. Made me banana bread to take home because she knew Allison was out of town." Shawn glanced my way and offered a sheepish grin. "Thanks again for not calling my wife. I sure did lose it for a while, didn't I?"

"I'm glad the real Shawn Cuddahee is back." I returned his smile.

"What about those boxes in her house?" Tom asked. "Was the house filled with them back then?"

"I did notice a few boxes and assumed it was cat food or a litter delivery. Other than that, the place was neat as a cat—like Mark Twain used to say."

My curiosity got the better of me. "What's with the boxes, Tom?"

"Don't know. We're fingerprinting all of them before we open them, though that may be a waste of energy. Who knows how many hands have touched them. If the first few are loaded with prints, our time will be better spent searching for other evidence." He turned back to

Shawn. "So, aside from when you adopted out this kitten, when was the last time you had contact with Mrs. Schultz when she didn't seem as confused?"

Shawn thought for minute. "Maybe nine months ago? She named off all her cats when we bumped into each other at Doc Jensen's clinic. She seemed fine."

Someone knocked tentatively on the door.

"What do you need?" Tom called.

"It's B.J. You might want to see this."

Tom sighed and whispered, "He's new at investigating. Pretty gung ho."

Tom opened the door and B.J. handed him a paper, saying, "I pulled this off the *Blue Sheet*."

The *Blue Sheet* was an advertising flyer for locals buying and selling used goods.

"Sum it up, B.J.," Tom said.

"Mr. Winston was advertising about cats that had been found, and there are descriptions."

Shawn stood abruptly. "What? The county never advertises about recovered cats in the *Blue Sheet*. Those cats are mentioned in the *Mercy Messenger*, pictures are put on Facebook and the county shelter has a Web site."

Tom gestured for Shawn to sit back down and Liam seconded the motion. "Come on, Shawn. Please don't get all worked up again. Let me do my job."

Tom stepped outside the interview room. Since I sure didn't want to see Shawn get agitated again, I reached across the table and took his hand in mine. "Hang in there. Trust Tom to get to the bottom of this mess."

Tom returned within a few seconds. "We're checking into the ad. Maybe Chester Winston helped Mrs. Schultz place it since she had so many cats and—"

"No way." Shawn shook his head vigorously. "She may be a few peaches short of a peck, but she would never do that."

Tom took a seat next to me. "You know her better than any of us, so I'm sure you're right. Tell me about the cats. Any idea where they all came from since you last visited the Schultz house?"

"Not a clue. It's crazy, because I'd recognize any of them that I'd adopted out. None of those newer cats came from my shelter." Shawn looked at me. "Is the poor lady okay, Jillian? This whole thing seems screwy."

"She's a tad confused. They're getting her a good doctor, though." I went on before Shawn could ask any questions about what *kind* of doctor. "She had that little tuxie with her when the police picked her up and he's at my place now."

"Otto?" Shawn said. "He was an imp—that's for sure."

"That's him." I smiled and sat back, not wanting to say anything to Shawn that I shouldn't.

I was surprised when Tom rested a hand on my knee before addressing Shawn again. From the tension I felt in his touch, I had the feeling this whole encounter with Shawn had been more difficult than he'd let on. Small-town policing was different from the larger police force in North Carolina where he'd been an officer years ago.

He said, "What do you know about the dead husband, Otto? What happened to him?"

Shawn said, "She once told me he died in a car wreck several years back. She said she missed him."

Tom pressed on. "Do you know anything else about Mrs. Schultz that might help? Ever meet any of her relatives? Her friends?"

"Never met anyone at her house when I went there.

There's some grown kids, and I remember her talking about out-of-town cousins. I was more interested in the cats, as bad as that sounds." He rubbed his forehead again. "God, forgive me, I should have paid more attention."

Tom sighed heavily. "You feel guilty. I get that, but it won't help us, Shawn. I need facts."

Liam said, "Tom's right. Let's get through these questions and then you can leave."

"I'll switch gears. What can you tell me about Chester?" Tom asked. "You've had plenty of interaction with him. When did you see him last? Aside from lying dead between those twin beds, I mean."

Liam sat straighter in his chair. "Shawn, since we're talking about the victim now, I'll remind you that you don't have to say anything."

"I've got nothing to hide. I didn't hurt him," Shawn said.

"But at one time you *did* hit him," Tom said. "That's why he took out the restraining order, right?"

"That was several years ago," Shawn said through clenched teeth.

"I know. But tell me about it," Tom replied.

"You don't have to, Shawn," Liam cautioned again.

"No, no. It was stupid of me and I want to answer. See, I called him to come pick up an injured dog—this was before I had any good way of dealing with injured animals. I thought he was too rough with the animal. We exchanged words. I only hit him after Chester got his rifle from his truck and was about to put the dog down. I had to stop him. That's not his job and he knows it. So I grabbed the rifle and maybe the rifle butt popped him on the jaw. Okay, it *did* pop him on the jaw."

I shook my head. I'd heard only part of this story. "But that was so wrong of Chester."

"Tell me about it. I didn't even hit him hard, but he fell down and acted like I'd killed . . ." Shawn's face flushed. "Anyway, he took out the restraining order."

"Why didn't you tell the judge about the rifle and how he was about to do something that he should have been fired for?" I couldn't hide my outrage. What Chester had done was despicable.

"Oh, I did. But the judge didn't believe me." Shawn looked at Tom. "And just so you know, I wasn't the only concerned citizen Chester pissed off. You might want to check that out."

"Do you have names?" Tom took a small notebook from his pocket.

"If you give me time to think on it, I can probably come up with a few people. It was stuff I heard from folks who came to the shelter to adopt. I see a lot of people in the sanctuary and right now I couldn't remember one word of any of them said to save my life." He raised his eyebrows. "Do I have to save my life, Tom?"

"Shawn," Liam cautioned again, "I am strongly advising you to stop talking. You've said enough."

Thing is, if I were in Shawn's position, I'd keep talking, too. Being suspected of committing a terrible crime would make me talk until I lost my voice in hopes that I'd be believed.

Shawn squeezed his eyes shut. "I *have* to cooperate. Otherwise Tom will think I did it." He rested his arms on the table and leaned toward Tom. "So, what else do you want to know?"

Tom said, "When as the last time you came face-to-face with Chester Winston?"

"In person? Longer ago than I can remember. The court allowed me to call him about reports I got from people who spotted strays or dead or injured animals. It was his job to take care of the ones I couldn't get to. We were allowed to communicate that way—on the phone about business. But I couldn't go near him."

"Do you have any idea what he was doing in Minnie Schultz's house?" Tom sounded as baffled as I was—probably as we all were.

Shawn raised his head and squinted over my shoulder, no doubt considering the question. Then he looked back at Tom. "It had to be about all those cats, right? That's the only thing that makes sense."

Tom said, "At least we're on the same page. The cats connect you, Mrs. Schultz and Chester. But what exactly does that connection mean, if anything?"

Shawn shook his head. "I have no idea."

Eight

After it was obvious even to me that Shawn had nothing more to share about Chester or Minnie Schultz, at least for now, Liam offered to drive him back to the sanctuary, probably so Liam could get a better feel for his client. After they'd gone, Tom gave me a much-needed hug.

"Thanks for helping out," he said. "I doubt Shawn would have calmed down if not for you being here."

"I don't know if that's true, but I refuse to accept for a second that he killed Chester."

He sidestepped this by saying, "One thing I'm sure of. He doesn't *believe* he did. But enough cop talk. I'm starving. Can you do me a favor?"

"Sure."

"I'll call in an order to the Main Street Diner for my folks since they'll probably be here all night working with me. Could you pick up the food? Candace uploaded the crime scene photos and—"

I held up my hand. "Remember? No cop talk. Consider your request done." We kissed good-bye, and as I left the building, I checked my phone. It was past five but I didn't feel hungry at all. I felt tired. The stress of this day had walloped me. Most of all, my heart felt bruised. No matter what kind of person Chester was, he didn't deserve to die so violently. As for Shawn? He didn't deserve to be handcuffed and treated like a criminal. That, however, could have been avoided. I couldn't blame Tom for doing his job. It was an unintended consequence and I sure hoped Shawn would cooperate from now on.

Before I drove to pick up burgers, chili dogs and fries, I sat in the van and pulled up my cat cam to glimpse what was happening at home. The kitties were awake and probably ready to play. "I'll be home soon, my sweeties," I whispered as I closed the app. Just seeing them move and stretch and nudge one another made me feel more serene as I drove out of the parking lot. Yes, all I needed was a hefty dose of my feline friends to set the world straight again.

Once I picked up and delivered the food, I still felt drained. I needed coffee—maybe with half the caffeine so I could sleep tonight. Belle's Beans, a little café with the best coffee in the world, was on the way home. I stopped in and ordered a half-decaf vanilla latte to go. The young woman behind the counter wore an oval name tag that said BELLE. Her real name, I knew, was Tina. All the baristas wore those tags. Belle Lowry, the owner, saw this as a way to make everyone feel comfortable in her lovely coffeehouse—as if they were being served by the person whose name was attached to this establishment. Soothing music emanated from overhead speakers, and at this time of day, most of the lacquered tables and stools were empty. I always enjoyed the bustle in the morning, but as I waited for my order,

I decided this atmosphere was so . . . pleasant. After a truly *un*pleasant day, I appreciated this.

I grabbed my coffee and was ready to leave when I practically ran smack into the real Belle as she was coming in through the entrance.

"Hey, Jillian," the white-haired Belle said. "You never visit at this time of day. Were you down at the police station because of the murder? Is Shawn really under arrest?"

Nothing that happened in this town got past Belle. But I had to set her straight. "He was never under arrest, Belle."

"But Jessie Turner told me he was in handcuffs and—"

"I promise you—he *wasn't* under arrest. He was troubled about the cats we found at Mrs. Schultz's place and didn't want to leave her house until every cat—"

"Ah, I get it. Your brand-new husband insisted he get out of poor Minnie's place and he wouldn't leave. Has Shawn settled down?"

"He has. Do you know Minnie very well?" I asked.

"Not well. Knew her husband, Otto, better. His death was such a tragedy." She shook her head, appearing genuinely down.

"Do you have time to tell me about him—and what you know about Minnie? See, I have this kitten that belongs to her. I'm keeping the little guy while she's hospitalized. It would help me to understand her better—and maybe understand little Otto, the tuxie kitten."

"I always have time for you, Jillian. Let me grab a cup of tea and I'll join you at a table."

She hustled by me, and I chose one of the low tables toward the back. I smiled at the thought of a woman who sold coffee for a living drinking tea.

Belle soon joined me, her pink lipstick applied perfectly—probably because she was wearing new glasses, the white frames studded with rhinestones. Before she finally gave in and visited the eye doctor, Belle's lipstick was often misapplied, either well below her lips or beyond the corners of her mouth. It always made me smile, but I couldn't bring myself to tell her when I saw her like that. Today, it wasn't a problem and I noted her linen outfit complemented her coloring. Belle was much older than I was, but her energy never failed to amaze me. Running a busy place like this certainly took plenty of stamina.

"What would you like to know about Otto?" Belle set down a single-serving teapot and a cup in front of her.

"Wait a minute. I need to hear about this first." I stared at her cute little teapot. "You own a coffeehouse and yet you drink tea?"

"My grandparents were born in England. We always had tea in the late afternoon when I stayed with them. It's a comforting tradition, a little bit of them to hang on to."

"Ah. I had no idea." I took the lid off my latte cup to allow my drink to cool. "Okay, about Mr. Schultz. You knew him?"

"He used to come in and buy coffee beans. Minnie was a bit shy, but she accompanied him on occasion. They never bought coffee drinks or pastries. They were pretty old-school. Then tragedy struck and I haven't seen Minnie since."

"You mean since her husband's accident?" I tested my latte with a tentative sip. It was perfect.

"Yes. Horrible wreck on a back road. He ran into a ditch and flipped over. They didn't find him for two days.

He wasn't wearing a seat belt, or he might have been all right. Anyway, that's what Mike Baca, our dearly departed former police chief, told me." She poured her tea and a sweet, unique smell wafted my way.

"How awful." I looked at the table, remembering the sudden death of my first husband, John, and how devastating it had been. It had taken me years to recover. I closed my eyes and put aside thoughts of John. "That tea smells wonderful, by the way," I said. "What is it?"

"Pomegranate green tea. Special blend I order online."

"I might have to try that—maybe flavor up my sweet tea. Back to Minnie Schultz. You haven't seen her in five years?"

Belle shook her head. "No, ma'am. She quit church and that was where I always saw her. I heard a few ladies on the bereavement committee reached out to her several times, but she never returned to the pew where she and Otto always used to sit. Sad thing, that."

"Tell me anything more you know about Mr. Schultz." I took a longer drink and hoped the small amount of caffeine would energize me.

"German immigrant—came here as a boy. Very polite. Such a nice man. He always dressed so formal with his vest and his pocket watch. He was a jeweler, and since his passing, we haven't had a fine jewelry shop here in Mercy. These days all the jewelry sold in town seems to be made for teenagers and comes from China."

"I had no idea Mercy once had a store like what you've described, but then I rarely wear jewelry, except for this." I held out my hand so we could both admire the diamond-studded wedding band now gracing my ring finger.

Belle took my hand and held it up for a closer look.

"Your Tom has such good taste." She continued to admire the ring for several seconds after I'd set my hand back next to my coffee.

"He does. Picked it out all by himself, but because of Mike's death, he didn't have it in time for our wedding." I smiled, remembering the night he'd made a romantic dinner all by himself and poured me a glass of champagne with this ring in the bottom of the flute, sparkling more than the champagne ever could. Then my thoughts returned to Minnie Schultz. "Did you know she's in the hospital?"

"Oh, for sure. One of my customers called the police and the ambulance about Minnie. He saw her wandering down Main in the early morning, right when I was coming to work. He said she looked so confused. I do hope she's okay."

I explained about how I'd been asked to retrieve the kitten.

Belle's forehead creased with concern. "So strange that she had a cat with her. My sweet Mocha kitty would have been out of that tote in a flash. It all seems so . . . *troubling*. A dead man in her house and poor Minnie wandering around all by herself in such a state? Bless the poor woman's heart. But she has a wonderful helper in you, Jillian."

"I'm not sure about that, though I do want to help."

Belle went on. "I have to say, no cat I've ever been acquainted with would ever tolerate a walk down Main Street." She shook her head sadly. "That poor woman— and that poor kitty cat. I will make it my business to get the church to try harder this time to engage her once she returns home. Her children certainly won't be much help." Belle raised a hand to her mouth. "Oh my. She might not want to return home, right? Not after what happened to Chester. What do you think he was doing there in the first place? Picking up stray cats?"

"Maybe," I replied. "I'm sure Tom will figure it out. But what's this about her children?"

"They're all grown—a girl and twin boys. They came from two loving parents and yet once they left home, apparently they rarely visited. Or that's what I hear." She sipped at her tea. "Could have been Otto's death that caused a strain, but from what I understand Minnie was the kindest woman in the world—just shy, is all."

"Do you know the children?"

"Just in passing. The daughter, Greta, married and moved to Welcome Path, not too far from here. The young men are named Harris and Henry. Lookers, those two. Used to charm the girls when they were teenagers. Always had young ladies with them when they came in here. I'm pretty certain all three of Otto and Minnie's children went to college because Otto told me once they had to pinch pennies with the children in school."

Belle drained her teacup, stood and picked up her dishes. "I wish I could chat longer, but I have a new applicant coming in. Don't even know her name, so I'd better get to my office and read up on her before she arrives."

I stood. "I should get home, too—before there's a kitty revolution. I've been away far longer than I expected, and tuna dinners are late."

We said our good-byes, and soon I arrived home to find four cats showing their disdain by offering a chorus of unhappy meows. I'd stayed away well past their dinnertime. Once I'd made sure Dashiell's blood sugar hadn't tanked and filled their dishes, I went to the basement to see about what was probably a very lonely kitten.

He might enjoy a little feline company as well as visiting with me, but the question was, would my crew enjoy him?

Otto purred up a storm when I picked him up. I played with him a bit so the other cats had time to finish their food. Otto had eaten well in my absence. His little belly felt warm and fat as I carried him upstairs.

After the usual hissing when I introduced Otto, most of it coming from Dashiell, I walked around the house so he could follow me and explore. That's when I wondered if they made a bed larger than a king-size to accommodate yet another cat. Little Otto would soon want to join his new friends at night.

Nine

For the first time since Tom and I married last fall, he wasn't home when I awoke the following morning. He'd stayed at the police station. But, of course, I wasn't alone. Four cats were staring at me, and Chablis took this feline attention one step further by kneading my chest. When I'd gotten up at about three a.m. to check on Otto downstairs, they'd all remained sound asleep. I'd put the kitten to bed down there since I wasn't sure he was ready to join the clowder. He'd been sound asleep like the rest of the cats in the middle of the night and I had no trouble getting back to sleep myself.

After the morning routine of feeding cats, showering and eating breakfast, I poured my second cup of coffee and decided to call Shawn. Yesterday had been so difficult for him, and I wanted to make sure he was okay. I sat on the couch with Otto and Chablis in my lap. The other three cats believed, as usual, that they needed to check out Mercy Lake and make sure that it had remained still and safe while they'd been napping and not keeping watch. They then turned their attention to the hummingbird wars currently being waged at the feeder hanging from the deck post.

Shawn answered on the third ring and sounded weary. "Oh, hi, Jillian. Hear anything about the murder?"

"Nope. I wanted to make sure you were okay. That's my biggest concern right now."

"I'm fine, but I never want to wear handcuffs again. I'm glad Allison wasn't around to see me shamed like that. Not that I didn't bring it on myself. I'm not sure I thanked you for helping me out. If you hadn't been there, I might have totally lost it."

"Shawn, you are one of my dearest friends and I didn't do much of anything but sit there. How did the shelter fare without your guidance?"

"Okay, I guess. No problems have surfaced. Once I was back in my office, I recalled a few names of folks who complained about Chester and I e-mailed them to Tom. I hated doing that, though. I felt like a snitch in a bad movie."

"He has to touch base with all potential suspects. We need to find out who committed this murder."

Shawn, still sounding down in the mouth, said, "I suppose. Thanks for checking on me. I have a lot of cats to examine. Doc Jensen is headed over here to help me out. It's tough to keep more than twenty cats in quarantine—mostly because I can't stand the racket. They're a loud bunch and used to being spoiled rotten, is my guess."

I heard the life come back into his voice as he spoke of the cats. Despite the situation, I was certain they would cheer him up. We said good-bye, and as soon as I disconnected, my phone rang. It startled Otto awake and he leapt off my lap. Blinking away sleep, he sat down and stared up at me. Gosh, he was so cute with that smudge of black on his pink nose.

I didn't recognize the number of whoever was calling, even though it was a local area code. I answered and offered a tentative hello, hoping someone wasn't ready to sell me something.

"Is this Ms. Hart?" a woman asked.

"I'm Jillian Hart. Can I help you?"

"You can. My name is Brenda Ross. I'm a doctor treating a woman named Minnie Schultz. She said a lady visited her yesterday and took a cat from her—one she loves. She said you would keep it safe. I got your name from the policewoman stationed outside Mrs. Schultz's door."

"You found the right person, but why is there an officer outside her door?" To myself I added, *And what, exactly, do you need from me?*

"I'm not certain if they suspect Mrs. Schultz of murder or if they feel the need to protect her. Deputy Jewel wouldn't tell me."

"No, she wouldn't do that." I smiled to myself. I felt fortunate when Lois Jewel shared *anything* with me. "How can I help?"

"I know Mrs. Schultz's home is a crime scene, but I told my patient I would gather a few of her things. She's quite agitated and I believe it would calm her to have familiar items within sight. It seems unclear when she'll be released. Can you help me with that? I have a list."

What kind of doctor didn't know when her own patient would be released? Added to that, what doctor would go to all this trouble? Then it dawned on me. Dr. Ross was a psychiatrist—at least that was my best guess.

"I might be able to help. I'll make a call. Can I reach you at this number in a few minutes?"

"You can. Thanks so much."

We disconnected and I pressed Tom's speed dial.

He immediately apologized for not phoning me first thing this morning, considering this was the first time we'd spent the night apart since our wedding.

"No problem, hon. You must be swamped. This is about Minnie's doctor. She just called me."

"Really? Did she tell you if they plan to commit Mrs. Schultz to a mental hospital?"

"No. Do you believe that will happen?"

"I don't know what to think about her. It's all so bizarre. Anyway, what did this doctor want?"

I explained Dr. Ross's request. Tom was hesitant at first, but after a few minutes of talking it through with me, he said the doctor and I could meet Candace at Minnie's house in an hour. He also told me to find out if Minnie had mentioned anything important to the doctor. I explained that it was unlikely Dr. Ross would say anything, considering she had to abide by patient-doctor confidentiality.

"I'm aware, but you could get our cats to talk if you put your mind to it. Please give it your best effort—but only if you feel comfortable."

"I'll try—but maybe whatever Minnie wants from home will tell you something about her."

"Good point," Tom said. "Candace will meet you over at the house. Good luck, Jilly. I love you."

Around ten a.m., Candace greeted me with a hug at Minnie's house on Mill Creek Road. The scent of spring, that fresh smell of new grass and blooming flowers, seemed in stark contrast to the yellow crime scene tape surrounding me everywhere I looked.

While we waited on the front sidewalk for Dr. Ross to arrive, Candace told me she'd uncovered names and addresses for Minnie's family yesterday and hoped to bring them all in for interviews today. "And get this. The ex-wife, one Marjorie Allen, already called a life insurance company about Chester Winston's policy—and they, in turn, called us."

I glanced at a small white SUV pulling into the driveway. It was probably the doctor. I turned my attention back to Candace. "You have a new suspect, then?"

"His kids are the beneficiaries, not her. As of right now, between the people Chester pissed off and his family, that suspect pool seems Olympic-size."

A woman exited the SUV. She looked to be in her thirties and wore a khaki skirt with a crisp rose-colored shirt. The color complemented her fair skin and short blond hair.

She introduced herself as Brenda Ross and shook hands with both of us. Dr. Ross turned a wide silver ring on her right hand around and around as Candace led the way onto the small front porch.

"I've never been to a crime scene before," she said. "In other words, I'm nervous."

Candace smiled reassuringly and unlocked the front door with keys I assumed she'd found yesterday. Unless they'd been in Minnie Schultz's possession and had somehow found their way to Candace.

The crime scene tape ripped apart as she opened the front door. Candace said, "Don't worry. The body is long gone. We might not even have to enter the room where the man died, depending on what Mrs. Schultz wants you to bring her from the house. I'll have to make notes on anything you take."

I felt claustrophobic in the narrow path of boxes the paramedics had made when they came here yesterday. They were stacked almost to the ceiling around us.

Dr. Ross reached into her bag and removed her phone. She put in her code and tapped an app and started reading. "A pair of slippers with cats on them. Her special toothpaste. Her moisturizer. A nightgown. Underwear."

I was standing between the two women, and knowing Candace as well as I did, I sensed her tension before she even spoke. Her eyes narrowed, she said, "That all sounds perfectly normal. Did Mrs. Schultz become lucid after a session with you?"

Dr. Ross smiled. "These are things she came up with after I suggested personal items would make her more comfortable. She actually first named off several of her cats when I asked her what I could bring her. She did mention a special quilt, though. It also has to do with the cats, from what I gathered."

"Ah." Candace blushed, understanding she'd made an incorrect assumption.

Meanwhile, I smiled at the mention of a quilt. Minnie Schultz might be a woman after my own heart.

Dr. Ross stared up and around at the wall of boxes. "Was Minnie in the process of moving out? Because she never told me anything about that—not that she would remember, considering her mental state. I know so little about her and—forgive me for saying this—but Deputy Jewel isn't exactly forthcoming."

"She's following orders from the police chief to share as little information as possible. Small towns are always populated by big mouths." Such a typical Candace answer. She was definitely in cop mode.

Dr. Ross seemed to stand taller and looked a little peeved. "Sorry, but that doesn't work for me. I understand you have a job to do, but so do I. Mine is to understand Minnie better. If she's moving—as in leaving a home she once shared with a now-deceased spouse—that can be very stressful. It could be related to her confused mental state."

Candace stared at Dr. Ross. "Okay, how about a little quid pro quo. What's wrong with Mrs. Schultz?"

I glanced from Candace back to Dr. Ross, feeling as if I were at a tennis match as they conversed.

"I'm not allowed to share much because I have to follow the law just as you do, but I understand you need answers. Once I've talked to the family members—when and if I can find them—and hopefully get a consensus on her treatment, I'll give you as much information as I can. I will probably be pursuing an involuntary commitment since Mrs. Schultz is a risk to herself, as far as I can tell from our first session. I *will* say there are other doctors involved in her care. I'm sure Deputy Jewel is aware of all the tests being run."

"We have the names of Mrs. Schultz's children. I can help with that," Candace said.

Why did this conversation have to happen in a cardboard tunnel? Maybe these two didn't have an ounce of claustrophobia, but I sure did. I cleared my throat. "Is there a roomier spot where we could talk about all this?"

"Sorry, yes," Candace said.

She led us through the maze of boxes down the hallway that led to the bedrooms and bathrooms. We entered what I assumed was Mrs. Schultz's bedroom. All the boxes in here had been shoved against one wall. The dated maple furniture—a double bed and a dresser—looked polished and scratch-free despite the fingerprint powder on almost every surface, including the windowsill. I could tell where prints had been lifted, and by my amateur estimation, Candace had found precious few of them in here.

A mint green chenille spread and white sheets sat in a sad mound in the center of the mattress—more evidence of how this house of cats, probably once comfortable and tidy, had been transformed. This makeover had to do not only with the murder, but with the decline in Minnie Schultz's mental health. I was beginning to hate these boxes surrounding us at every turn, even as my instincts shouted that they were probably important.

Candace whipped a wad of latex gloves out of her trouser pockets. She handed a pair to me and to the doctor and snapped a pair on herself. "Touch as few things as possible. We haven't opened any boxes yet because it is a monumental task and we'll need help. As for this room, I searched it myself, but I could have missed something." She pointed to her right. "She kept most of her clothing in the walk-in closet. The bathroom is in there." She gestured to a door straight ahead, the six-panel door also marred by black fingerprint dust.

If I looked past this cardboard jungle, I could see how Minnie's room must have been a comforting place for her. Several cat beds sat close to where the woman had slept and looked to be freshly laundered. Then I noticed the framed picture on her bedside table. Her wedding photo.

While Candace helped Dr. Ross gather the items on

Minnie's list, I examined the wedding photo more closely. From the style of Minnie's gown, I guessed the wedding had been in the late seventies or early eighties. The satin-and-lace dress reminded me of Princess Diana's, and Minnie's small fingers rested on her husband's arm. Her engagement ring sparkled as much as her eyes. Otto Schultz had worn a vested wool suit to his wedding and the chain of a pocket watch was clearly visible. He had kind brown eyes, as did Minnie. Their smiles reflected a sweetness I'd sensed when I'd met the woman yesterday. Yes, I'd found out firsthand that her kindness could not be disguised by any mental illness.

Finding the quilt that might bring Minnie some comfort was far more difficult than collecting clothing and toiletries. We were about to give up when Candace determined that there seemed to be more to the closet than she'd noticed before. She mumbled that the dimensions between the hallway and the bedroom seemed off. Sure enough, she was soon pushing aside the hanging clothes to reveal a panel secured by screws. She used a coin to turn those screws while Dr. Ross and I stood side by side watching with wide-eyed interest.

Candace removed a piece of thin plywood and set it aside. She said, "Pay dirt," so loud both the doctor and I started. Candace took a small but powerful flashlight from her utility belt and shined the light inside the compartment.

I bent to see what Candace was looking at and apparently my mind was on other things because I said, "I don't see any quilt. Of course, why would she keep a quilt hidden away? Maybe if it was a family heirloom she would have kept it locked up, but obviously it's not in there."

Candace looked over her shoulder. "Look at this stack of journals. And this." I could see what I assumed was a jewelry box.

Candace said, "The late husband was a jeweler. I wondered why I couldn't find anything he might have given Minnie. Bet this is the answer."

"Open it." I wanted to see inside as much as she did now.

"I'm inclined to bag all this as evidence and take it to the crime lab. The new ways of lifting DNA are beyond my expertise. But it is fascinating."

"Could I just peek at those journals?" Dr. Ross asked. "If I want to reach Minnie, those could offer valuable insight into her personality—that is, if she was the one who wrote in them."

"Sorry, Doc. Like I said, it's evidence." Candace stood. "We have a quilt to find, right? Then I'll bag and tag what I just found and we can get out of here."

Dr. Ross hadn't taken her eyes off the stack of small notebooks. They each had brightly colored floral covers and a few looked pretty tattered. She said, "I understand where you're coming from, Detective. But your find *has* given me a hint on how to reach into Minnie's clouded mind. I'll give her a new journal and see if she'll reveal something that way."

"Sounds like a great idea. Now let's find that quilt." Candace sidled past us.

"Do you have any idea what's in these boxes?" Dr. Ross asked as we continued the hunt for the quilt. "That might also offer insight into Minnie."

Candace hurried out of the room without answering. As we followed, I explained that the last time Shawn had been here aside from yesterday, there had been only a few boxes.

"That's odd. Maybe she'll write about this change in her life when I give her a journal." Dr. Ross seemed genuinely concerned about her patient, but like me, she was also curious.

We continued through the house, and on top of the washer we found a laundry basket filled with linens. I asked Candace if she'd seen anything resembling a quilt in the dirty clothes.

"I wasn't the one to search the laundry room, so—"

"There." I pointed at the basket. I saw what we were probably looking for through the slats in the plastic basket. "Can I get it out or do you need to do that, Candace?"

Candace took out her phone and snapped a few pictures. "Just to be safe," she said, "even though B.J. searched this area and had a camera with him."

Seconds later I was holding a small plaid quilt—one I recognized. As I held it, I mumbled, "I made this." I looked between Candace and Dr. Ross. "She probably got this from Shawn, since I make them for the kitties at the sanctuary all the time."

"*You* made that?" Candace stared from the quilt to me and back to the quilt.

I nodded, unsure how I felt about this discovery.

"You're connected to her, Jillian." Dr. Ross smiled. "That might prove to be a tremendous help."

"I—I guess." The hairs at the back of my neck prickled. A quilt is a special thing—I felt as if every single one I made and sent out into the world held a piece of me. I *was* connected to Minnie.

Dr. Ross touched my upper arm gently. "Can you be

there when I give this to her? It might be just the thing to orient her to reality. Right now she resides in a confusing and stressful world."

"Um, sure. Be glad to help." I glanced at Candace, who still eyed the box and the journals like a bird dog on a hunt. "Is that okay with you?"

"Is what okay?" Candace looked at me reluctantly. I'd interrupted her thoughts.

I explained about the hospital visit and she agreed it was fine. She seemed so distracted, however, that I wasn't sure she'd even heard what I said.

Dr. Ross typed the names of Minnie's children into her phone as Candace recited them. Then she said, "Can you bring the quilt to the hospital? You made it and it will mean more if she can connect it to you. Her room is on the third floor."

"Um . . . sure. I'd be glad to," I said.

Dr. Ross explained she had calls to make before heading to the hospital and also hoped to find a few blank journals to offer her patient.

She left the laundry room that led to the kitchen and we heard the front door close seconds later.

"Dr. Ross seems like a very caring person," I said.

Before Candace could reply, her phone rang. She listened to the caller and then said, "She's where?" Her free hand was on her hip and I saw her close her eyes in what I recognized as frustration. "Why did you *tell* her, B.J.?" She listened and then responded with, "Call Lois. She needs to be prepared. I don't want her to let the woman in to see Mrs. Schultz until I get there. I'm on my way."

She sighed heavily after she disconnected. "Come on and bring that quilt. The daughter has surfaced at the hospital and we need to intercept her."

Ten

Candace arrived at the hospital sooner than I did because, well, she had a vehicle with flashing blue lights and enjoyed taking advantage of the speed those lights permitted her.

I found her in the third-floor hallway taking a tongue-lashing from a very pregnant young woman who was angry—and to my way of thinking, understandably so. I heard her clearly state that she hadn't been informed about her mother's problems and she should have.

I walked up to them just as Candace said, "A man was murdered, Mrs. Kramer. You have to understand that our priorities lie with getting answers for the victim."

"I heard he was found in my mother's house." She sounded very angry, but at least she'd lowered her voice. "Why doesn't that make *her* family a priority—especially after she was discovered wandering around in her night-gown? Did she have blood all over her and you were trying to keep that information from us?"

This young woman, with a face so flushed the redness nearly hid her spattering of freckles, must have been Minnie's daughter, Greta. Her tawny brown hair was held back by clips, but many strands had escaped and surrounded her face. Her hair only added to how frazzled she seemed. This certainly wasn't a pleasant conversation for either of them, and the tension now spread to me. I don't do well with confrontations like this and I clutched Minnie's quilt to me as if it were a security blanket.

"I apologize." Candace tone was about as contrite as she could manufacture. But she didn't answer the question about the blood, and that had me wondering if there *was* a connection to the murder that Candace and Tom hadn't shared.

"Thank you for that, even if you didn't mean it." Greta rested a hand on her swollen abdomen and rubbed in circles.

Was she in pain? Was this tiff with Candace sending her into labor? I had the silly thought that it was a good thing we were in a hospital.

"Now, I want to see my mother." Greta had lifted her chin and the smug attitude didn't quite fit. I saw something in her dark brown eyes that told me she felt a tad guilty about her outburst. She might also be a little scared, if I was reading her right.

Deputy Lois Jewel, previously avoiding this clash from the safety of Minnie's room, stepped out into the hall. She straightened her shirt, tucking it more securely into her uniform trousers, all the while keeping her gaze on the floor. She spoke so quietly, her words were almost unintelligible. "Mrs. Schultz isn't in her room. She went for a scan. Don't know when she'll be back."

Greta glanced back and forth between Lois and Candace. "You have a policewoman in my mother's room? What's that about? And what kind of scan is she talking about? Who authorized it?"

Before Candace could address any of these questions, Dr. Ross came upon us so quietly I actually flinched.

She said, "The neurologist I consulted ordered a lot of tests."

Greta turned her attention from Candace and Lois. She looked first at Dr. Ross and then seemed to notice me for the first time. "And who are *these* people? What the heck is going on?"

Dr. Ross held out her hand. "I'm your mother's psychiatrist."

Greta stared at the doctor's hand, and after several seconds of awkward silence, she said, "You're a shrink? Does everyone who finds a body in their house require a psychiatrist?"

Dr. Ross dropped her hand. "When your mother was discovered on Main Street, no one knew about the dead man. She was very confused and I was assigned to her case because I was the doctor on call. She needs help, Greta."

The sincerity and gentle way she delivered this information had a calming effect on the young woman. Greta's features softened and she murmured, "Well, that's for sure," before turning her attention back to Candace. "Why are the police here? Is my mother under arrest?"

"We can answer all your questions in her room, okay?" Candace glanced at Dr. Ross as if seeking her approval.

The doctor said, "If Minnie returns to find a room crowded with people, I'm afraid that might upset or confuse her even more. We can go to one of the conference rooms."

"Let's do it," Candace said.

After giving Lois the personal items collected for Minnie, she instructed Lois to find Minnie and stay with her. The implication was she should have done this to begin with. Between Greta's arrival at the hospital and Lois's not accompanying Mrs. Schultz, my friend Candace was not a happy camper.

Dr. Ross led us to a frigid room on the first floor. A long, shiny table was surrounded by padded armchairs that rolled quietly on casters. The place smelled like . . . nothing. No sweetness from air fresheners, no disinfectant odors. It was a cold, sterile room with pictures of the hospital administrators on the wall. The aging unsmiling men's faces only added to the chill I felt in this room.

We took seats at the end of the table with Candace at the head. Greta and Dr. Ross sat to Candace's left and I sat to her right. I'd hung on to the quilt and folded it in my lap.

Greta stared at me with narrowed eyes. "First of all, who are *you*? Another police officer in plain clothes? Are khakis and cotton shirts the new uniform for the Mercy Police Department?"

Her caustic tone had returned, and I doubted she really wanted answers to her multiple questions.

Before I could speak, Dr. Ross responded. "This is Jillian Hart. From what I've been told, she helped the emergency room staff yesterday because your mother had a kitten with her. She refused to let anyone take it, but Ms. Hart has a way with cats and with people. She and your mother had a great conversation and she willingly gave the kitten to Jillian. I understand he's named after your late father."

For the first time since I'd arrived here, Greta opened her mouth to speak but no words came out. She blinked several times and glanced at each of us. Finally, she quietly said to no one in particular, "She had a cat named Otto with her?"

Candace nodded. "A young cat, from what I understand. That's partly why the doctors in the emergency room decided to call in Dr. Ross to consult on your mother's case. Mrs. Schultz is not . . . not—"

"All there?" Greta finished.

Candace blushed. "That's one way of putting it."

"Has she ever had an episode like this before? Where she wandered away from home?" Dr. Ross asked.

Greta leaned back in the chair and used both hands to soothe her belly with slow circles. "No. She's always been a little eccentric. She does have seven cats, a tiny fact that pushes her needle toward crazy cat lady, right?"

"She had about *two dozen* cats," I offered. Maybe I shouldn't have spoken, but this young woman needed *all* the information if she was here to help her mother.

"What?" Greta's gaze trapped mine with shock and disbelief. She then turned to Dr. Ross, who nodded in confirmation.

"I take it you haven't visited your mother lately?" Candace asked.

"I'll state the obvious." Greta's irritation had returned. "I'm pregnant. I shouldn't be around cats."

"Actually, you shouldn't be cleaning litter boxes, is all. This whole thing about . . ." I stopped myself. This wasn't why we were sitting here. "Sorry. I've veered off topic. The important thing is, I'll be keeping little Otto safe until your mother feels better. She seemed very protective of him. Now, I'm sure the doctor and Detective

Carson have more questions for you." I slid my chair back a little, determined to keep my mouth shut.

Candace began those questions and learned not much more than I'd heard from Belle yesterday about how Greta had lost her father and that she had twin brothers. It became obvious that Greta hadn't even *spoken* to her mother in months, a realization that saddened me.

"You have no idea why your mother suddenly started collecting cats in the last year?" Candace asked.

"Started? You don't consider seven a collection?" Greta said disdainfully. "My brothers and I wanted nothing to do with a hoarding situation, and that's why we limited our contact with Mama."

Candace looked at Dr. Ross. "Tell us about hoarding, Dr. Ross. Does it lead to confusion?"

Dr. Ross cleared her throat. "Hoarding includes pretty specific parameters. It's actually an obsessive-compulsive disorder—or *usually* is, I should say. Confusion is *not* a typical symptom. Even though I saw an excessive number of large boxes stacked in Mrs. Schultz's home, I'm not sure that I am ready to label your mother a hoarder. Her home was clean and pretty tidy. Hoarders are usually not tidy and organized."

"What boxes? And you've confirmed she had way more than seven cats. But you're saying she's *not* a hoarder?" It was Greta's turn to appear confused.

I thought about Shawn and how he didn't consider Minnie a hoarder, either—and he'd seen plenty of them in his time running his no-kill shelter.

Candace said, "You want a full explanation, I know, Mrs. Kramer. Let's try to keep this as simple as possible for today. I have a few more questions before you and Dr. Ross visit your mother."

Thank you, Candace. But how could she get answers with Greta presenting these multiple-question sentences every time she spoke? Maybe the woman was nervous and this was how she dealt with it. But aside from her irritation, she seemed almost . . . detached.

"I've told you about our family," Greta said. "I don't even know who's dead, so how can I answer questions about who my mother might have killed and why? Was it someone you think I know?"

I sighed inwardly. It seemed as if it might be impossible for Greta Kramer to *not* ask questions. Candace's tight-lipped expression told me she was losing patience.

"First of all," Candace said in a quiet, measured tone, "no one says your mother killed anyone. Second, the dead man's name was Chester Winston. Did you know him?"

"The name sounds familiar, but that's all. He's not a relative or anything." She glanced at the gigantic clock on the wall to her right. "Can we speed this up? I have errands to run before I return home. My due date is next week and I'm not sure I'll make it that long. I need to stock the pantry and fridge. But before you judge me—and I can tell that's what happening—I *did* come here to see my mother, not to be interrogated by the police."

I blinked, troubled by how she'd reacted to hearing a dead man's name. None of the emotions or lack thereof that Greta Kramer had displayed helped me understand her. Maybe the pregnancy and the obvious family estrangement had something to do with her behavior.

Perhaps once she saw her mother, she'd be different. Or so I wanted to believe.

Candace continued on, not swayed by Greta's demand that she hurry up. "Chester Winston was the animal control officer for our county. Did your mother ever mention his name—I mean, at a period in time when you *were* speaking to her?"

Dr. Ross sat straighter. This line of questioning seemed to interest her. Or perhaps she wanted to see Greta's reaction to Candace putting the young woman in her place—because she'd accomplished that much as far as I was concerned.

"Oh, *him*. No wonder his name sounded familiar. That's who died?"

I closed my eyes. I rarely get annoyed with people, but Greta's way of dealing with this interview was wearing on me.

"So you *do* know him," Candace said. "Ever meet him at your mother's house—I mean when you felt it was safe to be there?"

Before she could answer, the muted buzz of a vibrating phone made everyone focus on Dr. Ross. She looked embarrassed and said, "Let me just see what this is about."

She stood, took her phone from her trouser pocket and turned away from the table.

"Could you answer the question, Mrs. Kramer?" Candace leaned toward Greta, hoping to finally get somewhere.

But Dr. Ross interrupted with "Mrs. Kamer and I need to meet Dr. Patel upstairs. It's important."

"Who is Dr.—"

But this latest question from Greta was cut short by Candace. "The doc says move, we move. Let's go."

I actually believed she welcomed the end of this frustrating interview. I knew I did. I'd grown so anxious I'd wrinkled the quilt I'd been clinging to for dear life.

"I can come back later and bring Minnie the quilt if—"

"No. I think we should all go," Candace said. "According to Dr. Ross, you seem to have a rapport with Mrs. Schultz."

We rode on the elevator in silence, but I noticed that Dr. Ross trapped her lower lip with her teeth and was breathing a little too fast. Something was definitely wrong. Urgently wrong.

Eleven

Dr. Patel, a small man with delicate hands and thick lenses in his glasses, met us outside Minnie's room. His features seemed to indicate he was of Indian or Pakistani descent.

"I did not expect an entourage, Dr. Ross," he said pleasantly. "I must speak to you in private if this suits you."

"Of course. But this young woman is Mrs. Schultz's daughter. She needs to hear about your findings."

"Of course. I did not realize you had located her family." With that, Greta, Dr. Ross and Dr. Patel disappeared into a room at the end of the corridor, leaving Candace and me standing in the hall outside Minnie's room.

Seconds later, a scrub-suited aide, accompanied by Lois Jewel, wheeled Minnie Schultz toward us. She offered a "Why, hello there," as her wheelchair passed us and entered her room.

But despite the greeting, I saw no hint she recognized me.

As Candace began to follow them, I stayed back.

"I'll leave this to you. In fact, perhaps I should head home and—"

Candace used her best stage whisper, grabbed my arm and pulled me toward her. "Nonsense. The woman needs that quilt you're wringing the life out of, if nothing else."

By the time we entered, Minnie was settling herself in the bed. The aide finished pulling the white cotton blanket and sheet over her knees and left with the wheelchair.

Minnie pointed at me. "Where do I know you from?"

"We met yesterday," I said.

"Here at the hotel?" she answered.

Perhaps Greta Kramer came by her questioning conversational style via genetics, upbringing or both.

"We were downstairs in a different part of this . . . facility." I didn't want to upset her by telling her this was a far cry from a hotel.

"I'm Detective Carson, Mrs. Schultz—a friend of Deputy Jewel's." Candace nodded at Lois.

Minnie reached out for Lois's hand. "Then you're a friend of mine, too. Lois is the sweetest thing. She has been such a help." Minnie's smile grabbed at me. It was as if she couldn't quite remember how to form the expression—like it was hard work. "Could you get me a soda pop, Lois? I'd like a Cheerwine, please."

"Sure." Lois left the room as fast as a cat with its tail on fire.

I wanted out of here, too—before Dr. Patel reappeared. At this moment I fully understood that what he was now telling Minnie's daughter and Dr. Ross had nothing to do with mental illness. Something was seriously wrong with Minnie Schultz. The fact that

Minnie had no clue only added to how much this upset me. She could be dying. I managed to say, "I brought you something, Minnie," in as normal a tone as I could muster.

Her eyes traveled to the quilt I held out to her. This time she smiled from her heart. She recognized the quilt. Seeing something familiar did seem to help—but it felt like meager help. Dr. Patel, the neurologist, would deliver a truth I was certain I didn't want to know.

"Where's Otto?" Minnie asked. "Are you bringing me his quilt because something bad has happened to him?"

"No, nothing like that," I said quickly. I whipped out my phone.

When I showed her the live feed of little Otto curled up with Chablis, she cocked her head. "He's on TV? How did that happen?"

Candace glanced at the smartphone screen. "He's a cute boy and Jillian is taking good care of him. But right now I need to ask you a few questions about why you left your house."

"It had become uninhabitable—that's why. All those boxes everywhere. I suppose they have something to do with Chester, but I'm not quite sure what." Minnie squinted as if trying to remember. "Perhaps he thought he could take over my home since he started bringing me all those cats. I'm confused about that. Sure, he brought me some sweet babies, but that didn't mean I wanted to adopt Chester, too."

I almost laughed, but the seriousness of this situation reminded me immediately that even nervous laughter was wrong. Obviously she remembered Chester, but I doubted she understood he was dead.

"When was the last time you saw Mr. Winston?" Candace was pressing on, no doubt understanding her time for questions would soon be cut short.

Minnie searched the ceiling. Then her gaze trailed in the direction of the window. "Why, I have no earthly idea. He gave me that contraption he called a phone." She nodded at my hand. "Looked a lot like your little TV. I didn't understand it, especially when he said we had to talk through it. He seemed to think we didn't need to be connected to a real telephone and my words would travel through the air if I pushed a few buttons. Silly man."

Candace held out her cell. "He gave you something like this?"

She squinted at the phone. "Not exactly like that. But close. He said it was our secret. I do believe the man needed Dr. Ross's help more than I do. She's a psychiatrist, you know. Someone thinks I'm not parked close enough to the curb, if you know what I mean."

Candace smiled. "I know exactly what you mean. Where is that thing Chester gave you?"

"I couldn't tell you, and that's awful because I used to have such a good memory. Maybe it will come to me later." Minnie seemed troubled that she couldn't remember and my heart went out to her.

"How often did Mr. Winston visit you?" Candace asked.

"Lately it seemed like he was at the house all the time, bringing me one cat or another. Mind you, I *love* cats. They all deserve to be cared for, but I am getting overwhelmed. I might have to just say no the next time. It's so much work to make sure the place stays clean and all the kitties are well fed." Minnie turned to me. "Since you went to my home and brought me my quilt, you couldn't miss seeing how crowded all the poor animals are with those boxes everywhere."

"You're right about that," I replied. "You're saying you don't know what's in the boxes or where they came from?"

"They came from the UPS man and the FedEx woman—she's a pretty thing and strong as an ox. I was hoping my boys would come by and get rid of them." Suddenly her eyes filled. "Of course, Harris isn't strong enough to move much of anything. Henry isn't, either, for that matter. Why doesn't Greta visit anymore?"

The sudden change in direction, from the cold hard facts to the emotion of a woman missing her children, brought tears to my eyes as well. I took Minnie's hand and rested it on the quilt I'd placed on her lap. "We hope to find out." I looked to Candace for guidance.

She seemed to be at a loss for words. The switch in subject matter had gotten to her, too.

Our silence was interrupted by the entrance of the two doctors and Greta Kramer.

Minnie whispered, "Oh, my word," and stretched her arms out to her daughter.

Greta went to her mother's bedside and the two embraced. It was obvious Greta had been crying. What an emotional day for everyone.

Dr. Ross pulled a straight-back chair from the corner and set it next to Minnie's bed. "Greta, why don't you sit down?"

Minnie nodded. "Yes, sit, but I had no idea you were pregnant. What's your husband's name again?"

Greta glanced up at Dr. Ross before saying, "Aaron. Remember, Mama?"

Minnie smiled, but it was that strange look again, as

if she were being asked to understand a foreign language. "Yes. He's Aaron."

Dr. Patel introduced himself and then asked Candace and me to leave.

But Minnie said, "These people can hear whatever you have to say. They have been the kindest ladies and have helped me so much."

Dr. Patel glanced at Greta for her approval. She gripped both her mother's hands. "If that's what makes you happy, Mama."

"Go ahead, Dr. Patel." Minnie looked at her daughter. "See? I remembered."

"You have a medical problem that needs to be taken care of right away." Dr. Patel sure cut right to the chase. "You have a brain tumor, Mrs. Schultz."

I might have half expected this, but the doctor's delivery was so blunt, it shocked me. I supposed it was rather like ripping off a Band-Aid stuck fast—rip it clean and quick and it won't hurt as much.

Minnie blinked. "Well, then, let's get this taken care of." She said it so matter-of-factly, as if having a brain tumor was like having a paper cut.

"I have a few surgeons in mind who can do the procedure you need. Ethically I cannot play favorites, so you and your daughter will choose. My educated guess is that this is a nonmalignant tumor, but any surgery on the brain is dangerous."

Nonmalignant. Good. Brain surgery? Not so good.

Candace glanced my way. "Perhaps we should leave them to discuss the details?"

"Of course." I looked at Minnie. "If there is *anything* I can do for you, tell Dr. Ross. She has my number."

"What about Lois?" Minnie said. "Where's Lois?"

Dr. Ross said, "She's outside your room. I'll send her in to say good-bye."

"She won't be staying?" Minnie's eyes pleaded in Candace's direction.

"She'll be by to visit, but I hope you understand we really need her help at the police station." Candace patted Minnie's arm and left the room as quickly as gossip flew around Mercy.

"Um, can I give you a hug?" Though I wanted to get out of here before I started crying, I felt close to Minnie. I had the feeling Candace's hasty retreat was to hide her emotions as well. She felt connected to this woman, too.

Seconds later, I joined Candace and Lois outside Minnie's room. Lois held the Cheerwine soda tightly—so tightly, in fact, that I thought she might dent the can. Candace must have just delivered the news to her fellow officer because Lois was shaking her head sadly.

We started down the hall toward the elevator after Lois had hurried in and dropped off the soda. But we all turned when we heard Dr. Ross call, "Wait."

"I was afraid of this," she said after joining us. "She did not present as early-onset Alzheimer's. It wasn't a mental illness involving memory loss and confusion, either. I wanted you to know that I have agreed to assist Greta when she gets in touch with the rest of her family. Since her baby is due within the next week or so, she asked for my help, even though this is not a psychiatric issue at all. It seems she's not sure her brothers will want to be involved in her mother's aftercare."

Candace sounded irritated when she said, "Maybe they'll just have to step up. Your mother is your mother and you care for her no matter what. You can be sure they'll each get a chance to visit my interview room down at the station. I might have a hard time withholding that particular piece of my mind."

"Why wouldn't they want to be involved?" I asked.

"It doesn't surprise me," Candace said. "I've talked to them on the phone and I wasn't impressed with either of them. They didn't seem to care that their mother was in the hospital or that a dead man was found in her house." Candace lowered her voice. "This isn't for public consumption, but be very careful, Dr. Ross. Harris and Henry Schultz knew the dead man and his family. Seems Chester's kids and Minnie's sons went to high school together. I didn't let on that I knew this when I spoke to them. I'm waiting to see how forthcoming they'll be when we sit down face-to-face."

I could tell when Lois's mouth formed a surprised O that it was *big* news to her that the brothers had a connection to Chester's family. But Lois came from a big city, not small-town America, so these links between folks weren't as common there as they were here. I wasn't the least bit astonished that they knew one another. What *did* surprise me was that Belle failed to mention this—because surely she must have known.

Dr. Ross said, "Thanks for letting me know. Perhaps I'll let Greta handle this herself, after all. I would hope that learning their mother is gravely ill will make a difference to those young men." Brenda Ross glanced back in the direction of Minnie's room.

"Please don't mention anything else about Chester," Candace warned.

"I promise." Dr. Ross continued on her way.

As we entered the elevator, Candace said, "Guess it's time for me to pull those twins in for an interview.

Who knows? Perhaps they'll develop an ounce of compassion and come to their mother's bedside before her surgery."

"Maybe," I replied. But if they'd already shown that they didn't care, why would this change their minds? Unless they thought she might die and there was money involved. Money always had a way of changing certain people's minds.

Twelve

By the time I arrived home, my stomach growled in protest at being neglected. I'm not one to forget to eat, but I simply hadn't had an opportunity. But lunchtime was long past and dinner might have to be pizzas I delivered to the police station so I could share a little time with Tom.

The cats seemed pretty darn upset at my absence. They were getting used to me talking to them through the camera, but it would never replace being here with them. Feeling guilty, I sat in the middle of the kitchen floor and gave each one of them some much-needed attention.

Otto had been left alone too long, and after I slapped together a cheese sandwich with mustard, I retrieved him from the basement room where I'd put him before leaving the house this morning. He purred loudly but wanted out of my arms the minute I reached the kitchen. He walked right over to Dashiell, the only one of our cats who'd hissed at him, and rubbed against him. This little guy certainly had moxie and was rewarded with another hiss for his efforts. Dashiell walked off, but my other three were happy to sniff Otto all over and Merlot even bumped heads with him. This hit from my gentle giant sent poor Otto sprawling, but he quickly got up, and soon a game of chase between Syrah, Merlot and Otto ensued.

The happiness watching them bond, play and just be such typical cats relaxed me as the stress of the last two days melted away. Chester's murder was still a nightmare, of course, and if I could assist Tom and Candace, I would. What surprised me, however, was the strong need I felt to help Minnie Schultz. Maybe it was because her family's behavior bothered me. True, her daughter had been supportive once she found out about the brain tumor, but why had it taken such an awful diagnosis? I didn't know their history other than what Belle had told me. All I knew was that Minnie Schultz needed all the support she could get.

I decided to think through all that happened in the last two days by sitting in my sewing room and working on a quilt order that was nearly finished. I always thought better with needlework in hand. I'd already machine-sewn the bindings on the three plaid kitty quilts ordered by a returning customer. Now I needed to hand-stitch those bindings onto the back of each one. That was the last step, but the playful Otto wasn't about to let me be. I kept having to stop and get him out of a drawer or off a shelf. When he crawled up my leg—his little claws like needles through my khakis—I gave up. Otto needed attention and I didn't blame him.

He and I played for the next thirty minutes. He liked the feathers on a wand the best and chased the toy as I swiped it along the floor in the living room. Of course, what cat could ignore feathers on a stick? Soon all five cats took turns. Otto tired first, of course, and while I continued to sit cross-legged on the floor and play with my four kitties, the little one crawled up onto my shoulder and purred in my ear. He was soon asleep.

I held him gently against my cheek and grabbed a little quilt from the basket near the sofa. After laying it out on the sofa, I set him down. Otto curled into a little black-and-white ball and continued his nap.

Once all the cats grew bored with feathers, my thoughts turned to Tom. I was so used to having him call me frequently throughout the day or even come home and surprise me with flowers or kisses or just to chat about whatever they were working on. Not now. Not with a murder to solve. Gosh, I missed him.

But I could do a little something for him and the rest of those folks working the case. I texted him and suggested I bring pizzas around seven this evening. He quickly texted back and told me to call B.J. for details on what everyone might like on their pie. So I did, and once I had ideas for several different pizzas, I was free, at least for now, to finish binding those quilts.

Close to seven that evening, I walked past a lone man wearing dirty blue jeans and an equally filthy shirt sleeping on one of the benches outside the door to the police station. He didn't stir and I was glad the smell of pizza didn't wake him. I supposed I would have shared a slice or two had he asked, but I'd rather be talking to my police friends than with whoever this guy was. He could be waiting for a ride or, as was the case at times, he might be hoping to be arrested for loitering so he'd have a place to sleep in jail, a place only a tad more comfortable than the bench he'd chosen.

Once I was inside the waiting area, a young woman I didn't recognize stood and smiled broadly. She couldn't be more than twenty years old.

"Hey there. I'm Jillian Hart, Chief Stewart's wife." It still seemed odd to call myself his wife, maybe because it was rare that I had to introduce myself that way. Living in a small town made such introductions unnecessary most of the time.

"Oh, hi. When I met my dad for the first time, he mentioned you." She held out her hand.

Her fingers, long and thin, were cool to the touch and her skin was as pale as a winter moon.

"Your dad?"

"Mike Baca," she said.

I almost gasped in surprise. Mike had never mentioned a daughter. "I am so sorry . . . What is your name again?"

"Grace. Grace Templeton. I was adopted by my stepfather. He's gone, too. Heart attack. He was Mom's husband number four. Mike—my biological father—was number two. I only met him once, right before my mother called to tell me he'd died, too. I wish we'd had more time to get to know each other."

I blinked away my surprise and found I was struck by her smile. Yes, very much like Mike's, and here she was, talking about loss and pain and smiling the whole time. But her blue-green eyes told the truth. I saw sadness there and it tugged at my heart.

"We would have reached out . . . had we known about you."

She nodded knowingly. "I was getting ready to leave the country when we talked. He said I would need a proper introduction, that he wanted to surprise everyone here." She gestured toward the hallway lined with closed doors. "I wanted to come and make sure everyone knew—because that's what he wanted." There came Mike's smile again. It was eerie.

"He was one of the best men I ever knew." But terrible at choosing partners—a trait that had turned out to be a fatal flaw.

Meanwhile, the pizzas might be ice-cold by the time my friends were ready to eat. But there was so much I wanted to know about Grace. The questions, however, would have to wait.

She must have read my mind because she said, "Oh, the food. Everyone has been talking about pizza ever since you called B.J. Let me help you take them to the back."

I handed her the two top boxes. "You're assisting with dispatch?" We walked through the swinging half door that separated the waiting area from the rest of the police offices.

"Yes. Answering phones, taking messages, doing what I can to help. My dad must have been talking to me because I knew something was wrong here in Mercy. I called yesterday, the second after I had the dream, and talked to B.J. I dropped everything and came here. School will still be waiting should I decide to return, but there isn't much work for art history majors these days anyway."

"You quit school to come here?"

"I did. Sometimes you have to do what you're called upon to do."

We'd reached the break room—the *deserted* break room—at the end of the corridor. I set the pizzas on the small table in the center of the room.

"Chief Stewart has everyone in his office," Grace said. "I'll tell them the food is here."

With that, she went across the hall and knocked on Tom's door. Soon I was joined by Candace, Morris Ebeling, Lois and B.J. Morris, once Candace's partner, had gained a few pounds around the middle. Since he was pushing seventy, maybe Tom had him doing more desk work.

Grace took a slice of pizza and walked back to the waiting area and the ringing phone.

"What about Tom?" I asked Candace.

She already had her mouth full of cheese and pepperoni but managed, "Still working."

B.J. hadn't started eating yet and filled me in. They had just made a revised list of witnesses and possible suspects after Shawn offered his information, as well as tips from concerned citizens who'd called in. Tom was making the timeline more complete.

I put several slices of his favorite pizza as well as a cheese slice for me into an empty box and walked our dinner over to his office. That sandwich I'd eaten earlier hadn't quite done the job.

After I opened the door all the way, I saw that his blue eyes were shadowed beneath, his heavy lids showing his complete exhaustion. When small-town crime wasn't just graffiti and jaywalking anymore, the load on the officers was horrendous.

He glanced away from his computer and his smile erased some of the weariness at once. "My favorite person in the world carrying my favorite food. Doesn't get any better than that."

I set the box on his desk. He came around and pulled

me to him. The hug turned into a kiss that lasted so long
I almost lost track of where we were.

"I missed you," Tom said when the kiss ended.

"Same here. Yet it's only been one night without
each other. Now, time to eat and you can tell me about
Grace Templeton. What the heck, Tom?"

But Tom devoured one slice of pizza before saying
anything. I wondered if he'd been living on coffee all
day. Finally, after he wiped his mouth and swigged
water out of the economy-size bottle that had been sitting on his desk, he spoke.

"She just showed up. Said she was Mike's daughter
and knew she had to be here to help us. I didn't have
time for questions. B.J. needed relief and the last woman
we had in here just couldn't manage all the calls and
messages. When there's a murder, everyone believes they
have answers. The number of calls isn't as bad as when I
worked in North Carolina, but it's been close."

"What are people saying?" I placed my pizza crust
in the box and wiped my fingers on a napkin.

"Some are convinced that Minnie Schultz is a de-
mented killer, based on town gossip after her trek down
Main Street. But the victim's being vilified far more."

"They think they're helping to solve his murder by
calling up and saying terrible stuff?" I said.

"I suppose. It baffles me and makes for a slew of
information that we can't ignore. There could be a clue
in there somewhere."

"I'll answer the phone, too, if you need me to."

"I did plan to ask for your help, but not with that. We
have to go through those boxes in Minnie's house now
that we have a search warrant that covers absolutely

everything on the premises. I can't risk evidence being tossed out of court because we rushed a warrant—not with so much stuff in that place. I was wondering if you could keep an inventory as Candace and B.J. go through them. One of them will dictate into their recorder, but I want written documentation as well. But I do have to warn you about that room where we found the body."

"Oh." I paused to consider this. "I'd have to go in there?"

"Probably. There's not much room to move boxes around. Here's the thing. Chester wasn't dead right after he was hit on the head. Head wounds bleed profusely and—"

"Would he have lived if someone called nine-one-one?" The thought horrified me. What an awful way to die.

"He might have survived," Tom said. "We don't know for certain since the autopsy isn't in. We did find evidence of what criminal profilers call 'undoing,' but I'm not sure about that."

I squinted at him, not understanding.

He read me and went on. "Some people—like a good defense lawyer—might say the killer had shown remorse. Maybe we should leave it at that." Tom stood and picked up the pizza box.

My gaze followed him as he walked around his desk, ready to leave the room. "Wait a minute. You're obviously troubled. You need to tell me what's wrong. That's what this marriage thing means—that we share whatever upsets either one of us."

He sighed. "I never saw anything like this before, Jillian. The killer poured cat litter over Chester's head."

My hand went to my lips and I whispered, "Oh my

gosh." I swallowed hard before speaking. "That's just dreadful."

"Maybe it was remorse, maybe it was anger. We simply don't know. Most of the tips we've received show how many people disliked Chester Winston—and the word *dislike* is being kind. Unfortunately, that expands the suspect pool to oceanic proportions."

"I guess you have to ask that question Candace always mentions. Why did this person have to die?"

"And why now?" He glanced at his watch. "Where has the time gone? I have to get back to work."

I followed Tom out of his office and saw B.J. hurrying toward the waiting area. I was used to seeing him casually dressed and behind a desk. Of course, I knew he was over six feet, but the khaki stripes down the sides of his dark green uniform pants made him seem even taller.

Grace waited at the end of the hall holding the phone out. Concern clouded her wide eyes.

B.J. took the cordless phone, but he turned away from us so I couldn't hear what he was saying.

Tom went on into the break room with the pizza box, but I stayed behind. They were used to crises here, but I had a sick feeling in my gut.

When B.J. turned around, I saw his grim young face and knew something bad had happened.

He nodded at me as I stood in the hallway feeling as if my legs were stuck in concrete. I wasn't sure I wanted to hear what he was about to tell the others.

But I was so close to the door I couldn't help but hear when he said, "It's that shrink. She's been in a bad wreck. They don't know if she'll make it."

Thirteen

Even though I'd been told that Dr. Ross had been rushed into surgery, I decided to head to the hospital anyway. The spitting kind of rain we'd experienced this evening had now intensified into the real thing, and though I didn't have far to run to my van, my short hair was wet and plastered to my head by the time I slid behind the wheel. I was hoping I could talk to Dr. Ross's family and offer support. I felt the need to do *something*. In the short time since we'd met, I realized I liked and respected her.

Meanwhile, I'd heard that Tom and Candace would be heading for the spot where the accident had occurred. Apparently the county sheriff's deputies who responded to the accident said something was wrong at the scene—but that was all I knew. I couldn't hear any more of the whispered conversation between B.J. and Candace.

I didn't get a chance to tell Tom I planned to drive to the hospital. By the time I reached my destination, the sky was pitch-black with rolling charcoal clouds and thunder rumbling angrily. Though I'd spent far too much time in that hospital in the last two days, I'd felt such a strong pull to return here for Dr. Ross. Once I'd parked, I pulled up the cat cam on my phone and activated the chat feature. I felt renewed guilt at leaving my kitties alone so much since the murder.

I could see the cats, but they could only hear me when I said, "Calling all kitties," into my phone. To my surprise Otto showed up first. He'd caught on right away to this camera thing, it would seem. We'd had a black-and-white barn cat at my grandparents' farm named Jezebel, and I swore that cat could read minds. She was loving and the best mouser we'd ever had. Yes, tuxedo cats were quite smart. I took several screenshots of Otto and saved them to my camera. That guy was so darn cute.

Syrah came next and sat looking up at the camera and our little speaker. Otto rubbed up against Syrah as if asking him to explain this weird phenomenon. Soon the whole clowder was listening to me tell them where I was and that I would be home soon. No, they couldn't understand, but I felt better just seeing their faces so acutely interested in hearing my voice.

By the time I shook my umbrella as dry as I could outside the hospital, I wondered if Candace and Tom had learned anything about the doctor's accident. The halls were oddly deserted, the bustle of the day gone. I asked at the information desk about the surgery waiting room and was directed to the second floor.

One man sat alone in a corner, his balding head down as he stared at his clenched hands. I chose a seat on the green vinyl couch not far from his chair and set my damp umbrella on the floor. My hair was nearly dry, thank goodness, or I would have caught a serious chill in this cold place.

The man glanced up when I sat down. His eyes showed fear—and those eyes were so like Dr. Ross's I knew at once he was a relative.

I spoke softly before he could look down again. "Are you here for Dr. Ross?"

He pulled in his lower lip and nodded. "Do you know her?"

"We only just met, but I felt so . . . so comfortable in her presence. When I heard about the accident, I wanted to offer my support."

He squinted at me. "You're a patient of hers?"

"No. I'm simply a new friend."

"How did you hear about this? Was it on the news?" He glanced at his watch. He then mumbled, "No. The news doesn't come on for a while yet."

"I was at the police station when I heard. My husband is the police chief in Mercy."

His expression showed he understood. "You met her because of the lady they found in Mercy, the one Brenda was helping?"

"That's right. Will she be okay?"

His face grew grim again. "She suffered a head injury, internal injuries and broken bones. Several doctors scrubbed in on the operation. I wanted to be in there, too. I'm a doctor as well, but since I'm her brother, they sent me out here with very few facts. This is a hard place for family members to wait. I have a new appreciation for what they go through."

"I'm Jillian Hart, and you're . . . ?"

"Peyton Ross." He tilted his head and pointed at me. "You're the one who took the cat from Brenda's new patient. She told me what she could about that situation, but I don't know the woman's name, just yours. Confidentiality and all that."

"Yes. The woman is still here in the hospital and—"

"Jillian?" I turned to see my stepdaughter, Kara, striding into the room. Her umbrella had done a good job keeping her dry. Her long dark hair wasn't wet, and her trousers and shirt bore not a spot of rain.

I stood and we hugged before I introduced her to the other Dr. Ross, explaining his relationship to the woman in surgery.

"I am so sorry, Dr. Ross," she said. "I was following up on the accident for the newspaper. I'm the editor. How is your sister?"

He shook his head slightly. "I appreciate your concern, but I doubt Brenda would like anything written about this . . . *if* she pulls through." His voice cracked as he went on. "She's my only family."

Kara sat on the edge of the chair next to him. "If I write about her and what happened, maybe someone will come forward. There could have been witnesses."

He squinted again, accentuating the lines worn into his face. "Why do they need *witnesses*?"

Kara blinked.

I swallowed hard. He obviously had no idea there was anything suspicious about what had happened to his sister.

"No one told you this might not have been an accident?" Kara said.

He drew back. *"What?"*

"From the initial examination of evidence at the scene, the police believe she was run off the road."

He collapsed back in his chair, looking confused,

tears welling. "It could have been one of her patients," he mumbled. "People never quite understand that therapists can be at risk."

"Did she mention any patient she thought might direct violence toward her?" Kara asked.

"She would never tell me; she would never tell anyone unless the situation was so serious she feared for others. She *never* feared for herself."

"Sounds like a special and dedicated doctor," Kara said. "You do understand I'm here to help, to get the story out there. Anything I report might prompt a witness to come forward."

"Shouldn't I be talking to the police rather than a reporter? I mean, you seem like a perfectly nice person, but I'd prefer to hear from the police first."

Time for me to speak up, I decided. "Kara is my stepdaughter, and I can assure you, she would never put anything out there if my husband, Chief Stewart, didn't give his approval. I don't know if you're from Mercy, but Kara is responsible, honest and wants the news to be in the public interest." It sounded like a speech, and an unconvincing one, at that.

He glanced back and forth between us. "My practice is in Columbia, so I live there. Here's what I'm willing to tell you. Brenda only moved to Mercy so she could be closer to this hospital and the surrounding rural towns. She believed she could help in this area of the state better than in an urban setting. There's very little psychiatric care around here." He took a deep breath. "That's the kind of person she is. Write about that."

Kara offered a small smile. "She has a mission. She's one of the good guys. You want people to know that, right? You want to find out why this happened."

"I do. But only after I speak with the police." He looked at me. "Is your husband the one investigating?"

I nodded. "He went out to the crash scene after getting a call from the sheriff's deputies who responded. He'll know everything they do by now. Do you want to speak with him?"

"Yes. Absolutely."

So I called Tom, explained where I was and then handed the phone over to Peyton Ross. The two had a short conversation, and once he disconnected, he told us he'd been assured that Kara was telling the truth and that any publicity would be helpful. He added, "I understand what you're saying, but I'm not sure how I can assist you."

Kara had taken her computer tablet from her leather bag and readied her stylus. "When did you last speak with your sister?"

"This morning. She said she had met with the police about a client. I know Brenda was troubled by this particular patient. But she couldn't say much, just had a little rant about how families made things so difficult for her to do her job sometimes. Then she texted me later, but I couldn't make sense of it." He reached into his pocket and pulled out his cell phone. After tapping his phone several times, he read, "'Something not right. Must go . . .'" Then his eyes widened in horror. "Oh my Lord. Could she have been texting and driving? Sending me this unfinished message right before the accident?"

I said, "Do you know if she drove hands-free?"

He pressed the heel of his palm into his forehead, eyes tightly closed. "Yes. Of course. How could my mind have gone there? She would take calls from patients at all hours of the day and night and always went hands-free in the car." He glanced at the phone again. "Wait. The time on the message is much earlier than when I got the call about the accident . . . or *incident*. She must have been in her office . . . or here."

I wanted to rest a hand on his forearm but didn't. Something told me he wouldn't be receptive and that I might disrupt his thoughts.

"I wish I knew what the heck she meant," he mumbled.

Kara said, "Did she have a receptionist? Someone who knew her schedule and could help you understand this message better?"

"No. She handled everything herself and purposely never carried a high patient load. You see, she dealt mostly with patients in this hospital waiting for transfer to psychiatric facilities or with those clients who ended up committed for days or weeks. Psychotic or bipolar patients can go off the deep end and need their medications readjusted. That was her specialty. She was damn good at it, too. She knew how to talk to folks like that, knew how to persuade them to do what was best."

I smiled at him. "I could tell from the short time we spent together she's good at her job. As far as Mrs. Schultz—that's the name of your sister's patient—I might be able to help both you and Kara, since I don't have doctor-patient confidentiality issues." I went on to explain about our visit to Minnie's house, about the brain tumor diagnosis and meeting Minnie's daughter.

Kara fixed a long strand of hair behind her ears. "A brain tumor? Wow. That's pretty awful. Of course I won't say anything about her medical condition in my piece. What did the doctors say? Will Mrs. Schultz come through this okay, Jillian?"

"I have no idea. But I did hear that the tumor wasn't malignant." I turned to Peyton Ross. "Getting back to Brenda. Can I call her that?" It seemed strange to call her by her official name when she was fighting for her life in a surgery suite.

"She'd want that. And please call me Peyton."

I took a deep breath. "I hate to ask this, but what did the doctors tell you about your sister when they called you? About her . . . chances?"

"Not much. Just that they were doing everything they could. See, they know her. They care about her, too. She's such a good, decent person." His eyes filled again.

"You know, your sister met with Minnie's daughter. Even though this turned out to be a medical rather than a mental health issue, your sister was right there to support Minnie. That says a lot about her character."

"She would have stuck with her no matter what her diagnosis. Psychiatric and neurological issues are not that far apart," Peyton said.

"One thing I do remember," I said. "She planned to get a journal for Minnie to write in." I stopped short of sharing what I knew about the evidence we'd found in Minnie's little hiding spot. "Maybe she was on her way to buy one? Maybe that has something to do with the message? She had to go to the store, maybe?"

"Could be," he said. "Or her text message could mean nothing." He paused, the squint back. "She kept notes on her phone. Sometimes she'd leave herself voice memos and sometimes she'd dictate into her note program. Thing is, she didn't feel they were safe to keep there, so she would erase them regularly after transferring anything pertinent to a patient's file."

Kara said, "Did they give you her things? That phone could be important in figuring out what happened."

"No. That's not uncommon, though. A patient's belongings are not what's important during an emergency. Since they knew Brenda in this hospital's ER and knew me, too, they probably called me without having to go through her things."

Kara turned to me. "Can you tell all that to Tom? The phone could be invaluable in finding out what happened." She readied her stylus again. "And if you have a picture you can share for me to run with my article, that will help. Also, since I haven't been to the scene, tell me about the make and model of her car. I know where this happened, so I've got that covered."

I stood and picked up my umbrella. "While you two are talking, I'll call Tom and then check on Minnie."

Kara and Dr. Ross nodded and refocused on each other. He looked far calmer than when I'd arrived. Perhaps this interview would take his mind off the possibility of losing his sister—at least for a few minutes.

Tom didn't pick up when I called him, so I left a message about Brenda's phone and the unfinished text. As I headed toward the elevators, I could have sworn they'd lowered the thermostat in the hospital to about sixty degrees. Of course, my clothes were still damp, and that made it seem colder. I had goose bumps on both arms as I exited the elevator on Minnie's floor. It seemed like I'd spent the last two days exclusively in this hospital.

But all of a sudden the silent hallway became anything but quiet. I heard the pounding footsteps first and then was nearly knocked on my butt by two security guards racing down the corridor past me.

I gave myself a second to take a few deep breaths and wondered what the heck had happened. But as I neared the circular nurse's station on this wing, the sound of raised voices grew louder the closer I got.

Then I saw the commotion. The security guards now faced each other, arms spread, holding back people screaming at one another right near Minnie's room. And I mean *screaming*. A few patients who were able to get out of their beds stood in the hall watching all this. It was reminiscent of a *Jerry Springer* episode. Since all four people were shouting at once—two young men on one side, a man and a woman facing them—it was impossible to understand what they were saying.

Then I noticed Minnie's daughter, hanging back in her mother's doorway, gnawing at her index finger. I was nearly knocked over again as a woman in scrubs, stethoscope draped around her neck, marched toward the fracas. She glanced back at me, saying, "This isn't a Broadway show. Go back to see whoever you're visiting here. They might be upset by this commotion."

This woman parked herself between the two guards. She never raised her voice, but there was plenty of finger-pointing. After the people she was admonishing finally stopped shouting, the security guards escorted the three males and one female in my direction. Since I stood in the middle of the corridor, frozen by what I'd witnessed, I guessed I was fair game. The woman, who looked to be in her late twenties, with bright red hair and a tattoo of something I couldn't make out on her biceps, gave me the dirtiest look I'd ever received. "Get out of the way, bitch."

I blinked and watched the security guard grasp her a little tighter.

He said, "That's the police chief's wife. You really don't want to be saying that stuff to her."

They were gone quickly, leaving me with a heart beating so fast my chest ached.

Fourteen

Unsure whether this was the best time to visit Minnie, I almost turned and left. But then Greta, still standing in her mother's doorway, gestured for me to come her way. If I were that pregnant, I'd be sitting, not standing right now.

When I reached her, Greta whispered, "Two of those fools were my brothers. They never even made it in to see Mama because Chester Winston's relatives had apparently followed them here—at least that's the gist of what I heard them arguing about."

I glanced back toward the elevators, but the argument had obviously been taken elsewhere. "Why were Chester's relatives here?" But then it dawned on me. "Oh. Do they think your mother killed Chester?"

Greta shrugged. "I guess. I wanted nothing to do with all that. I have a baby inside me to protect."

"You were smart to stay out of it," I said. "I hope all the noise didn't upset your mother too much."

"She was already upset. Mama's been asking about

Otto—the cat, not my father. She's really getting agitated. Can you help me calm her down?"

"Where's Lois?" I asked as I followed her into the hospital room. But then I remembered Tom had said Minnie didn't need a guard anymore. So I was surprised when I saw Lois sitting by Minnie's bed, holding the woman's hand.

She mouthed, "I'm off duty."

She'd taken quite a shine to Minnie and I was glad Lois had because Minnie's expression told me the hall incident just might have terrified her. I would have thought the roles would have been reversed—that Lois would be observing the argument in the corridor and Greta would be by her mother's side. But then, little in the last few days had made sense.

Suddenly, Minnie broke into a grin. "It's you. I forgot your name, but it is definitely you."

I had to smile. "Hi, Minnie. It's Jillian."

Lois said, "Must be the security guards finally showed up, since it's quiet again. I called them at least ten minutes ago. No one needs to be acting like a fool around all these sick people."

"There are sick people here?" Minnie said. "I had no idea."

"Mama, you're in the *hospital*. Of course there are sick people here." Greta's reaction was patient, though. She didn't seem irritated with her mother like she'd been before. Maybe she finally understood how ill her mother was.

I might have been an inadequate substitute for Brenda, but I needed to help out here. "People forget names all the time, Minnie. It's okay." I remembered the photos I'd taken off the cat cam and pulled out my phone. "Otto is doing fine at my house. I thought you'd like to see a couple of pictures."

I brought up the pictures and showed her. As soon as she saw the tuxie, her features softened. "Is he getting along with his sisters and brothers? He and Marlowe were good friends, but Archie was quite jealous of my newest baby. The girls, of course, ignored him for the most part. Especially Minous."

Minous was the gray cat Shawn had recognized first. The other names probably belonged to her other cats, the seven or so in residence before the influx of so many others began. I chose to consider my own bunch as the "sister and brothers" and said, "They're getting along just fine. You'd be so proud."

"That is such a relief to hear." She took the phone from my hand and leaned back against the pillow. "I'm proud of all of them."

Lois's big dark eyes captured mine and she shook her head slightly, saddened, I concluded, by the symptoms produced by this awful brain tumor.

Greta had taken a chair beside Lois. "I hear there were a lot of cats carried away. What happened to them?"

Thank goodness Minnie was still staring fondly at Otto's picture and didn't seem to be paying attention to anything else.

I knelt by Greta's chair and whispered. "They're all fine. We don't want to upset certain folks who aren't aware of the situation." I glanced her mother's way.

Greta's eyes widened in understanding. "Oh. I shouldn't—"

I put a finger to my lips. But I had a realization myself. How would we know which cats originally belonged to Minnie and which ones were the new arrivals? Chester

Winston might have known, but he would never speak again. Then I had a thought. Shawn's adoptees were chipped. Plus he'd know the cats he'd adopted out to Minnie. As for the rest of them, maybe they had microchips as well and could be tracked back to other owners.

My mind seemed on overdrive now. Why were there suddenly so many additions to Minnie's clowder? I had a sense that knowing this piece of information was important. Shawn might have answers. But knowing Tom, he had probably thought of this already and was on it as a clue.

After Minnie reluctantly handed me my phone, I told her she needed to rest and I should get home and give Otto a kiss for her. She liked that idea. Then Minnie did something unexpected. She held out her arms for a hug.

I readily gave her a gentle squeeze and told her all her kitties would be well cared for. When I walked out, I was surprised that both Lois and Greta followed.

"My mother perks up when you're here, and I wanted to thank you for visiting," Greta said. "It took her mind off the argument."

Lois said, "That was Winston's family and Greta's brothers, from what I heard. Those Winstons seem to think Mrs. Schultz is a murderer."

Greta looked at Lois, then at me. "She's cleared, though. She would never do that."

Lois said, "We're looking at everyone, but your mother probably didn't have the strength or the stamina to kill Chester. From what the chief told me, your brothers went to school with Mr. Winston's son and the son's wife."

"Oh. I had no idea," Greta said. "My brothers and I are several years apart."

I'd heard this from Belle. "They have a lot of nerve

coming up here to confront a poor woman in her hospital bed."

Greta shook her head. "I wouldn't want to meet either of them in an alley."

Lois said, "In your condition, you need to be staying away from alleys in general."

We all smiled—and it was a rare thing to see Lois smile. Minnie and, yes, even Greta had really touched her.

I was ready to leave but wanted to stop back at the surgery waiting area to check for any news on Dr. Ross. I supposed now was as good a time as any to share what had happened with Minnie's daughter.

"Please don't mention this to your mother, but you should know Dr. Ross won't be in to visit." I told her about the wreck and how the doctor was currently in surgery.

Lois nodded knowingly. "I heard. It must have happened right after she picked up that new journal Minnie was writing in."

"Have you even left here, Lois?" I asked.

She nodded. "Finished my shift and came right back. My dog has gone to some major training facility, so where else do I have to be?"

Greta smiled. "You're so sweet to stand by us, but it's a horrible thing about the doctor. Bad things just keep happening. It's about time I apologized for being so . . . *full of myself* when we first met. Being estranged from my mother was wrong. I'm just sorry it took her wandering in the streets and having a brain tumor to bring me to my senses."

"We all have family issues at one time or another." I patted her shoulder and smiled. "You're here now, and I know that means the world to your mother."

"Her surgery is tomorrow. They say it will take a long time according to what the docs saw on the scans. I only hope this baby waits until we can get through this. Someone needs to be here for Mama, and my brothers can't be counted on—because from what I could tell, they might have had a little too much to drink before coming here."

"I'll be around as much as I can." Lois started back into the hospital room but turned and said, "The alcohol explains a lot. I'm guessing Winston's family might have had one too many themselves. Good night, Jillian."

I said good-bye to Greta and took the elevator down to the second floor. Kara was sitting on the ugly vinyl couch and Peyton stood talking to a tall man wearing surgical scrubs, a paper mask dangling around his neck.

I hung back until the doctor turned and headed back down the hall. Kara stood and rested a hand on Peyton Ross's shoulder. I joined them and was told Brenda was in a medically induced coma to help relieve the swelling on her brain. She would be transferred to ICU in about an hour.

Kara and I said our good-byes to Peyton, who at least had some color back in his pale face since the last time I'd seen him. Brenda had made it through the surgery and there was hope.

The two of us walked to our cars together and Kara told me that she'd heard everything the doctor said and they thought Brenda had a good chance of recovery. I was happy to drive home with that piece of good news after such an awful day.

I was surprised to see Tom's Prius in the driveway when I arrived home. I found him with his legs propped on the ottoman, his head resting against the sofa cushions. His eyes were closed and his jaw was slack. I tried to be quiet and lure the five cats past him so as not to wake him, but he stirred before I could make to the hallway leading to the bedrooms.

"Hey there," he mumbled.

"Darn. I was hoping not to wake you." I sat on the chair across from him, and Chablis and Otto immediately jumped onto my lap. Otto clawed his way to my shoulder and I winced. He nestled his head into my neck and began to purr as I stroked his back.

Syrah perched on the sofa behind Tom and he reached back and scratched his head. "They sure miss you when you're gone. So what about the doctor? The accident scene was . . . *bad*."

I told him what I knew and also gave him the scoop on what happened outside Minnie's room.

Tom sat up and put his feet on the floor. "The families were there and they had an argument? Whoa. Those brothers denied being in town, so I'm calling them on that lie tomorrow, when they told me they *might* be in Mercy."

I sat beside him and immediately felt Dashiell rubbing against my shins. Merlot lay on the Oriental carpet nearby so he could look back and forth between us. "What about Chester's family? Have you talked to them already?"

Tom rested a hand on my leg. "They're coming to the station tomorrow, too. The daughter-in-law asked if they needed a lawyer. It should be so awesome visiting with those folks if they're as pleasant as Chester *never* was."

I smiled. "Greta Kramer, Minnie's daughter, said her brothers were drunk and maybe Chester's family was, too. I don't envy you interrogating any of those people. I had a thought when I was visiting Minnie and—"

"Is she going to be okay?"

"Her operation is tomorrow. Brain surgery sounds scary, but the good thing about her condition is that she probably won't realize what's happening."

"Somehow that last part sounds scary, too," Tom said.

"She's a sweet lady and I hope the doctors can work some magic," I said.

Tom put his arm around me and I leaned close to him. "Enough sad talk," he said. "Shawn told me to call him first thing in the morning because he should be done examining all of Minnie's cats. Only about seven are her original cats. We know those felines have something to do with the case. We also hope the contents of the boxes will shed light on what was happening inside Mrs. Schultz's house in the last few months. We need to leave no stone unturned."

"Before I head over to Minnie's place tomorrow, I'll call Shawn and see if he can return Minnie's kitties to her by the time she comes home from the hospital. She'll need her friends with her. That is, if she can even care for them."

"Whenever you're ready in the morning is fine," Tom said. "We're getting a warrant for not only Chester's financials, but Minnie's as well. My instinct tells me there's a connection between all those boxes and Chester's interest in Mrs. Schultz. We can match purchase records to the contents of those packages in her house. Many of them seem to have come from big-box stores."

"Before I forget, Minnie was vague about this, but

she said she had a cell phone—or thinks she had one—
and that it came from Chester."

"Okay, I'll make sure Candace is on the lookout for
more than one cell phone when y'all are over there tomorrow. Lydia told me Chester did not have a phone on
him, which I found odd and not understandable. He had
to have one for his job. Where the heck is it?"

"That *is* weird. I can see Minnie not having a phone
since she believes mine is a miniature television. But
Chester? That makes no sense."

"We can't find his work phone, either. Worst-case
scenario is the killer took the phones—maybe even
Mrs. Schultz's phone—because he or she was worried
they would connect him or her to Chester."

"What about those journals Candace found. Are
they helpful?"

Dashiell decided that since Tom didn't seem about to
get up, he could settle in his lap. As soon as Tom stroked
him, Dashiell closed his eyes and began to purr. "Yes,
the journals. We haven't had time to thoroughly look
through them. Unfortunately, the last one she dated was
about three weeks ago and completely filled with scrawl-
ing cursive that made no sense. She must have already
been falling apart."

I sighed. "That is so sad. No leads there, I take it?"

"There could be journals missing. As I said, they were
dated, and there seems to be a gap from her making perfect sense to making no sense whatsoever. There's another
thing to add to the list for tomorrow's search—missing
journals."

"Lucky us," I said with a laugh. "Either you or Candace can give me a call when you need me. But what

about Morris? Will this make him feel like I'm taking over something he could be doing?"

"Morris will be heading to Chester's apartment to do another, more thorough search. We need evidence connecting him to Mrs. Schultz—evidence aside from the cats. Meanwhile, I'll be interviewing both the Schultz and the Winston families. Those twin brothers have to provide me with a plausible explanation for lying about their whereabouts."

"I'd say they'd been visiting some bar, from what I witnessed at the hospital. And by the way, Lois is spending her off duty time visiting Minnie. I do believe she's quite fond of her. I'll bet she'd like to be around when the poor woman comes out of surgery."

"Mrs. Schultz has become a key witness rather than a suspect, so maybe she needs protection if she comes out of that brain surgery and remembers what happened the other day. I mean, who knows what she might say that could put her in danger? Still, it will be difficult sparing Lois to stay there. I have only two officers on the night shift right now."

"Well, maybe Lois doesn't need to be there tomorrow. Minnie's daughter will probably be at the hospital all day. Could be her sons will show up there too, that is, if they're allowed back after their shenanigans. I understand it will be a long operation. She'll surely be in ICU afterward, and getting in there is like trying to keep your eyes open when you sneeze. That's a pretty safe place."

"Okay, maybe Lois could stay at the station and help with interviews for a day or two. I could sure use her help to sift through all the tips we've received. As for Mrs. Schultz's sons, if those young men are hanging around at the hospital, I'll interview them there. They aren't wiggling out of a *long* talk with me." Since Dashiell was now sound asleep, Tom reached back and stroked Syrah. Our Abyssinian began to purr so loud the neighbors across the lake probably heard him.

Then I had a thought. "Will asking me to help out at Minnie's house come back to bite you? Jeopardize the case? I'm *not* a police officer, last time I checked."

Tom smiled and the weariness in his eyes was evident. "I pretty much can make the rules. Police chiefs in small towns who are good friends with the mayor can do that. We did give Candace the title of detective, didn't we? Now your new title is citizen volunteer—and a volunteer I can rely on."

"I'm a willing one. Did I tell you I met Dr. Ross's brother Peyton at the hospital? He told me he got an unfinished text message from his sister. He was hoping you found her phone. He said she often left messages to herself on that phone. Maybe there's a clue there."

"Why all the missing phones? This is so weird because her phone wasn't with her belongings. Wow. Coincidences like this should *not* exist in a murder investigation."

"Do you think someone stole it from her wrecked car?"

"Maybe," he said. "Pretty cold to leave an injured woman at death's door while you dig around for her cell phone."

I shuddered at the thought. "Okay, enough talk about awful people doing terrible things. You, my sweet Tom, need sleep. But I'm not sure if five cats will allow you to rest. I can take the fur friends into the guest room if you think that will help you rest better."

Tom lifted Dashiell and held him close. "Are you

kidding me? I've never slept better in my life since we got married. Without you and all these guys with me, I'd be tossing and turning all night." He stood. "Let's get on with our routine. Treats first."

Routine was important, that was for sure. The thought of Tom close to me tonight had me grinning like the Cheshire cat I'd become since we'd married.

Fifteen

Tom left home in the early-morning hours, about the time the cats first wake us. We usually go back to sleep, but not today. I finally got out of bed after Chablis sat on my head and Otto snuck under the covers and began biting my toes. Cats *will* have their way.

Because of Dashiell's diabetes, I could no longer leave out a dish of kibble at night. He would devour any food he could get his paws on. Once I gave him his insulin, all the cats sat happily on the floor chowing down—all except Dashiell. I fed him his special diet in the pantry with the door closed. Though Dashiell had learned to leave the other cats' food alone, I wasn't sure that Otto would leave poor Dashiell alone to eat in peace.

While they ate and coffee was brewing, I called Shawn, updated him on Minnie's medical condition and asked about her cats.

He said, "I have them all accounted for except one. I microchipped the ones she adopted from me, so I have the records."

"Exactly how many cats are definitely hers?"

"Six. Unfortunately, there's one missing. A ginger Persian named Simon. He's young, so if he passed away, something bad happened suddenly and I was never told. She only got him from me maybe eighteen months ago, when he was a kitten."

"Uh-oh. I don't believe anyone should tell her about that. Let's keep it to ourselves for now."

"She won't hear it from me. Those cats were like her children, Jillian. But if she gets well enough to come home in the near future, someone needs to tell her we couldn't find him."

An uneasy feeling mushroomed in my gut. "You think I should be that someone?"

"If you wouldn't mind. You know how I am about delivering bad news."

"But Simon might turn up, right?" Before he could reply, the call waiting sound beeped in my ear. "I have another call. Talk to you later, Shawn."

It was Candace telling me to meet her at the Schultz house in an hour. That gave me plenty of time to get dressed and eat a piece of toast. When I left the house, the stares from our cats as I closed the door said it all. *You will pay for leaving us three days in a row, human.*

Just as I arrived at Minnie's house, a Mercy PD squad car swerved into the driveway from the other direction. I pulled up to the curb in front of her place. Candace and B.J. exited the cruiser and B.J. had an expression my grandma used to call "the green apple nasties." Candace's driving *will* do that to a person.

I hugged each of them as the scent of honeysuckle wafted toward us. I realized I hadn't even noticed the pale pink flowers and vines creeping toward Minnie's roof the other times I'd been here. Too many disturbing things had been on my mind. Unattended, those vines would take over the front of her house. I wondered who had helped her care for her yard as her mind began to shatter. Chester? The thought made me shiver with distaste. He died as no one should die, but I couldn't deny that I had never liked the man.

B.J. took a small video camera from the trunk of the car and Candace grabbed her evidence satchel. As she unlocked the front door, I hoped these boxes would reveal something—anything—about why Chester had inserted himself into poor Minnie's life.

I felt claustrophobic again once we were inside. Thank goodness the cardboard corridor would be coming down. It couldn't happen soon enough. Candace pulled a folded sheet of legal paper from her pocket and handed it to me, along with a pair of latex gloves.

"Here's my plan for this search. First, I need a more thorough examination of that cubicle cut into the back of her closet. As long as we're in that room, we can unpack the boxes there. After that, we follow my list. But any evidence we find might change the plan." Candace held her evidence kit with two hands in front of her so she could fit through the narrow space leading to the bedrooms.

B.J. stayed back and recorded our progress and then joined us in Minnie's bedroom. We were intruding into the woman's most personal space.

"Does it ever bother you?" I asked.

"Does what bother me?" Candace snapped her gloves on and I followed her lead.

"Going through people's things."

B.J. seemed to be all ears, waiting for Candace's answer.

"Not anymore. Used to, but I'll bet when a doctor has to stick his hands inside a person on the operating table, that feels even weirder. It's the job."

"Ah." I nodded. "That makes sense."

Candace began narrating into her handheld recorder, and her voice was loud enough that B.J. could pick up the sound on the video camera.

I got a better view of the cubicle where the journals and jewelry box had been stashed. The space was wider than I'd realized and the ceiling matched the height of the closet. There was no light in there, and though the front closet light was on, it was impossible to really see into the corners of this back closet. Candace's solution was to stick a small LED light onto the wall and also turn on the Maglite from her bag.

I knelt so B.J. could record the closet and the space behind the closet. Soon Candace was on her hands and knees, her flashlight focused on the farthest corner.

"B.J., hand me my tweezers and a couple of small evidence bags."

She put something in the first bag—I couldn't tell what—and next she picked up something with her gloved fingers and deposited it in the second bag. It appeared to be a pink button. She wrote on the bags after sealing them using a Sharpie she'd taken from her pocket.

"Take these and put them in my satchel, Jillian." She handed me the bags.

"Are those torn fingernails?" I said before stashing them carefully away. They actually looked like *chewed* fingernails bearing tiny specks of blood.

"That's my guess." Candace continued to examine the floor and the walls for anything else that might offer a clue into this mystery within a mystery. "Maybe Mrs.

Schultz hid in here to write in her journals. But why hide in your own home?"

"Could she have been hiding in here from Chester Winston?" B.J. asked.

"From him or from whoever killed him. I sure hope we get to ask her." Candace glanced back at me as I wrote down what evidence had been collected in the notebook I'd taken from the evidence kit.

Candace refocused on the corner. Using the tweezers again, she picked up a few ocher-colored cat hairs.

Anticipating her need, I pulled out another small evidence bag and held it open. She dropped them into it. "Cat hairs, I assume. I'm surprised that there aren't more. Why is that, cat expert?"

As she wrote the date on the bag, I said, "For a woman with so many cats in residence, this place is amazingly clean. My guess is, Minnie Schultz spent her days vacuuming up behind her babies. Like all the time, every day."

"Maybe these cat hairs will be important at some point in the investigation, or they could be useless." Candace handed the bag to me and I put it with the others.

"Shawn told me that a ginger cat is missing," I said. "One that belonged to Minnie before two dozen more came to live here. This feline business is all so strange, Candace."

"I'll say." B.J. had turned off the camera briefly. "Maybe this missing cat is important. Perhaps the entire case revolves around the cats."

Candace nodded. "You could be right. But all these boxes have to be important. We need to get busy."

The closet seemed to have given up all its secrets and we moved out into the crowded bedroom itself. First, Candace numbered all the unopened boxes, but just as we moved box number one away from against the wall, the doorbell rang.

Candace, kneeling and ready to cut the tape with her pocket knife, sighed in frustration. "B.J., would you please see who that is and get rid of them? Curious neighbors are not on the agenda for today and your uniform will be persuasive. We'll wait."

We waited in silence, though I knew Candace was dying to slit open the box.

But when B.J reappeared, he wasn't alone.

"Deputy Candy Carson, right?" It was a big man in a Mercy County Sheriff's Department uniform. He had a baritone voice and graying temples. Either he had visited a tanning salon or he'd already taken advantage of the sunny spring days. My guess was the latter. The fact that he'd called Candace by her most hated nickname did not bode well. Didn't the man realize she was holding a knife?

"Yes, I'm *Detective Candace* Carson." She squinted at the name tag above his blue uniform pocket. "How can I help you, *Deputy Sheriff* Osborne?"

"Actually, it's Captain Osborne, head of the county's criminal division. Are you new to plainclothes? I remember seeing you in uniform at Chief Stewart's formal swearing in."

There was only one phrase for what was going on here in a tiny room that had become suddenly quite cold: *Pissing contest.*

"Promotion." Candace's tone was clipped and as chilly as the room. "What can I do for you?"

I noted that B.J. had taken a spot where he was almost completely obscured by one of the larger boxes. I stayed where I was, feeling like a surgeon who should be holding her hands up to keep them clean while unwanted conversation kept me from my operation. Instead, I grasped my hands behind my back.

"First of all, can you introduce me to your officers—oh, wait a minute." He grinned at me, his teeth all whiter than white. I had to admit he was a good-looking guy, maybe about Tom's age. But his cocky attitude was off-putting to say the least. He said, "Aren't you Tom's new wife?"

I almost put out my hand to shake his, but instead thought better of offering latex fingers. I also felt a tad guilty for not remembering him. "Yes, I'm Jillian Hart. Nice to meet you. But I didn't catch your first name." Maybe first names would help settle the tension that had taken over this room.

"Brad. Nice to meet you." He turned his attention to B.J. "Deputy? Or has everyone at Mercy PD risen in the ranks?"

"Deputy B.J. Henderson, sir."

I saw Candace close her eyes briefly. Knowing her, she didn't think this guy deserved a title like *sir*. "Again, what can I do for you, *Captain* Osborne?"

"I'm here to make you an offer you won't want to refuse. We can take over this case and—"

"What are you talking about?" Candace's disdain had turned to hostility in a nanosecond.

"Detective Carson," he said. "Surely you realize we have far more resources than Mercy PD. Chester Winston worked for the county and that technically makes this our jurisdiction."

"In whose *technical* world, Captain? This property, this house where a crime occurred, is in *Mercy*. This is *our* case. This is our jurisdiction, *period*."

Osborne took in the room, his gaze darting from one

corner to another. "You've called in a volunteer, that much is obvious." He looked at me. "No offense, Mrs. Stewart."

"None taken." I smiled a smile that was as fake as it probably appeared. "And it's Ms. Hart, though I prefer Jillian."

"Sorry. Don't tell on me when you talk to Tom. You're a strong, modern woman. I totally get that."

No you don't, I thought. *Not for a minute.* But I kept my smile as earnest as I could, hoping to warm up the cold war between him and Candace.

"We don't need the county's help," Candace said. "Especially since we've done all the work to get warrants for Chester's financials, for all this merchandise and for searches. As you can see, we're kind of busy right now, so if that's all you came for—to offer to take our case away—mission accomplished. But we'll handle this and we'll solve it."

Osborne sighed heavily. "I hoped to avoid this, but maybe I should speak with Tom."

Ah. Time for me to play the wife card, I thought. I pulled my phone for my pocket. "I have a direct line. I'll call him for you."

"No need. I'll stop by the department and—"

"Hey there, Tom." Speed dial is a wonderful thing. I already had him on the line before the guy could blink. "I've got Captain Brad Osborne here from the sheriff's department and—"

"Let me guess. He wants the case."

"He does," I said solemnly, trying not to give away the irritation I'd just heard in Tom's voice.

"Let me talk to him. He's got a hell of a nerve."

Not long after, Captain Osborne was gone with hardly

a good-bye, his expensive white teeth hidden by a frown and his earlobes red with anger. Now I remembered a conversation I'd had with Tom a couple of months ago about territorial issues between Mercy PD and the county officers. His pleas for them to be respectful and share resources, to not simply take over whenever they wanted, always fell on deaf ears. If the case was one they wanted, one that would grab headlines, it was all or nothing for them. Now I'd seen it unfold before my eyes. Would this be the last we'd see of that condescending man? I had no idea, but I sincerely hoped so.

With B.J. once again behind the camera, Candace finally used her pocketknife to slit open the first box.

Her expression changed from surprise to confusion. "What the heck?" she said as she leaned back on her heels.

Sixteen

I peered into the large box. "Why would Minnie have a box of universal TV remotes? I didn't even see a television in this house, now that I think about it."

Candace shook her head in confusion. "Exactly. Yet there must be two dozen in here."

"You want to take one out?" B.J. had shut off the camera. "See if a remote is really what's in those smaller boxes?"

"Yes." Candace nodded. "Who knows? Maybe Minnie Schultz was smuggling drugs via discount stores."

But as I wrote down the number of remotes as Candace carefully opened each sealed package to check the contents, they were indeed remote controls. She even checked the battery cases to make sure nothing had been stashed inside. They held batteries and that was all.

This weirdness only continued as we went about the business of opening more boxes. One held late-model cell phones—though not the very newest ones. Another box was packed with Crock-Pots. There were laptop computers and digital tablets, as well as toasters, blenders and food processors. One particular box in the hallway was quite heavy, and Candace needed help moving it to an area where we had room to open it. It was packed full of robotic vacuum cleaners.

While I dutifully recorded everything in the notebook, Candace droned on about the contents into her recorder and B.J. videoed the process. By lunchtime we were tired and baffled. Maybe the exhaustion came from not understanding why a woman who didn't even know what a cell phone was had packed her house full of electronics and appliances she probably wouldn't know what to do with—at least in the state she was now.

That thought was a reminder of Minnie in the hospital, probably undergoing brain surgery as we rifled through her house. At least writing down the contents of these boxes had kept my mind off her and poor Dr. Ross. But right now, everything seemed wrong—from a man like Chester befriending a sick woman, to a house full of cats and retail items, to a car accident that was *not* an accident.

"Let's get food in our bellies and try to make sense of this," Candace said. "I'm beginning to feel as if I've been on a shopping spree at Sam's Club."

B.J. and Candace took the squad car, and though she offered me a ride to the Main Street Diner, I told her it was better if I drove my van in case they had an emergency that needed their attention.

Candace gave me a look that said I wasn't fooling her for a second. She knew how I felt about her NASCAR-esque driving style. I did feel sorry for B.J., but he'd have to get used to it because Candace wasn't about to change.

Before I turned the key in the ignition, I pulled up my

cat cam on the phone and spoke with the clowder. I was pleased to see that Dashiell seemed alert since he'd had his breakfast a little earlier than usual today. When his blood sugar plunged, he'd pass out, but only after wobbling around on shaky legs. I saw none of those signs. Chablis meowed for treats and Syrah showed his contempt for this method of remote communication by walking away. He would much rather I stayed home. Little Otto batted at the microphone as I spoke to them, and Merlot watched him do this. I sure hoped Merlot didn't get any ideas, since he was big enough to bring the whole camera and microphone down if he put his mind to it.

I said good-bye and took off for the diner. Minutes later, I walked in and passed the stainless art deco–style eat-in counter with its red leather stools. I joined Candace and B.J. in one of the old-fashioned wooden booths at the back of the restaurant. They'd already ordered and Candace asked me what had taken me so long.

"First of all, I observed the speed limit," I answered with a smile. "But I also needed a dose of kitty love." I looked up as the waitress appeared. I ordered a salad, sticking to my quest for a healthier diet. Sweet tea is a good thing, but too much sweet tea for a middle-aged woman can make buying new clothes a necessity rather than fun. Besides, Kara had convinced me I'd feel more energetic if I reduced my meat intake, and she was actually teaching me a few vegetarian recipes that I could manage. I wasn't much of a cook. In fact Tom enjoyed playing chef more than I did.

But I did order sweet tea today, figuring I'd be canceling out the sugar by eating salad. My comfort drink seemed a necessity at this juncture.

Candace's face grew solemn as she checked her messages. Then she set the phone down. "Mrs. Schultz went into surgery at eight this morning. They expect the surgery to take seven or eight hours."

"Holy crap." B.J. reddened. "Sorry. I meant *holy cow*. It's that bad?"

"Delicate surgery," I offered. "She doesn't have cancer, though, so that's a good thing." I looked at Candace. "And Dr. Ross?"

"Still in a medically induced coma, but she made it through the night with no further emergencies."

The waitress appeared and placed fries, chili dogs and hamburgers in front of B.J. and Candace. The young woman looked my way. "Be right back with that salad."

B.J. used a knife and fork to attack his hot dog, probably because he wasn't about to sully his new uniform with chili sauce.

Before Candace could take a bite of her hamburger, she focused over my shoulder, her eyes widened in surprise. "*Morris*. What the heck happened?"

I turned in the booth to see Morris Ebeling striding toward us. He had a lump on his forehead about the size of an egg and it was already turning reddish purple. I slid over so he could sit.

"That gosh-darn Winston family." He touched his forehead and winced. "They didn't much take to my searching Chester's apartment again."

Candace's cheeks flushed with anger. "I hope whoever did that is in a holding cell right now."

"Nah. Grief is strange thing. You know that as well as I do, Candace. No matter what kind of man Chester was, these folks actually cared about him. I got an apology."

My salad arrived, and as the waitress set it in front of me, I asked her for an ice pack.

She looked at Morris and gasped. "Why, Deputy Ebeling, you surely do need some ice, honey."

She returned with it quickly and brought with her a steaming mug of black coffee. Morris was a regular here. He thanked her, and once he'd pressed the ice-filled plastic bag gingerly to his forehead, Morris let out a small sigh.

"You could have a concussion," B.J. said.

I wondered if he was rethinking his decision to become a police officer as he stared at Morris.

"This hard head? Are you kidding? My problem is, I found nothing in that apartment that remotely looked like evidence of his involvement with anyone. I'm heading to his office next." Morris readjusted the ice pack. "I hope that girl who answers the phones doesn't have a temper."

Candace had pretty much ignored her food even as B.J. continued to eat. "Who hit you and with what? 'Cause you do remember our victim was smashed over the head, too."

"It was the daughter-in-law. I was bent over in the bedroom going through a pile of stuff on the bed. She snuck up behind me and asked me what I thought I was doing. When I turned, she hit me with a wine bottle. I'm just lucky it didn't break."

Candace was shaking her head with disgust. "She must have seen the squad car in the driveway, not to mention your uniform. She had to know who you were and what you were doing."

"My impression of that particular woman is that she ain't quite hooked up right."

"You're going soft in your old age, Morris. Five years ago you would have thrown that woman in jail without a second thought. I take it this is the daughter-in-law who was in the altercation at the hospital last night."

"One and the same. Lucinda Winston. She's pretty worked up about Chester's death, while her husband— that would be Chester's son, Earl—just stood behind her looking like he didn't have any more sense than a melon sittin' in the field."

B.J. had just taken a sip of his tea and nearly did a spit take after hearing this description. He quickly dabbed tea off his chin with a napkin.

Morris said, "You called me to meet you three here, so tell me what's in all those gosh-darn boxes over at Mrs. Schultz's abode."

Candace summarized between bites of food, but she managed to eat only about half of her burger before pushing her plate to the side. I, meanwhile, cleaned my salad bowl, not realizing just how hungry taking inventory at a crime scene could make a woman.

Morris finally set the dripping ice bag on the table. "That is strange as strange can be. You think Mrs. Schultz got herself addicted to the Home Shopping Network? I heard that can be a problem for shut-ins. And she sure seemed like a shut-in."

Candace pointed at Morris. "You're right. She *was* a shut-in. We need to figure out when that all started and add it to our timeline leading up to the crime. We also need to know what she planned to do with those purchases and what Chester Winston's part was in all of it. Maybe nothing. But I sure as hell am certain he had something to do with those cats."

"Shawn can help with that," I said. "He'd chipped all of Minnie's cats himself, but I didn't get the chance to ask him if any of the newer cats at the house were microchipped by different shelters or veterinarians. That information could lead to something, right?"

"It sure could. But it's like we have too much evidence, the pieces all jumbled together like an unsolved giant jigsaw puzzle." Candace sat back, looking tired and a little confused.

"You gonna eat your fries?" B.J. asked Candace.

She pushed her plate toward him. "Hurry up, B.J. There are a bunch of boxes still waiting for us back at the house."

When they finally got up to leave, I picked up the bill and said I'd pay. Meanwhile, the waitress returned. She squeezed Morris's shoulder. "You feel like eatin' now, honey?"

Morris stood to let me out of the booth. "I'm starving. Bring me breakfast for lunch. My regular."

I hurried after Candace and B.J. and told them I would meet them back at the house before stopping at the register. I sure hoped we'd find something important this afternoon.

Soon I was on my way back to Minnie's neighborhood, but before I was halfway there, my cell rang. The caller ID identified Shawn.

I answered and before I could get out so much as a hello, Shawn started talking so fast I almost didn't understand him. "Those cats we took from the house, Jillian? Those cats all have homes. That Chester Winston was a liar and a thief."

Seventeen

Shawn had apparently figured out on his own that the microchipping could be important. He went on to say that most of the cats were indeed chipped and he was able to find the names and phone numbers for the owners. Two people he'd phoned confirmed they had called county animal control to report their cats missing. I thanked Shawn and told him I would notify the police since I was working with them today.

But I remembered that Morris said he would be heading to Chester's office next, so I made a U-turn at the last stoplight in town and headed back to the Main Street Diner. Morris never answered his phone unless Candace was calling—especially if he was eating.

I found him mopping up fried egg with toast and he was surprised to see me. "You forget something, Jillian?"

"No. I just talked to Shawn and there's something you should know before you head to Chester's office." I went on to tell him about the cats that had been reported missing to Chester and how they'd been now located as ones found in Minnie's house.

He continued eating as I sat across from him. He polished off his brunch in what I considered record time and now sat back with a freshly filled coffee mug in hand. "Okay, so you're implyin' he mighta found those cats and given them to Minnie Schultz? Why in the heck would he do that?"

"I'm not sure. Something else was going on. Chester should have scanned those cats for microchips first chance he got. He would have had access to their information and been able to return them to their owners. Why didn't he do that?"

Morris appeared a tad confused for a second. "So these microchips can be traced back to the owners? Like GPS or something?"

"That's not how it works." I went on to explain to Morris, who was very tech-challenged, that the tiny chips were injected under a cat's skin, either by a vet or by the shelter. "Companies like HomeAgain maintain a database with all the owner information in case the cat ever gets lost. All my cats are chipped."

"Ah. I get it. And you think there might be evidence at Chester's office telling us why these cats weren't returned home?"

"Maybe." But now I wondered if he'd find anything there. "I suppose if he was doing this for some nefarious reason, he wouldn't keep records, would he?"

Morris sipped his coffee before speaking. "That's what I was thinking. This may sound far-fetched, but what if he fancied Mrs. Schultz? What if he realized she was sick in the head and thought taking care of lost cats would make her feel better? I mean, you always say your cats can mend your heart when you're blue."

I sighed, understanding what he was saying but not

really believing that's what happened. "That's one explanation. But it sure doesn't fit with what Shawn believes about the guy. He was pretty darn angry about Chester not returning these cats to their owners." I pulled out my phone. "After Shawn told me this, I saved the names and addresses of two people he'd spoken to with cats found at the house. One of them lives in Minnie's neighborhood." I held the phone out so he could read the names.

He took out his pocket notebook and jotted down the names and addresses. "I'll look for records about these two folks, maybe call Shawn and get more names if he has them. Meanwhile, you go back to the Schultz place and tell Candace. Maybe she'd like to pay this one person a visit since they live in Mrs. Schultz's neighborhood."

I said good-bye and left again, facing more questions from Candace once I arrived at the Schultz house.

When she let me in, she said, "Why did it take you so long? I was worried. You and that Dr. Ross got chummy and I was afraid maybe whoever hurt her had their sights set on you, too."

"Sorry." I went on to explain all that had happened in the short amount of time I was missing in action.

Candace's interest was certainly piqued. "Why don't we pay this cat owner a visit?" Leaving me standing in the tiny foyer of Minnie's home while she went to give B.J. instructions about what to take care of in her absence, I suddenly heard a little scratching noise. I looked to the ceiling, thinking maybe there were raccoons in the attic. This was a wooded neighborhood like my own. Raccoons can do some serious damage to a house.

Then I realized where the noise was coming from—inside the hall closet. Not sure what I would find—a rat, a 'coon or even a possum that might have wandered inside when doors had been opened frequently during the last few days—I was careful to only crack the closet door.

When I heard a pitiful meow, however, I flung the door open and knelt. A ginger Persian cat lay on the closet floor, one paw extended and touching the inner doorframe.

I scooped him up and realized this was probably Minnie's cat Simon, the one who had been unaccounted for. I sat on the floor with him in my lap, making sure he wasn't injured. His mews grew louder as I stroked him, and when he struggled to get away, I clung tighter to him. I didn't want him disappearing again. He stopped resisting when I stood and made my way to the kitchen. I ran into Candace, who had just emerged from the hall.

"Another cat? You have *got* to be kidding me." She reached out and stroked the baby's cheek. He began to purr.

"He was in the hall closet. He's got to be starving," I said.

Candace smiled at the hefty boy. "We had every door in this place opened and closed several times, especially on day one of the investigation. He was probably slinking around and no one noticed, then took refuge in that closet."

She followed us into the kitchen and I asked her to find a dish and a can of cat food. I wasn't putting this fella down until he had something to eat. Once this was accomplished, he had interest only in the food and chowed down voraciously.

I filled another bowl with water. Though I didn't want to leave him, I *really* wanted to talk to this neighbor with the missing cat. Any cat in trouble was important to me. B.J., who has a cat and dog of his own, was quite happy to cat-sit Simon while we went around the block to the neighbor's house. I got the feeling anything seemed better to him than numbering endless boxes.

Much to our surprise, Shawn's pickup was parked in front of the address I'd noted on my smartphone. Candace pulled into the driveway so fast I had to hold on to the grip on the roof.

"This isn't an emergency," I muttered.

Candace heard me. "But Shawn's here. He's talking to a potential witness before I can get information first. I don't like that."

"Oh, I can tell." I said this under my breath, but she must have a dog's hearing.

"I heard that, too. Hurry up."

I had to smile. Her intensity and dedication to her job were amazing. Who could stay irritated with a woman like that? Even if I'd nearly had my head slammed into the passenger window.

The man's name was Ferris Humphrey and he greeted us with a smile so big he knew sunshine helped build strong bones and teeth—because the sun sure was shining on him in more ways than one. The cat he held in his arms was a brown tabby with green eyes.

I saw Shawn standing behind Ferris, also wearing a huge grin. This was the best part of his job.

"I'm Detective Carson with Mercy PD, Mr. Humphrey. Can I ask you a few questions?"

He stood aside to allow us to enter and kept staring at me. "You're the police chief's wife, right? The one who helps cats? Mr. Cuddahee was telling me about you."

Shawn offered a shrug, palms up.

"That's right. Jillian Hart. What a beautiful cat." I wanted to pet this baby, but Mr. Humphrey was clinging to the cat so tightly, I thought better of it. This one, like the others, had been stressed mightily in the last few months.

We walked into a house with a layout similar to Minnie's. But it was cluttered by so much furniture rather than by boxes that it seemed very different.

Shawn backed up and took a seat in a leather recliner. Two cups of coffee sat on the small table situated between the recliner and an easy chair. The men had apparently been chatting.

"What's your kitty's name?" I asked as Mr. Humphrey gestured toward matching brocade wing chairs opposite the recliners. A love seat in gaudy floral was parked against the front window.

"Princess." He looked down at her with a doting smile and stroked her. The man was perhaps midsixties and bald with tufts of unruly silver fringe. Princess seemed to be getting restless in his arms, but he held fast to his recovered pet.

Candace sat on the edge of one wing chair and I eased into the other one. She took her smartphone from her shirt pocket and poised the stylus over the screen. "I'm glad you have your cat back, Mr. Humphrey. You must be so relieved."

"*Relieved* isn't the word." He stared down adoringly at the cat. "But I think she's a bit tired of me fawning over her." He set the cat down and she scampered into the hallway. Ferris Humphrey had no South Carolina drawl. He sounded like a Yankee despite the Southern-sounding name. "How can I help? Because Shawn has been telling me that Minnie had other cats that didn't belong to her. No surprise, though."

"Why is that?" Candace asked after sending a withering look in Shawn's direction.

"That awful animal control man answered Minnie's door when I passed out flyers in the neighborhood right after Princess disappeared. He didn't have to be so rude. I mean, I'd already told Chester Winston when I'd called animal control and reported Princess missing that I'd pay twice the recovery fee."

Shawn's eyebrows knitted and his smile faded to straight, tight lips. "What *recovery fee*?"

Candace held up her hand. "Shawn, I understand your passion for animals, but you've returned the cat. Perhaps you could leave now? I need to question Mr. Humphrey and—"

"I'm not leaving." Shawn sat back, arms folded across his chest. "But I'll be quiet—if that's okay with Ferris."

"You can move in if you want, I'm so thrilled you brought Princess home. You, my friend, are a hero." Mr. Humphrey certainly looked more than happy and I would have felt the same way.

Shawn, true to his word, kept quiet as Candace questioned the man about this recovery fee, his relationship to Minnie Schultz and also if he had any knowledge about other pets going missing.

While he related that he didn't know Minnie all that well, but that she used to take wonderful care of her garden and lawn up until about six months ago, Princess sauntered back into the room and jumped into my lap.

"You're a cat person and she knows it," Mr. Humphrey said. "She's a very affectionate kitty, and since my wife died, she has been my saving grace."

Candace said, "Did you see Chester Winston in the neighborhood often?"

"You mean the dead man? He made regular rounds in that prison on wheels he drove. But if he was questioning Minnie, that means he was onto her. If he'd lived long enough, perhaps I would have gotten Princess back several days ago."

"Onto her?" I blurted. I quickly said I was sorry, that I'd keep my mouth shut.

"Thanks." Candace's tone indicated I wasn't in as much trouble as Shawn, thank goodness. "You believe Mrs. Schultz stole your cat?"

"Of course she did," Mr. Humphrey said. "Shawn informed me there were dozens of cats in her house and that they were probably also stolen. What was that woman doing? Or maybe she and the animal control man were splitting the recovery fees."

Shawn flushed to his hairline. "That's not what I said, Ferris. Mrs. Schultz is ill and—"

"Shawn? *Please?*" I could tell Candace was using up every ounce of what little patience she possessed.

He stood. "Maybe I *should* be going, but there's one thing everyone in this room needs to know. The county does *not* charge a recovery fee for reuniting owners with lost pets. Your taxes pay for that."

He stomped out, with Ferris hot on his trail. But Shawn was too fast for the older man and I heard him revving the engine of his truck and the squeal of his tires as he took off.

Eighteen

Ferris Humphrey could tell Candace little more than the gossip now making the neighborhood rounds that more than implied Minnie was a murderer. She set him straight and informed the man that she had been ruled out as the killer. Right before we left his place, he apologized profusely for misinterpreting Minnie's involvement and said he would spread the word that she was innocent.

As we drove back to the Schultz house, Candace asked me to call Shawn and ask him not to visit any more of these owners who'd lost pets until she could at least speak with them over the phone.

"Can I wait on that? Knowing Shawn, he'll need time to calm down."

"Not for long. I don't want him heading back to his shelter and making more phone calls. We'll take charge of the list, and once Morris is done searching Chester's office, he and Lois can start calling people."

She opened Minnie's front door and B.J. met us with Simon in his arms.

"Maybe B.J. could make those calls?" I suggested. "Morris isn't exactly an animal lover and Lois will be back at the hospital if she isn't already."

"Jillian, I don't have to tell you that Morris is far more experienced in questioning witnesses. These supposedly *lost* pets and this whole recovery fee thing is a new angle. If need be, I'll do it myself and Morris can take over box duty with B.J."

B.J. looked like he'd been kissed by someone with the plague. Morris was a serious curmudgeon who had no patience for someone brand new at the job.

B.J.'s reaction didn't go unnoticed. Candace said, "Okay, okay. We'll work it out. After Jillian calls Shawn." She turned my way and stared at me pointedly.

"I think this is a job for Superman." I took out my cell and called Tom. After filling him in on what we'd learned and how upset Shawn was that he couldn't reunite every cat with its owner within the next hour, he said, "I'll have Shawn bring me the list and we can make the calls together. But this is an intriguing lead. Good work. May I speak with Candace for a second?"

I saw Candace blush and smile a tad at whatever Tom had said to her. He'd probably praised her for what had been uncovered with Shawn's help. Then it was back to recording the contents of boxes, which was far less fun than anything I can remember in my recent life history.

We kept documenting retail purchases for hours, and finally I told Candace we should stop for the day. I couldn't leave my kitties alone any longer.

"What about the extra cat?" she said.

Simon had followed us around the house and now, as we worked in the living room, he slept on a club chair we'd relieved of several boxes. I was pleased to see another one of my quilts protecting the chair from cat hair. Since I was the designated feline person, I happily volunteered to take Simon to the sanctuary so Shawn could check him out. "I'll need a carrier, though I haven't seen any. Maybe in the garage?"

B.J. said, "I saw quite a few stacked in the basement the day we started searching."

I groaned. "Oh no. Does that mean there are more boxes down there?"

"Nope," Candace said. "And that strikes me as odd. The basement is big enough to have handled three-quarters of this stuff. Storing all the merchandise upstairs tells me the contents of these boxes might have been headed elsewhere."

Her wheels were turning but mine definitely were not. I felt drained. "I'll get one of those carriers and be on my way. My kitty amigos might make me pay for being gone so long yet again."

The basement was as tidy as Minnie probably had kept the upstairs before Chester came into her life. I noticed a shelf full of home-canned peaches and toma-toes. There were also several cat boxes filled with litter. She had a Litter Genie and I stopped to clean the one box Simon had probably been using. Then I made my way past them to where cat carriers were neatly stacked against one wall. I wondered exactly when Chester had latched onto Minnie. Though the boxes we'd searched upstairs had been addressed to her, with all the invoices inside naming her as the buyer, we all suspected this was somehow Chester's doing—that he had convinced a confused woman she needed all sorts of tech stuff, televisions and small appliances. But to what end? Candace suspected he planned on selling it and that seemed like the only logical explanation.

I grabbed one of the larger carriers and made my way back upstairs. I set it on the kitchen floor and opened the top door, readying it for an unwilling traveler. I wasn't sure there was a cat on the planet who enjoyed being crated. Just then, the doorbell rang.

I heard Candace's footsteps cross the hardwood floor in the living room—the polished hardwood uncovered after we'd rearranged the boxes we'd searched to allow us to move freely. Since crime scene tape still surrounded the yard I wondered if Captain Osborne had returned. Who else would dare to interrupt a police investigation?

I hung back in the kitchen doorframe but had a good view of the front door. Yes, I was as curious as my cats.

"Is Chester here?" came a man's voice.

"I'm Detective Carson. What's your business with Mr. Winston?"

I stepped quietly into the living room and saw B.J. leaning against the entry to the bedroom hallway. He was interested, too.

The young man, who was maybe in his early twenties with shaggy, dirty blond hair, held up his hands. His eyes were trained on the gun at Candace's waist. "I'll come back. I'll—"

"You'll stay right where you are," Candace said. "Name?"

"I didn't do anything wrong," the guy said.

"No one said you did. And that's a very strange name." Candace took his forearm and pulled him inside. "Let's chat." She kicked the door closed with her foot and, still hanging on to his arm, led him into the living room.

"Hey, you can't do that," the guy said, shaking free of her grasp.

"But I did. See, here's the thing. You can't cross a police barrier, and the fact that you did tells me a lot about you. For instance, you're not afraid and you don't care if you break the rules. What kind of person is that, Mr. . . . ? Oh, that's right. Mr. *I didn't do anything wrong.*"

"The crime scene tape was already broke and I was curious, is all. What's going on here?"

Candace stared him straight in the eye. "I'll ask the questions. What's your name?"

"Joshua Meyers." The young man's gaze darted around the room at the boxes.

"Okay, Joshua Meyers. Why are you looking for Mr. Winston here? This isn't his residence."

As Candace spoke, B.J. had quietly come all the way into the room. He made his way past Candace and Meyers, taking a spot so he could guard the front door.

"He told me this was where I could pick up my order. I already paid him half, and I *want* my order."

"So, stepping over crime scene tape was worth whatever you paid him? Even though it was obvious that officers were on the premises?" Candace's tone was more measured, less abrasive. There was information to be had, and her tough attitude might not get her what she now wanted.

"I paid him a lot, so yeah."

"How much?"

"A thousand."

"And that was half?" she said.

Was Chester Winston running a *store* out of Minnie's house? How did that happen? But then, her mental state had made her ripe for exploitation.

Meyers was nodding. "Bargain prices for headphones and smartphones. Do you know how much those go for?"

"If I run your name, I won't find any priors, will I, Joshua?"

Meyers flushed. "Minor possession. A few speeding tickets. But I swear, that's all."

"Nothing like receiving stolen goods?" She sounded deceptively sweet now, pleased that this idiot had rung the doorbell.

"No. I *swear*. Would I come here if I thought this stuff was stolen?" Meyers glanced around the room again, but this time I didn't believe he was looking for his merchandise.

"You forgot the part about *me* asking the questions." She looked over Joshua's shoulder at B.J. "Joshua, you and I and Deputy Henderson are taking a trip to my . . . *office*."

Joshua backed up and nearly ran into B.J. "Whoa. You can't do that."

"There you go again with the memory problems. Remember the part about crossing a police barrier?"

He swore under his breath.

Candace looked at me. "Would you mind taking care of the cat and locking up?" She pulled the keys from her pocket and tossed them to me. "Give those to Tom tonight."

I sure hoped he'd be home, but if not, I'd take the keys down to the station this evening.

Once they were gone, I picked up Simon and put him in the carrier, which he treated like an act of betrayal by meowing so loudly I was sure they could hear him down the block.

Turned out, this sweet, loving boy quieted as soon

as I started the engine. When I arrived at the sanctuary, Shawn recognized him right away, but scanned his microchip to make sure this was indeed Minnie's cat. He also checked to see if Simon might be dehydrated after hiding for three days, but he was fine. He'd probably been hiding under beds and chairs or even down in the basement before hunkering down in the closet.

Problem was, Shawn had no room to keep Simon and so he came home with me. I could now be considered Mercy's newest cat collector. How would the new fur friend be greeted? I would soon find out.

On the way home, I thought about the conversation Shawn and I just had concerning the cats who were chipped and who had owners in the area. He told me that after e-mailing the list to Tom, he made calls to a few owners out of curiosity—no surprise there—and the story was the same every time: that darned fake recovery fee. Looked like Chester was a crook in more ways than one, charging people a hundred dollars each to reclaim their beloved cats.

What did Minnie have to do with this scheme? I couldn't imagine her willingly participating—that is, unless she had been convinced by Chester that it was all on the up and up. It wasn't, of course, but in her state of mind, she might well have believed anything the man told her.

Nineteen

Bringing Simon into a house with five cats already in residence proved more difficult than I'd imagined. Since so many cats had been in Minnie's place, I believed this would have been a smooth introduction. The hissing game started the minute I walked in the back door with yet another feline in tow.

Maybe my crew had just about all they could take. How could I blame them? I'd been absent for three days running, and during that time, they'd had to put up with a very energetic Otto. My absence meant little petting or conversation—both of which were quite important to my kitties. Since marrying Tom, I had become a home-body for the most part, having given up many of my craft show attendances. Instead, I did almost twice as much quilting and sold everything from home. My projects were selling online just fine. And my feline friends enjoyed this change.

Dashiell's negative response to Simon was especially strong, so I decided the new baby and Otto could hang out downstairs in the cat room since they were familiar with each other already. Once they were settled, I sat on the kitchen floor with my four sweet kitties. I offered treats, played with them, and after scarfing down another salad, I lay down on the sofa for a little rest. It had been a tiring day. Chablis couldn't have been more thrilled. She jumped onto my stomach and settled down for a much-desired cuddle. I was soon surrounded by the other three and their collective purring put me right to sleep.

I awoke in the darkened living room to the sound of Tom opening the back door. At least I *hoped* it was him. I sat up carefully, not wanting to disturb the slumbering Chablis. The other three were no doubt greeting Tom, hoping for double treats from him and lots of scratching on their foreheads.

"Jilly?" came his stage whisper.

I reached around and turned the lamp on. "Hey, hon. What time is it?"

"Past nine. You sound sleepy." He came into the room carrying his buddy Dashiell. "Why not head to bed and get some good rest? I hear you were plenty busy today."

"I've been asleep for at least two hours, which means I'll be awake for a while. Guess I can catch some late-night TV. What did you learn from Joshua Meyers?"

Tom settled into the easy chair across from me and put his feet on the ottoman. "Joshua Meyers, my dear, is a fence."

"Why in the heck did he ring the doorbell at Minnie's house knowing the police were there? Seems rather . . . *stupid.*"

"Regardless of what you see on TV, criminals are not known for their intellect. The Joshua Meyers of the world believe they can lie their way out of anything, even if they're talking to a police officer."

"Meyers was there to pick up stuff to sell and actually thought he'd leave with a truckload, huh? That is pretty dumb. Why did Minnie buy all that stuff for Chester in the first place? What could he have told her to make her believe it was okay?"

"We don't even know if *she* actually did the buying. Those boxes remain a bit of a mystery. From my little talk with Joshua, he only heard there was merchandise that he might be able to buy cheap and sell high. We have no proof he gave Chester Winston any money at all; in fact, we have no proof he even *knew* the dead man. Word on the street travels faster than a three-legged chicken, and my guess is Joshua heard about Minnie's house and what was inside. I doubt we'll get a straight answer out of him as to exactly who he heard this from."

"Gosh, I was hoping him showing up would be the break you needed."

"We're holding him for a few more hours, but he's only guilty of being as dumb as a box of rocks. I have to head back to the station, but I wanted to check on you. I turned on the cat cam and saw you were asleep, but you'd hardly moved a muscle every time I looked at you."

"Ah, the cat cam is also a wife cam, then?"

He laughed and pointed at me. "Right. So don't get any ideas. Actually, when you didn't answer my text, I got a little concerned."

"I never heard it. Can I fix you coffee before you leave?" I picked up a limp Chablis and held her to my chest as I stood. She was out like she hadn't slept in days. She nuzzled into my neck and began to purr.

"Coffee would be awesome. Mind if I chill out with old Dashiell? This chair seems a lot more comfortable than I remember."

"I don't need help making coffee. You have to be more exhausted than I was. How much sleep have you had in the last three days?"

"Doesn't matter. I'll catch up when we clear this case."

I made the coffee strong and Tom accepted his mug with a grateful smile. I also handed him the keys to Minnie's house and he dropped them into his shirt pocket. Meanwhile, the cats decided I needed watching, probably figuring I could disappear again at any moment. The original three amigos gathered around me and Merlot even sat on my feet when I settled on the sofa.

I said, "Do you believe that Chester's hitting up pet owners for those recovery fees turned him into a victim?"

"Could well be, but we need to start from the center and work out. Most murder victims are killed by an angry or mentally unstable family member. If I clear those folks, then as I mentioned before, the suspect pool becomes a whole lot bigger."

"Alcohol could be involved in whatever happened. Seems Minnie's twins were drunk when they got into it with Chester's family at the hospital."

"Alcohol and drugs are kind of what I meant when I used the term *unstable*." He smiled.

I nodded. "This case is all over the map. Fake recovery fees, a fence hoping to cash in on murder, a woman with a brain tumor who was probably taken advantage of and a doctor run off the road and nearly killed."

"Hold on," Tom said. "We don't know if Dr. Ross's crash is connected to this case. Remember—she deals with mentally ill folks all the time."

"Of course. You'd think I wouldn't jump to conclusions by now, but something tells me it *is* connected."

"Maybe." He sipped his coffee and offered nothing more, which made me believe he knew something he wasn't saying.

I decided to change the subject. "That Captain Osborne offered to help. You wouldn't have an issue with that man, would you?" I smiled, knowing immediately from his expression that I'd hit the nail on the head.

"He's arrogant and he wants to move up the county police ranks. Remember that big meth lab we had our sights on a couple of months ago? The one just inside Mercy town limits?"

Chablis jumped into my lap now that she'd decided I wasn't getting up again. "I recall you were determined to gather everyone involved and put them in jail."

"The county sheriff's officers who joined us in the investigation made the bust too soon. We lost out on arresting several other players. We'd had to pair with the sheriff's department since so many bad guys were on our radar. I'm certain Osborne was the one who jumped the gun."

"You never told me, Tom." I stroked Chablis and she closed her eyes and purred.

"I was embarrassed. Half of those drugged-up morons have moved out of Mercy because we didn't complete our investigation. I'm glad they're not here anymore, but they'll be setting up somewhere else and spreading their misery."

"That's pretty sorry. Osborne did that so he could take the credit?" I asked.

"That's my guess. I've worked with people like him before. They act like an invading army, ready to claim territory that doesn't belong to them."

"You sound frustrated and I don't blame you. Speaking of frustration, what about Chester's family? Are they cooperating? I mean, one of them hit Morris in the head. They had a loud argument in the hospital corridor with Minnie's sons. The daughter-in-law was the one who attacked Morris. Who *are* these people?"

"Them." He closed his eyes, breathed deeply and let out the air with a huge sigh. "The daughter-in-law is Lucinda, married to Chester's eldest kid, Earl. I haven't met the daughter, but she goes to school in Tennessee and isn't around. The ex-wife might have had a beef with Chester. Her name is Marjorie Allen. She's been married and divorced four times. They've all lawyered up. After how they've acted, that's actually a smart move. Makes my job harder, though."

"Have you spoken with them at all?"

"Yesterday, before the head-bashing and the hospital incident. They all alibi each other for the day we found Chester, but who knows if that will hold up considering we don't have a time of death closer than within the last five days. I had to call the coroner today and, of course, guess who answered the phone?"

"Lydia Monk. How did that conversation go?" From my brief encounter with her at Minnie's house the other day, her animosity toward me seemed to have ratcheted up a notch.

"Actually, she was helpful for once. Polite, even. She told me the autopsy was scheduled for tomorrow. They had to ask a medical examiner to come here from Columbia to do the job. The lady doc they've been using is sick with pneumonia."

Syrah jumped onto the back of the sofa near my

head and rested a paw on my shoulder. I reached back and petted him. "Is it weird that I enjoy talking to my husband about murders and suspects and autopsies?"

"That's my world. I promise to enjoy a quilt discussion in the near future."

"Are you kidding me?" I laughed. "Quilting is never that exciting. No adrenaline rush. It is, however, relaxing and comforting."

"That's why I want to talk to you about it. Besides, isn't a quilt like a puzzle that you have to put together?"

I laughed. "It is. It becomes even more puzzling when I make a mistake and have to figure out how to fix it without undoing hours of work."

"I believe that's why you like to hear about my cases—because you're a puzzle solver at heart." Tom lifted Dashiell, stood and walked over to the sofa. He set his sleepy boy down next to me. "I have to get back to work. I'm trying to take on the reports for everyone working the case. The two night shift officers are picking up a lot of slack. We do have other crimes to handle but nothing major. They're pulling twelve-hour shifts."

"And you're pulling twenty-four-hour shifts."

He put his hands on either side of my face, bent and kissed me. "As long as I can spend a little time with you every day, I can manage."

My phone, sitting on the coffee table in front of me, rang. I was ready to let it go to voice mail so I could say a proper good-bye to Tom, but I'd asked Kara to update me on the two women in the hospital. I didn't want to miss that call.

Tom picked up the phone and handed it to me so I wouldn't disturb the cats surrounding me. Merlot had completely stretched out on both my feet to make sure I didn't move.

"It's Kara." Tom blew me a kiss while I answered the phone.

She said, "Jillian, it's good news. Minnie's operation took longer than they thought, but they got the whole tumor. As soon as the swelling goes down in her brain, they'll start to wake her up."

Relief washed over me. "Great news. What about Dr. Ross?"

"Her brother tells me she's out of the woods. In fact, they could start bringing her out of *her* coma as soon as tomorrow."

"I am so glad. Maybe she recognized whoever ran her off the road."

"Her brother said she will probably have no memory of what happened right before the wreck. Who's working her case, by the way? I'd like to talk to them for my piece about her. I've learned she's quite a remarkable woman."

"You know, I have no idea. Tom mentioned the two night shift officers—that's Clancy and Fowler, I believe—are picking up the slack while everyone else works on Chester's murder."

"But chances are, this is part of the Winston case, right?" Kara sounded a tad disappointed.

"That's what I thought, but Tom said we can't jump to that conclusion. There's no evidence connecting her incident to Chester's murder."

"What if we could find that evidence?" she said.

"Are you saying that you miss that investigative journalist job you had in Houston and feel you can start over right now?"

"Do you truly believe that her accident so soon after she took on Minnie as a patient was a coincidence?"

"No—and I don't think Tom believes it was a coincidence, either, but he said they have to start in the center and move out. That means investigating family members first."

"Okay, so while they're doing that, we can at least try to gather information about the hours before the accident. Maybe we'll find a connection."

"We shouldn't interfere with Tom's investigation, Kara."

"Her brother is torn up, Jillian." She was almost pleading now. "All they have is each other, and she was intentionally targeted."

"You've been away from big-city journalism for too long. Peyton touched your heart, didn't he?"

A short silence followed. "Yes," she almost whispered. "Like I said, all they have is each other. For years before my dad met you, all *we* had was each other. I felt an instant connection to him."

"Okay, I get that. But can you do the digging around and leave me on the fringe of your personal investigation?"

"I know you, Jillian. You care as much as I do. But I'll make it easy for now. Tell me everything you know about Dr. Ross's interactions with Minnie."

Twenty

I lay in bed an hour later feeling as if I were hiding information from Tom that he needed to know. Once Kara set her mind to investigating something, she wouldn't quit. I'd distracted myself from this reality by taking care of the "downstairs kitties" before I got ready for bed. I'd found them snuggled together sharing one of my quilts. I'd quickly run upstairs to get a few more so Otto and Simon would be nice and comfy. They'd probably have to stay in the kitty room through tomorrow, as I wanted to visit my hospitalized new friends—or at least show my support to their families. Visiting them probably wasn't an option.

But as I awaited sleep, I had nothing to do but think about Kara's plans. When I sat up and turned the lamp on, my four cats all raised their heads and looked at me as if I'd lost my mind. They'd been sure I was down for the count.

I called Tom, but he didn't answer, and I chickened out when his recorded voice asked me to leave a message. It would be a stammering and probably incoherent recitation about how my stepdaughter would soon be crossing the line into his police territory. He was already irritated with Captain Osborne for doing exactly that.

But not leaving a message turned out to be a worse mistake because within seconds Tom called sounding panicked. "Are you okay? You always leave a message."

"No. I'm fine. I decided it could wait until morning." I leaned against the headboard, eyes closed. It *could* have waited. Kara wouldn't be out with her tablet and stylus hunting down witnesses in the middle of the night.

"It doesn't have to wait now." The tenor of his voice alone could soothe me.

"Promise you won't be angry?" I said.

"Jilly, you are the last person on earth who could get me riled. What's going on?"

"It's Kara. She's got a soft spot for Dr. Ross's brother. To help him get answers, she wants to figure out who might have run his sister off the road and at the same time prove to you it's connected to Chester's murder." I went on to explain more about our conversation.

Tom sighed. "I can't say I like that. We're dealing with a killer, and if she does make the connection between the two crimes, she could become a target. I'll call and warn her off this tomorrow."

"I'm sorry. I should have been more forceful with her. But you're right. She could be putting herself in danger."

"Actually, this isn't anything you did, so no need to apologize. She's a big girl and no matter what you said, she probably would have stuck her investigative nose in all this. I love Kara, but I hope I can convince her to wait this out for a few days."

I said, "The stubborn adolescent I met years ago has

grown into an even more stubborn adult. I wish I knew how she planned to *investigate*."

"That's the question I intend to ask her tomorrow." After Tom told me to get some sleep, we both said, "I love you."

I had another fitful night and by morning I thought maybe I should be the one to convince Kara to let the police do the investigating, especially after she showed up at our back door looking as tired as I felt.

Once we both held mugs of coffee and she'd greeted each cat, we sat looking out on the still lake.

She said, "Tom called me very early this morning. I guess you told him how interested I was in Dr. Ross's case." Chablis had squirmed into Kara's lap, even though the edge of the table made it a tight fit.

"Guilty as charged. I asked if he thought the cases were connected. I'm sure he told you exactly what he told me."

"That he has to focus on the families as suspects first, and he cannot try to fit Dr. Ross into the equation right now. I get that. Most people are murdered by someone close. Blah, blah, blah. But I've already started checking on those family members. Chester's daughter, the college student, was on campus all week. It's midterm time."

"How did you find this out?" I asked.

"I know people all over the country from my days working at the *Houston Chronicle*. These are folks willing to check stuff out for me. The professor in charge of the school newspaper where she attends? I know him. He immediately called a student who knew someone who knew someone else. Took me thirty minutes last night to discover she remained on campus all week."

"Did you tell Tom?"

"He thanked me, though he'd already checked her alibi and knew where she'd been. The others are far trickier. I mean, who can vouch for where *you* were every minute of the day and night yesterday or last week or . . ." I started to speak but she held up a hand. "I take that back. You're not a good example. You're married to the police chief. But what about me? Where was I? How much of my time can you or Liam account for? If I lied, would either of you back me up if you had knowledge that I wasn't telling the truth? Because that's what happens in families. They protect each other."

"You have a point." She seemed so worked up, I decided to simply listen and not dispute what she said. Tom could interrogate with the best of them. I often believed he could get the truth out of a stone, so at some point he would make the connection between the crimes if one existed.

"Meanwhile," she went on, "Brenda was run off the road and her case is sitting on the back burner because this small police department has way too much on its plate. And there I go mixing metaphors, which shows how tired I am."

I smiled at my frustrated stepdaughter. "You care a lot about Brenda and her brother—and you haven't even met the woman."

"Like I said back when Peyton was talking about her, she's one of the good guys, Jillian. He is, too. I spent a lot of time sitting in the surgery waiting room with that anguished man. I've had enough experience interviewing people to be a pretty good judge of character. Brenda cared about the mentally ill. She cared about her patients almost to the exclusion of all else. What happened to put her in harm's way? That's what I need to find out."

I looked at Kara over my raised mug. "The sheriff's department offered to help. Should Tom have taken them up on that?"

She raised her eyebrows and appeared interested. "Who offered?"

"Captain Osborne."

"Oh. *Him*." Kara sounded dismissive. "I've run into him when I've been to crime scenes outside Mercy boundaries. He *is* a take-charge kind of guy, so I suppose I shouldn't be surprised. A few deputies under his command responded first to Dr. Ross's wreck, but her crash was within Mercy city limits, just like the murder. It was our paramedics and our fire department that took care of her. It's a Mercy PD case."

"You didn't answer my question. Should I try to convince Tom to get over his animosity toward Osborne so the sheriff's department can help with documenting all the evidence and even do some interviewing?"

Kara seemed distracted now. "I never got a good vibe from Osborne when I would run into him while covering a story in the county. He's, well, kind of *obstructive*. Since I once worked for Tom when I first came to live in Mercy, I'm certain he can handle the job of finding out what exactly went down in Dr. Ross's case—but with my help."

"You seem worked up. What is going on, Kara?"

"I have knowledge and experience to dig around in what happened to Dr. Ross, yet I feel Tom ignored my offer. There's no political or territorial agenda for me. All I want is answers." She smiled for the first time since arriving. "But now that the coffee is kicking in, I know what I have to do."

"And what's that?"

"Put on my big-girl newspaper panties and interview people. We still have freedom of the press last time I checked." She set down her mug and stood. "About time I got busy."

Before I could say anything but "Wait," she was gone. No one could stop Kara once she put her mind to something. Unfortunately, one of those people she was about to interview might be a killer. Though it could be considered intrusive of me, I decided Liam had to know what Kara was about to do. He still had his finger on the pulse of the criminal elements in our county. I'd seen that reckless look in Kara's eyes, the same look as when I'd first met her so many years ago.

I decided to call Liam's office after his cell went to voice mail. Sue Ann answered with "Liam Brennan, attorney-at-law."

"Hey there, Sue Ann. It's Jillian."

"I see that from the caller ID, but I am sticking with the professional approach. What's up, Jillian?"

"Is Liam available? His cell went to voice mail."

"He actually has a client. Not exactly his *kind* of client, but money is money."

"Darn. I wanted to give him a heads-up about Kara. I'm a little worried about her—though I'm probably being overprotective."

"He's kind of overprotective about her himself. One day, my prince will come, too." She laughed. "Can I take a message?"

"Ask him to call me when he's not busy."

"Oh, that would be ninety percent of the time. For now, anyway," she said.

"Does that mean more clients are on his agenda?"

"Didn't he tell you the other day? He's joining forces with students from the local law school—and *local* here means what? Fifty miles away? Anyway, he wants to create something similar to the Innocence Project in this area of South Carolina."

I smiled. "Getting justice for people falsely imprisoned sounds like something Liam would embrace."

"He also wants Kara on board. She's a great investigator and has contacts everywhere."

"She was quick to remind me of exactly that this morning," I said with a laugh.

"I'll have Liam call you, Jillian."

I disconnected, thinking how that project sounded like something the two of them would be quite good at.

I was due back at the Schultz house to help Candace and B.J., but I wanted to fit in a hospital visit. Plus I had two cats downstairs who needed a little more human interaction. When I went to the basement, I found Dashiell crouched at the door to the cat room. Maybe they'd been playing the paws-under-the-door game, a kitty favorite around here. Before saying good morning to Simon and Otto, I cleaned litter boxes that belonged to the upstairs crew. I couldn't help but hear Dashiell's continuous low growl. No paws-under-the-door game, then. Not yet. Merging cats while I was away today obviously wasn't an option.

I gathered up our grouchy tabby and took him upstairs. A stressed-out Dashiell could mean his blood sugar would rise, so when I went down again to visit with Simon and Otto, I closed the basement door to keep him distanced from his obsession with the cat room. A half hour later, I returned upstairs, having satisfied myself that the two newest additions were content to stay with each other in the basement—at least for now.

The trip to the hospital seemed to take longer than ever. It wasn't until I arrived at the information desk that I learned Minnie was also in the ICU, her bed perhaps right alongside Brenda's. I took the elevator to the third-floor ICU waiting room.

Greta sat with two young men who had to be Henry and Harris, since they looked exactly alike aside from their hair. One had his pulled back in a messy bun with strands loose around his face. The other twin had a preppy style with clean-cut sandy hair. He wore a thin V-neck sweater over an expensive-looking collared shirt. Long-haired guy wore a T-shirt and jeans. Despite the difference in grooming and style, their features told me they were identical twins.

A coffeepot sat on a small table against one wall. The grimy liquid inside the glass container looked like it might grow mold right before my eyes if I stayed here for the next hour.

Greta waved at me, looking weary. She had her feet propped up on the seat of a straight-back chair and I saw that her ankles were swollen. Long-haired brother whispered in her ear while staring at me.

Might as well deal with this straightaway, I thought. I didn't like people whispering about me while I was five feet away. I walked over and introduced myself, glancing back and forth between the two young men. I learned that Harris had the bun and Henry was the preppy type.

"Greta says you're the top cop's wife," Harris said. "Did you come here to finish what he started?"

"He was here?" I ignored his question, sensing I might be ignoring much of what he said if he didn't take the insolence out of his tone.

"You just missed him." Greta slapped Harris's knee. "And be nice. She's been good to Mama."

"How is your mother doing?" I asked Brenda.

"They got the whole tangled mess out of her head," she replied. "It took them a long time but apparently the swelling in her brain will go down and she might be her old self again after rehab."

I smiled. "What a relief for all of you." *Even if y'all pretty much abandoned her when she needed you the most,* I thought. I could never picture Tom or Kara or Candace or Liam or any of my family . . . well, they'd never do what these siblings had done.

"Greta says you're taking care of Otto," Henry asked. "He was small the last time I saw him. I'll bet he's grown."

So we talked about Otto, obviously a safe subject, until Peyton entered the room. His rumpled trousers and wrinkled shirt, not to mention his unshaven face and tired eyes, told me that he probably hadn't left the hospital.

"Hi, Jillian." He eased into a chair on the other side of the room and patted the chair next to him. "Can I give you an update?"

Harris said, "What are you? Hospital lady? Do you know everyone here?"

I wasn't about to explain the relationship between these two families. I found myself wondering if Tom realized they'd all been here together.

I sat next to Peyton and turned my chair so I could see his face. "Did Brenda have a good night?"

"I just went in to see her. She's still in the coma but they will start bringing her out today. It's great news."

"Did you get to talk to my husband and tell him this?"

"Yes. Captain Osborne, right?"

I must have appeared as confused as I felt because Peyton said, "No. I've mixed things up. I haven't slept and—"

I rested a hand on his arm. "My husband is Chief Stewart, but the mix-up is understandable. You're saying Captain Osborne came here?"

"His deputies were the first to respond to my sister's accident. He was concerned. I told him they probably saved her life. But your husband came after the other police officer left. I saw him in the hallway and we talked briefly. I've spent a lot of time trying to walk off this haze of exhaustion created by worry. It didn't work, I'm afraid."

Henry Schultz had approached us so quietly, he surprised me enough to stop me from replying. I blinked in surprise as I glanced up at him.

He took in Peyton and then said, "You're here for the doctor who helped my mother?"

"Yes. I'm Peyton Ross, her brother." He rose with effort and extended a hand.

The two men greeted each other.

"I'm Henry Schultz, Minnie's son. I saw you sleeping in that corner when we arrived but I had no idea you were related to the woman we've heard about. She's the one who figured out Mama wasn't nuts."

I watched as Peyton recoiled at the word *nuts*. "My sister takes care of those nut jobs pretty well." He nodded, his lips tight with irritation.

Henry reddened. "Sorry. But you know what I mean."

"Yes. Brenda is an excellent physician. Went to medical school and everything." He looked down at me. "This lady here was quite a help to your mother and to my sister as well. She's here visiting all of us waiting for good news." He refocused on Henry. "By the way, I don't know anything about your mother's case aside from the fact she actually had a medical issue rather than a psychiatric one."

"Brain tumor. In a coma. But they say the operation was a success."

The chill between them seemed to recede. Meanwhile, Harris busied himself by playing a game on his smartphone and Greta leaned back against her balled-up sweater, hands resting on her pregnant belly. It dawned on me I hadn't ever seen her husband. Perhaps he was caring for other children or simply hated hospitals.

Henry went on to say, "I'll leave you two alone now. I wanted to make sure my guess was correct. Thank your sister for helping Mama."

Peyton offered a weary smile. "I'm grateful that I'll get the chance to do that." He sat down again.

"Remember how you talked about Brenda's phone?" I said quietly. "Did anyone ever bring your sister's belongings to you?"

"Oh, Captain Osborne took them—but there was no phone. I mentioned this to Chief Stewart, by the way. He seemed a little bothered about the whole thing, said something about chain of custody being down the toilet now."

"What did you give Captain Osborne?" I asked.

"Bloody clothes and shoes. Nothing more."

"I remember Brenda said she wanted to give Minnie a journal since she seemed to be a woman who liked to write everything down. Her daughter said Brenda may have picked up one that Minnie had been writing in while she was in the hospital, a notebook that I assume Brenda gave to her. They didn't find anything like that in the car?"

"Not that I know about. The car went to wherever they take wrecked cars that might be considered evidence. Maybe something like that got left behind or was even tossed from the vehicle during impact. I hear it was a twisted mess. Seems she went off the road and hit a gigantic tree. But that darn tree saved her from careening into the creek not too far down the embankment. She would have drowned." His lip quivered with emotion.

I leaned forward and put my arm around his shoulder. "But she didn't. It wasn't her time."

His swimming eyes met mine. "No. Not her time."

Twenty-one

On my way back to Mercy, Kara called. But if I thought I'd get away with warning Liam about her quest to make sure Brenda's case received as much attention as Chester's Winston's death, I was wrong.

"Jillian, I know you mean well," came her tinny voice through the phone. "But I will be fine. Liam even offered to help, if it makes you feel better."

"The reception on this call is pretty bad, Kara. Where are you?"

"Liam and I are at the scene of the crash. Pretty isolated area. I've also learned where the wrecked car was taken—a garage Mercy PD has a contract with—and we're headed there next."

"I'm glad Liam is with you. Sorry to be a worry-wart, but someone tried to kill Brenda and—"

"I understand. You love me and you care and that means a lot."

I said, "One thing I learned when I went to visit the hospital patients—or rather offer support to their relatives—is that Captain Osborne came by and he took away the clothes Brenda was wearing when she got run off the road."

"I know. When I called Tom he told me Osborne dropped them off at the station."

"Oh. That's good, right? But there was no phone or anything else? Things that might have come from Minnie."

"Nope. Just clothing. Apparently even her purse was missing, so Tom thinks she could have been robbed. Since Osborne brought everything to Tom straight-away, I may have judged him too harshly," Kara said. "He *is* trying to help and Tom told me that even though Osborne still believes this is his case, if he's relegated to the sidelines, that's okay."

I smiled. "Tom's pretty good at steering people to his way of thinking."

"He sure is. Listen, we have to get moving. I promised Tom that all I would do is talk to the wrecker drivers who pulled Brenda's car off that tree. I don't want to mess with evidence. But those drivers see every kind of smashed-up vehicle and they might tell us a lot about exactly what they think happened."

"I'm glad you're working with Tom and keeping him informed. I'm certain that's all he wants."

"We're family, Jillian. We talk things through. I would never do anything to damage the honesty we all share. Tell Candace what I'm up to when you see her. I did a little venting to her last night on the phone and she'll be relieved to know I've taken her advice and let Tom know up front what we're doing rather than after the fact."

"I will. I'm on my way to meet her at the Schultz house now. I'm glad Liam is with you. Still, you know me. I'll worry no matter what."

Surprisingly enough, I beat Candace to the Schultz

house, but then again, I'd left my house early. It gave me a chance to pull up the cat cam and watch Merlot and Syrah wrestling while I considered the twin brothers I'd just met. No doubt Tom had talked to them since that's why he'd gone to the hospital, but had they given him any real information? There'd been no mention of any conversation, even though they knew who I was. That seemed odd. But then, the twins had been elusive since day one. I didn't trust those two, even if Henry tried his best to seem friendly.

Candace and B.J. pulled up and I noticed B.J. was driving. How had he *ever* convinced her to let him take the wheel of her squad car? But B.J. could be charming in a naïve sort of way.

Candace held two to-go cups of coffee bearing the Belle's Beans logo. Maybe B.J. had said the coffee would be all over the place if she drove—and that was definitely the truth. I met them at the front door and she gave me a vanilla latte bearing my name in black marker on the side of the cup. They knew what I always ordered and I couldn't have been more grateful. Peyton Ross's outpouring of emotion had sapped me after such a sleepless night.

"Let's hope no more cats are hiding in closets," Candace said as we entered the house.

I was pleased the corridor of boxes was gone. Yesterday's items had been hauled away to Mercy's evidence locker. The house almost seemed huge now.

"What will we find today?" B.J.'s mustache of foam from his coffee almost made me laugh. "I'm hoping for the latest video games."

"Which will all head to the evidence locker, too," Candace warned.

"Of course," he said. "But I might see something I don't know about yet and will have to buy."

We headed to the kitchen, our first room to tackle today. It smelled so fresh and clean—like the lemon verbena cleaner I used myself—despite the fact this home had housed dozens of cats in the last few months.

"I swear Minnie spent all her time cleaning." I set my already half empty coffee on the kitchen table.

"Something that makes our job more difficult, unfortunately," Candace said. "We found almost no fingerprints, although the lab called and said they definitely matched Chester's in various places."

"That's not a real surprise, is it?" I said. "The man was found dead here, after all."

"Those prints showed that he'd been in almost every room, though," B.J. said. "It confirms that he made himself at home."

Candace perused the kitchen, probably wondering where to start. "Too bad those prints could have been left anytime. How I wish we had a way to time-stamp fingerprints. Maybe that technology is in the works. It sure would help clear cases quicker."

"Do you believe that all the cats helped Chester insert himself so completely into Minnie's life?" I asked.

Candace walked over to a stack of boxes in front of what looked like a baker's rack. "Yes, it seems the cats are telling us the story."

B.J. followed her, fiddling with his video camera.

"Because of those microchips, right?" I couldn't help but smile at the idea of kitty assistance.

She nodded. "Thank goodness Shawn matched the microchipped cats to their owners. An added benefit is that his doing this also revealed *when* the cats disappeared from their homes. Some of them weren't even outdoor cats. Two of them were apparently taken from outdoor kitty apparatuses after the mesh was cut open."

"Holy cannoli. That's pretty bold," I said. "And who would the owners report this to? Chester Winston, of course."

Candace nodded again, more emphatically this time. "Exactly. Then he hands them over to a woman who couldn't say no because she was confused. Somehow Chester convinced her this was a good thing. Obviously he couldn't take those cats to the county shelter. There would have to be documentation for any cat Chester supposedly *found* and hauled there. I'm wondering how much money he made on those fake recovery fees. We haven't got his financials or his phone records yet."

"Why is it taking so long?" I asked.

Candace checked her notebook and then marked the largest box in front of the baker's rack with the number twenty. "It always does. But now that we have proof Chester committed fraud, we can get those records today. Just because someone died violently doesn't mean their bank or credit card records are freely available. Judges are pretty careful about issuing warrants. But Shawn has made our job a whole lot easier because the victim himself committed a crime. He was basically extorting money from those cat owners."

"Ah. I see. But what about Minnie's bank and credit card records?"

Candace was about to open the box with B.J. and the camera ready. But she stopped and turned to face me, head tilted. "*Minnie's records?* You believe Minnie was complicit in the fraud? We found no evidence that—" She put her hands on her hips and looked at the ceiling. "*Wait *a minute.* We simply collected her financial documents and they've been sitting at the station. I never thought to see if she was the one who actually *bought* a case of cell phones. Or any of this other stuff. In our defense, that's because until yesterday we had no idea what was in all these boxes." She waved her arm around the kitchen.

"Those bank and credit card statements are on your desk at the station," B.J. said.

"Along with about five thousand other things. We ruled out Mrs. Schultz as far as committing murder, but what if Chester talked her into helping with this other scheme of his? Maybe he promised her all the cats she ever wanted if she'd buy stuff he could sell for a profit?" Candace unclipped her phone from her utility belt. As she punched numbers she pointed at me. "Thank you, my friend. I should have thought of this yesterday, but I am overloaded with evidence and suspects."

I almost laughed out loud at that one. All I did was ask a question. She figured out the rest.

Because Tom wasn't available, Candace had Grace fetch the documents from Candace's desk. She listened while Grace apparently read things to her. When she disconnected, she said, "All of this stuff—or let me be careful—*a lot* of this stuff was purchased with Minnie's credit card."

"Oh no," I said. "Does that mean she's a criminal, too? Will she be arrested? Because—"

"Hang on to your heart, Jillian. If Chester inserted himself completely into that poor woman's life, he probably had access to everything, including her credit cards. With her family distanced from her, who was paying attention to her spending habits? No one—including Minnie herself."

"All this stuff was probably purchased over the Internet, right?" B.J. said. "No signature required."

"Exactly," Candace said. "I can't wait to see how much money Chester made off selling what were probably stolen goods—no doubt bought and paid for by a woman who had no idea what was going on."

"But where was he selling this stuff?" I asked.

B.J. said, "When I canvassed the neighborhood the day we discovered the body, that guy across the street told me there were plenty of deliveries here. That made sense considering all these unopened boxes. But what if there were pickups, too?"

Candace grinned. "*Both* of you are geniuses. Getting information out of those delivery companies isn't easy. But pickups are scheduled and the delivery company would require payment. All we need is the name of one buyer and that might open a floodgate of information."

"But if you need a warrant for the delivery company records, that could take time," B.J. said.

"The computer we found here, the one taken to the tech lab, was a new laptop. Grace just told me Minnie's credit card statement indicates she bought that computer from an online electronics retailer. Maybe those postage and pickup fees were also charged but just haven't shown up on the statements we've collected so far."

"But she didn't even recognize what a cell phone was," I said. "She wasn't capable of using a computer in her condition, so all of this had to be Chester's doing."

"Perhaps with the help of the person who killed him. Maybe this was more than a one-man operation and tempers flared. Along with the laptop, Morris took another one in after searching Chester's apartment. If he was buying and selling online, the information could be on that computer, on the one Minnie supposedly purchased or both—even if he thought he'd covered his tracks by deleting the money trail."

My turn to nod in understanding. "I see."

"Catfishers sometimes use a similar scam," B.J. said. "Hook an unsuspecting *love interest* online, create a *fake* credit card, order merchandise just like what we're seeing in this house, have it shipped to the love interest, who turns around and ships it overseas as instructed because they think they're doing a good deed. This is a little different since an authentic credit card account was used, but it's a similar scam. Or perhaps Chester was using both methods."

"Right," Candace said. "B.J., we need Tom's clout right now. I want you to hunt him down, explain this theory and have him call the computer forensics lab where we sent those computers. Even if Chester or someone else deleted information, knowing what might have been deleted will make the lab's job easier. Pressure from the police chief will be more effective than if it came from me."

"I'll get right on it." He set the camera on the kitchen table and was gone so fast I hardly had time to blink.

Candace already had box number twenty open.

"Should I operate the camera?" I asked.

"No. That would create problems if this case goes to court. I'll do it. But you can number boxes. Start in this room with number twenty-one and then all we have left is the living room and dining room, thank goodness. This has been tedious, but evidence work has to be done right."

"I got that message the first day we met," I said with a smile.

I finished numbering the boxes in both areas and returned to the kitchen to find Candace dictating into her phone. The particular box she was inventorying was filled with new toasters—and not cheap ones, either.

Candace shook her head and looked down at the toasters. "I swear Chester was starting his own big-box store."

"There are online stores, you know. It's not just eBay anymore. I have my own online site for selling cat quilts with 'buy' buttons."

Candace gave me that look again, like her mind was going a hundred miles an hour. "Craigslist isn't the only game in town, either. This could be nationwide, and that means transporting stolen goods across state lines. If Tom thinks Captain Osborne is a pain about butting in, the FBI is about a million times worse. For now, why don't we keep this to ourselves until the computer forensics come back?"

My heart sank. "If Minnie had knowledge of what Chester was doing, could she be arrested by the FBI?"

"That's a worst-case scenario, Jillian. A woman with a brain tumor who was so confused she wandered away from her house wouldn't be considered a criminal mastermind."

"But that means there *is* a criminal mastermind. And whoever it was came into this house and killed a man. Why?"

"Because despite that quote from Proverbs about honor among thieves, it simply isn't so."

Twenty-two

When B.J. returned to the Schultz house, Tom accompanied him. The two brought sub sandwiches, bottled water, and a carafe of sweet tea as well as a bag of paper cups and plates and a mountain of napkins.

I'd missed Tom so much in the last few days, but if he did end up taking the police chief job permanently, I would have to get used to him spending long hours when cases like this landed in his lap. Thank goodness it probably wouldn't happen often.

I found a tablecloth in the dining room sideboard and we spread it out on the kitchen floor. Tom and I sat with our knees touching. I was happy to spend even a small amount of time near him.

After I swallowed down the first bite of a veggie sandwich—and it tasted so good—I said, "Any luck on the computer front?"

"Don't I wish," Tom said. "I called in a few favors with the bosses and they've put a rush on it. We still have no idea if there's anything of value on that laptop. Chester's work computer is at the lab, too, so we're dealing with three computers now. Morris took almost everything from his office and booked it as evidence."

"Everything?" Candace asked.

Tom picked up the second half of his sandwich. "There wasn't much to take. I spoke to Sara Jo, the young woman who answers the phones at the county shelter and relays calls to Chester about animals in need of care. She says she found his office unlocked the day he died. *That* was unusual. So far, we haven't found his work keys. They weren't in the jeans he wore the day he died. My guess is, the killer took them and went to the office. Any piece of evidence on Chester's body that would lead us to our murderer was probably removed by that person—phones, keys, who knows what else."

"Are Minnie's sons still suspects? Because I saw them when I went to the hospital this morning," I said. "I hear you were there, too, Tom."

"Though I had to talk to those brothers, I didn't want to interrupt them in the waiting area while their mother was having brain surgery. Thank goodness the hospital that early in the morning is pretty quiet and I was able to conduct a short interview. They both swore they've had little contact with her mother since she went—what was the medical term Harris Schultz used? Oh, that's right. *Bonkers.*"

I shook my head sadly. "Why are those twins so unkind when it comes to their mother's condition? Do they think she was confused and taking in cats because she was simply eccentric?"

Candace wiped mustard off her lips. "Mental health issues are so misunderstood. A lot of times I think people are plain scared and don't know how to react. Even cops sometimes freak out around the mentally ill. It's because there's an unpredictable element and cops hate that."

I shook my head. "That doesn't excuse those twins' behavior. I spoke to them and I heard Harris use the word *nuts* to describe Minnie."

B.J., who'd been quietly finishing off half a sandwich, said, "I take it you didn't like them, Jillian?"

"I hate to say I didn't *like* them, seeing as how I only just met them. They're an odd pair, though. They upset me because Minnie is really so sweet. Let's say they made me uncomfortable."

"I'll second that," Tom said. "But I found out something important when I talked to Greta alone. She believes her brothers were more interested in their mother's money than her well-being. They kind of abandoned Mrs. Schultz when she wouldn't write them any more checks for weekend parties at their apartment. But now that they understand how seriously ill she's been all this time, Greta Kramer saw hints of remorse."

"Minnie has money?" I glanced around the room. "She lived pretty simply."

"The daughter might not be the best person to inform on them," Tom said. "She said her parents always favored the boys. To quote her, they were 'spoiled rotten' growing up and she sounded jealous. As far as this money? I'm not saying she was a millionaire, but we'll know soon enough. The bank promised me a full report of all her accounts this afternoon."

"Finally," Candace said.

Tom said, "She's not dead, so it makes it more difficult to get financial information, especially since there are relatives involved. I had to convince the bank that Mrs. Schultz was a suspect. Now it seems she could *still* be a suspect considering all this merchandise in the boxes."

I shook my head emphatically. "I don't believe it for a second, Tom. She was hoodwinked into whatever was going on here by Chester. She's *not* a criminal."

"I trust your intuition, Jilly. I do. But we have to eliminate Mrs. Schultz with hard evidence. The possibility of the FBI sticking their nose into our business has me more bothered than Osborne being so persistent. I'm beginning to wonder if he knew about this and wants to come off as the hero if the Feds do have to come to town."

"How would he have known, Chief?" B.J. asked.

"Captain Osborne's been a cop for a long time. He has an informant network that I can't begin to access yet. It takes several years to get all your crooks in line—the ones who would be good candidates for informant duty. If he knows something, I sure wish he'd share it."

I laughed. "Get your crooks in line? Really?"

"That's how it works," Candace said. "Unfortunately, most of the idiots I approach to help me out with info either hit on me or declare their sincere hope I'll become more than just a cop seeking information one day in the future. You don't know how much I hate that."

"Oh, I believe I have a good idea." I smiled at her and noticed B.J. nodding emphatically. He got it, too.

Since we'd finished eating, we gathered the trash and refolded the tablecloth. I opened the drawer in the sideboard, ready to put it away, and then wondered if I should take the cloth home and wash it first. But was I allowed to remove anything from the house? I was about ready to ask Tom, who was still in the kitchen, when I noticed the corner of something in the drawer in the middle of a thick pile of place mats. It looked like paper. Surely they'd gone through all these drawers looking for evidence.

But I remembered this sideboard had been completely blocked off by boxes before we started clearing the room. Could they have missed searching these drawers? I decided whatever it was, I didn't want to risk touching it.

"Um, Tom? Could you come in here?" I called.

Maybe something in my tone cued all three of them, because Candace, B.J. and Tom responded to my plea.

I pointed at the tiny corner of what looked like white paper. "I didn't want to touch that."

Candace was quick to respond. "Could be nothing, but I'll get my camera."

She'd brought her evidence satchel into the kitchen this morning so we could have extra gloves as we went through boxes. She fetched her camera and took several shots of the paper. Meanwhile, Tom had pulled gloves from his trouser pocket and snapped them on. Once Candace was finished, he carefully lifted off the ivory quilted place mats.

B.J., craning to see over my shoulder, said, "Those look like the same journal pages Minnie had in those books we carted off."

"That's exactly what they are," Candace declared. "Look at the date on this top page. Last month. *Yes.*" She pumped her fist and then took more pictures.

Tom picked up the top page with his now-gloved hand and Candace photographed the second one. It looked as if there were three in total. He was reading the first page and said, "This will take some time. Obviously the woman wasn't in her right mind when she wrote this—if these pages are hers, that is. She's writing about naming cats."

"Wow," I said. "But could she even keep track of all those kitties in the state she was in?"

"I don't know. You've actually spoken to the woman," Tom said. "What do you think?"

"Maybe it was a way to cling to her sanity," I offered. "She only had two things in her life—Chester coming around and the cats. I'd take comfort in the cats, and one way to do that is by making them special, by giving them a name she could recall."

Candace stared at one of the pages. "Can't assume, Tom, I know, but I saw the writing in the other journals and though this is scrawled, it's very similar."

"And seems to make little sense," he replied. "Let's hope we can decipher what she felt she needed to write down."

"There could be nuggets of truth hidden in these pages, especially since she felt the need to keep these pages separate." Candace set down her camera and opened one evidence bag for each page. The writing was easily seen through the clear plastic and I was sure Candace would devote all her concentration to deciphering whatever she could.

I said, "Maybe when Minnie is out of that postsurgical coma, she'll offer an insight. That is, if she even remembers writing any of this."

Tom put an arm around my shoulder and pulled me to his side. "Nice job, Detective."

"I'll bet when I took the tablecloth out of the drawer, the top place mats slipped a little and that's why I saw what I did."

B.J. grinned. "Thank goodness for a woman who needs a tablecloth for a take-out lunch."

But I could tell Candace wasn't happy these pages

had been missed. Her facial muscles were tight and her frown was fierce. "I'm sorry, Tom. We should have found this right away."

"Are you kidding? Sometimes it takes a half dozen searches to find everything, especially in a house this jam-packed with merchandise. The most important thing is that we did find them. Do you consider yourself perfect, Detective Carson?" He was smiling.

I saw her features relax a tad. "No. Far from it. These could be important and I am certainly happy we have the pages."

"What's your best guess on why these particular pages were torn out and hidden?" B.J. asked.

I said, "Though she was muddled thanks to that tumor, Minnie did have moments where she was almost lucid. Maybe she knew something wasn't right about Chester and wanted to document it as best she could."

"That makes sense even if these pages don't." Candace still appeared a little troubled by the delayed discovery.

But I was grateful Tom had made her at least feel a little better.

It was clear to me he was the right the person for the police chief job. If he were my boss, I'd ecstatic. But, of course, he wasn't my boss. Our relationship didn't have one.

Twenty-three

Since new evidence had been found, Tom, Candace and B.J. took off for the police station. I gathered the trash we'd accumulated and took it with me, but as I drove down Main Street toward home, I saw Kara's car parked in front of Belle's Beans. I pulled into a spot not far from her SUV.

The day had started out shrouded in fog, but the sun shined brightly now. This pleasant, clear weather made me feel cheerful despite the unsettling events of the last few days. Or maybe it was the smell of coffee as I approached the entrance to the café that was having that effect. I loved this little spot of heaven.

I headed straight to the counter and ordered a decaf latte before turning to look for Kara. I found her toward the back of the room, deep in conversation with Liam and Captain Osborne. As I approached I saw that Osborne wore a polo shirt with the sheriff's department logo on the chest. I assumed they were discussing Brenda's accident, since Kara had her tablet sitting in front of her on the table.

"Hey there," I said when I was practically standing over them.

They all looked at me and Kara stood to give me a hug. "Hey. What are you doing here?"

Just then the Belle of the Day—I think her real name was Joy—called out that my latte was ready.

I smiled. "Be right back. Anyone want anything?"

They all shook their heads no.

Soon I was sitting with them, my hands clutching the warm to-go cup. "Have you heard anything about Brenda's progress?" I asked Kara.

Kara's eyes showed her excitement. "She's out of the coma. She even said her brother's name. Of course, she's still sedated with painkillers, but she is definitely on the road to recovery. Peyton is over the moon."

I sighed with relief. "That's the best news I've heard all week."

"I take it you know Kara in a special way since you two share a last name? Sisters, maybe?" Osborne said.

I noted that Liam was sitting next to Osborne, but he was back a ways so Osborne couldn't really see him. I caught him roll his eyes. I was guessing that Osborne knew exactly how Kara and I were related and Liam was silently calling him on it.

But I played along. "I'm her stepmother."

"Ah. I see. I'm giving an interview to these fine people, so perhaps . . ." Osborne let his words trail off as he glanced toward the entrance. Apparently he wanted me to leave.

"Are you concerned I'll tell my husband something you don't want him to know?" I said.

My words got everyone's attention and they all seemed

to lean toward me. I'd surprised even myself by being so bold.

"I have no secrets, Jillian." Osborne ran his hand through his thick, salt-and-pepper hair. "Since my officers are busy doing police work, I agreed to share what they reported about Brenda Ross's accident."

"Not an *accident*," Liam said.

"No. You're correct. We determined that almost at once, but since Chief Stewart has claimed jurisdiction, I don't know much more than how we rescued Dr. Ross and—"

Kara held up a hand while looking at her tablet. "Let's be clear so I can report this correctly. It was Mercy Fire Department equipment that pulled her car to safety, right?"

"Yes, with help from my officers. Mercy PD didn't show up for a full fifteen minutes and the firemen had already hauled the car away from the tree." Osborne looked pointedly at me. "This town is woefully low on a police presence and Dr. Ross's tragedy proves it."

"Maybe you could make a plea to our town council for more funds," I said, trying to sound calm and kind despite not liking this man one bit.

Kara pushed her iPad away and set her stylus down. "I thank you for your time, Captain Osborne. We have a clear picture of what happened the other day and I am certain Mercy PD is grateful for your department's assistance. I'm only sorry we couldn't meet with the officers who responded to the crash. Maybe in the near future?"

Osborne recognized a dismissal when he heard it. He smiled at Kara. "As I told you, they're busy protecting the county. I've read your work, Ms. Hart. I trust you to report honestly, completely and without bias about this terrible incident. I know everything my officers know, so you have what you need." He stood and shook hands with Liam. "We have plenty of perps in the county lockup looking for good lawyers. I can throw some work your way."

Liam simply smiled and nodded.

Osborne looked at me. "Jillian, please give my regards to your husband."

He left quickly and I noted with much chagrin that his strides reminded me of a cat's—quiet, graceful steps, like someone who knew he was in charge of the world. I didn't like the comparison, but it was obvious to a person like me, who'd watched cats move her entire life.

"What a jerk," Liam said the minute the door closed behind Osborne. "And do they really say *perps* at the sheriff's department? Because I've never heard even one of their officers use that word."

Kara rested a hand over his fist. "Maybe he thinks we only understand television terms. I used to believe that advances in technology would make these kinds of territorial disputes between local police a thing of the past. But it all boils down to individuals. Some people are just, like you said, *jerks*."

I hoped these two had learned more than what everyone already knew about Osborne. "Did he provide anything new about Brenda's wreck?"

Kara nodded. "I have to say, he was forthcoming about the details and filled in a few gaps. But he wants me to write about his heroic officers more than about Brenda. That's not how it will be done."

Liam shook his empty cardboard coffee cup back and forth in a nervous gesture. "We went to speak with the wrecker who towed Brenda's car before we met with Osborne, so we had a good idea about what probably happened. The guy said it was a miracle she survived. He also said she'd been wrapped around that tree long enough that her engine had cooled down. Thirty minutes or more."

"Wow. That's a long time," I said. "Where did this happen again?"

They told me and I was familiar with the winding, narrow road. "Someone was probably following her, then. Because otherwise who could have found her on that road to try to take her out?"

"Exactly," Kara said. "The wrecker driver said there was white paint on her gray bumper. Not very helpful in the short term, but once Tom has time to investigate her case, I'm certain every paint has unique tints. They might be able to match it to a specific vehicle make and model."

"She was probably coming from seeing Minnie at the hospital. She told me she wanted to give her a journal and see if writing would help jog her memory about anything in her immediate past. Someone came into Minnie's house and killed Chester, after all."

Kara cocked her head like she always did when something piqued her interest. "A journal? Did you see anything like that when you visited Minnie?"

I considered this for a few seconds before answering. "Her daughter told me Minnie wrote in one, but Dr. Ross took that one with her when she left. Then Brenda was run off the road not long afterward. But we could ask Greta. She probably gathered the items from Minnie's hospital room when she was taken to surgery, and I recall Brenda saying she would buy a few journals for Minnie. Could be there's another one in those belongings."

Liam said, "Can you call this daughter?"

"I don't know her number and they do ask you to shut off your cell phones in that ICU waiting area. She's probably still at the hospital. She was there this morning."

Kara stood. "Let's try to find her, ask her about this journal."

We took Kara's SUV and she kissed Liam good-bye when we dropped him off at his office. He had another client and was pleased to have billable hours twice today. Since I'd left my van in front of Belle's Beans, I took time while Kara drove to engage with the upstairs cats. I only wished I'd remembered to turn on the camera in the basement cat room so I could check on Simon and Otto, too.

I could tell more than ever that I would have to make up yet another absence with lots of playtime tonight. I watched as Merlot sat and stared at the camera next to a meowing Chablis. Syrah wouldn't even look in the direction of my voice and Dashiell seemed tired but perked up when I said his name.

Once we'd parked in the hospital lot, I said good-bye to my amigos. Kara and I walked in the sunshine to the hospital entrance. When we arrived in the ICU waiting room, however, Greta wasn't there, nor were the twins. Only Peyton, it seemed, had remained steadfastly supportive. He looked pale and fatigued, but brightened when he saw us. He seemed especially pleased to see Kara. She *had* spent a lot of time with him talking about Brenda when no one was certain she would survive.

I glanced around at the empty chairs where Minnie's children had sat only this morning and Peyton must have read my mind.

"The guys left. The one with the short hair actually

has a job and I don't know about the other one. Maybe they drove here together. Anyway, in bigger news, Greta went into labor." He grinned. "Nice to have a doctor in the room when a woman's water breaks. It's her first and she was pretty anxious. I calmed her down, called the husband and had them bring a wheelchair to take her to labor and delivery."

"Wow," I said. "How exciting."

"Woke me up—that's for sure. But now I'm fading again. Did Kara tell you Brenda is awake—well, sort of awake?"

I glanced at Kara, who was smiling. "Yes, and that's great news."

Kara cleared her throat. "Did you notice if any of Minnie's children had a bag of her belongings? We're looking for something your sister might have given her."

Peyton reflected on this for what seemed a long time but was probably less than thirty seconds. "There *was* a clear plastic bag with a robe and slippers, maybe a few other things. One of the sons took it—can't remember which one. Greta was staying for the five-minute visiting time coming up, so at some point before she started having the contractions she handed the bag to one of her brothers."

I glanced at Kara. "Greta might know what was in it."

"Why is this so important?" Peyton asked.

Kara said, "If there was a journal in that bag, your sister gave it to Minnie. It could be a small connection between Brenda's case and the murder at Minnie's house, but right now, we'll take anything we can get. If we can link the cases, it might lead us to whoever ran your sister off the road."

"I wish I could remember more, but you can go up to labor and delivery to talk to Greta. It's her first baby. She probably hasn't delivered yet."

"But we're not family, so how can we talk to her?" I said.

"Oh, but we *are* family," Kara said firmly. "Isn't that right, *Dr.* Ross? And you could call up to that floor and say we ran into you since both you and Greta have patients in ICU and we're looking for our . . . *cousin*."

Peyton grinned. "I'll walk you up there myself."

Twenty-four

The floor that housed labor and delivery was a welcome breather from the rest of the floors I'd visited in this hospital. I knew this place so well I almost felt as if I worked here.

Dr. Peyton Ross sweet-talked us right in to see Greta, and this was a far cry from any other hospital room I'd been in. The place resembled a comfortable bedroom. But Greta looked less than relaxed. Her forehead was dotted with sweat and she tightly gripped the hand of a man sitting in the chair by her bed. She wore a hospital gown and a printed comforter was draped over her knees.

Thank goodness Greta owed Peyton a debt of gratitude for his help when she went into labor. She seemed more than happy to welcome us into this very private time after he'd pleaded for assistance concerning his sister. He'd left us quickly, saying he didn't want to miss any of the meager visiting time they offered him in the ICU. He promised Greta he would check on Minnie while he was in with Brenda.

Greta introduced us to her husband, Aaron, a thin

man wearing a shirt and work pants. The logo on the pocket indicated he worked for a local heating and cooling repair company. He was all smiles. You could have brought a marching band in this room and the guy probably wouldn't have minded. As he was quick to point out, his son would arrive today and he was "proud as a goat with four horns."

I almost laughed out loud at that one, but something about this room demanded calm and quiet, so I simply congratulated him.

Kara got right to the point, seemingly unimpressed by an impending birth. She was focused on her story and that was all that mattered. "We heard from Dr. Peyton Ross that one of your brothers took the bag with your mother's belongings. Is that right?"

"Yes. I had Henry take it because I kind of knew I might be needing my room here today. I'd felt funny all night. Do you know we had to reserve our spot months in advance, since there's no other hospital with a birthing center anywhere near where we live?" But before either of us could reply, her face suddenly transformed, twisting with pain. She raised her knees and said, "Oh, here we go, Aaron. Another one coming."

She sat up straight and Aaron put his face close to her ear and began whispering while at the same time pressing the nurse's call button.

"Rub my back, babe," she said.

A woman in lime green scrubs that were covered in cartoon characters bustled in. "Another one, huh, Greta? You're doing good, sweetie." She glanced our way and smiled. "Would you mind stepping out for a second?"

It wasn't really a question, and I, for one, was happy to leave.

Kara paced in the hallway as we waited outside Greta's closed door. "What if she's ready to deliver? Does that mean we have to hunt down Henry Schultz for information?"

"I guess it does. I can assure you he won't be as cooperative as she's being."

A minute later the nurse came out, her hospital smile still in place. "You can go back in."

Greta was leaning against the pillow now, recovering from the last contraction. She looked pale, and though there was a brief period of time when I'd wanted children of my own, it wasn't to be. I got the feeling I probably wouldn't have handled this part of a pregnancy all that well.

"You wanted to know about Mama's things?" Greta said.

"You mentioned a journal to Jillian. Was it among the belongings you gave to your brother?" Kara asked.

"Maybe. She was happy to have it and was scribbling away after the doctor told her about the surgery. Too bad that none of what she wrote seemed to make much sense."

"You read it?" I asked.

"Not the one Dr. Ross left the hospital with, the first one, but yeah, I did," she said. "I was hoping she'd come to her senses. But it was just a bunch of random words."

Aaron used a tissue to dab at the beads of sweat on Greta's forehead.

"Okay, seems there were two journals. Can you remember any of those words?" Kara asked.

Greta closed her eyes and bit at her lower lip. I was worried this was another contraction, but it turned out she was thinking. "She'd written something like . . .

asked Chester why no uniform. Then there was something about Simon being scared. Yes. Now I remember. She'd written *Scaredy Simon* and it seemed like she was trying to make a poem about him. Simon's the orange cat she got a while back, I think. I could never keep them all straight."

"That's it?" Kara asked, sounding disappointed.

"I'm not exactly in a frame of mind to be remembering . . . ohhhhhh, Aaron. This is a bad one." Greta sat straight up again and no one had to tell us to leave this time.

"Apparently Brenda Ross had one of the journals with her," Kara said. "Guess we have to hunt the brother down to get our hands on the other one."

We started down the hall but hadn't even made it halfway to the elevators when we heard Aaron calling my name. When he reached us, he said, "Greta wanted you to have Henry's address. He's the one who has Minnie's things."

I took out my phone and typed the address he recited into my contact list. He also gave me Henry's work number. "Thank you, Aaron, and thank Greta for us."

"No, she says it's you who need thanking—you and Dr. Ross—for bringing her and her mother back together."

As Kara and I entered the elevator, I blinked back tears. Minnie would have the love and support she needed as she recovered, and that would mean so much to a woman I never thought would become so important to me.

I told Kara I had to spend time with my kitties, so she dropped me off in front of Belle's Bean's, where I'd left my van. I made her promise not to contact Henry Schultz by herself. She said she was headed to her office to begin writing what she'd learned from Osborne and wanted to begin her personal interest story on Brenda Ross. Apparently she was still doing research on Brenda's past work.

Syrah gave me the cold shoulder when I arrived home. Though the other three cats were happy to greet me, he sauntered into the living room. I had been a poor kitty mom—that's for sure.

I checked Dashiell's blood sugar before doling out treats, but my guess was he'd probably been sleeping most of the day. Sure enough, his blood sugar was perfect. I then went into the living room and sat on the couch, hoping Syrah would get over his snit. It didn't take long, especially when I tempted him with a catnip mouse on a wand. It was his favorite toy and we sat on the floor and played for a good twenty minutes.

The other cats knew better than to interrupt Syrah's playtime. They waited for their turn. Merlot was more of a bush cat, which meant he liked lying low, hiding and pouncing. Syrah was a tree cat. He preferred high spots— like the top of the entertainment center—and he was also quite the jumper. As for Dashiell, he was getting on in years, but did pay close attention to what the other cats were doing. Chablis preferred lap time to playtime any day. She curled up on my legs as I teased the other cats with toys.

Once they tired of all this, I went downstairs. Simon and Otto had eaten every bite of their kibble. I refilled their bowls and decided after they ate, I'd try to integrate Simon upstairs. Maybe Dashiell would be mellower now.

I left them to their food, making sure to close the door to the cat room or Dashiell would find his way down and steal their meal. I was mounting the stairs when I heard the doorbell ring.

My good friends never ring the front bell, so I was curious. Who could be calling on me? My stomach growled as I made my way to the front door. That lunch at Minnie's house had been a long time ago.

Merlot and Syrah followed me to the front door and sat waiting to satisfy *their* curiosity. I looked through the peephole just as Lydia Monk pressed the doorbell again. Someone was standing directly behind her. What was this about? Did I have the energy to deal with her and her companion right now?

But like my cats, curiosity got the better of me. I opened the door.

As usual, Lydia marched past me. She waved her cohort to come right in as if she owned the place. I hadn't even uttered a word of welcome. Harris Schultz at least made eye contact—and I noticed the whites of his eyes were bloodshot and most of his shoulder-length hair had escaped the elastic he used to hold it back. His lids were so heavy I guessed he was exhausted.

"Come right in," I mumbled as I followed them into my living room.

"Watch out for the cats," Lydia said. "Especially the sneaky one with the big ears. He's vicious."

She was talking about Syrah, who was far from vicious, but who took great delight in tormenting Lydia when she visited here.

"Um, have a seat." I gestured at the sofa.

"Just know you'll be covered in cat hair by the time you leave here," Lydia told Harris as the two sat side by side. She added an extra dose of snide as she said this.

I took the overstuffed chair across from them.

Syrah, I noted, was already eyeing the fringe on Lydia's eggplant-colored tunic top worn over patterned leggings.

Dashiell had taken a keen interest in Harris's pant leg and was sniffing it almost like the guy had filled his rolled-up jeans cuff with catnip. Approaching a stranger so quickly was unusual for him. Merlot stretched out between the sofa and my chair, almost as if he was creating a barrier between us. But that barrier already existed in the form of Lydia's hostility. I'd never done a thing to her—not once. But I *had* married Tom. Lydia still clung to the delusion that he was her soul mate.

Since I hoped this visit would end quickly, I didn't offer them anything to drink. Glancing between them, I said, "What can I do for you?"

Lydia said, "This young man needs assistance since he believes the police suspect him of harming Chester Winston. Tom is apparently too busy to take my calls and because Harris tells me he invoked his right to a lawyer—he is an intelligent young man—I'm here to find out what the heck is going on."

"Why do you think *I* can help?" This was the most messed-up thing Lydia had done since I'd first met her. What was she doing helping a murder suspect? She wasn't a lawyer or a victim's advocate, last I heard. How had Harris Schultz ended up talking to *her*?

I wondered then if Tom truly believed Harris was a suspect. I had no idea. What would be his motive to harm Chester? Obviously I didn't know everything about the investigation and that was as it should be. So should I even engage in this conversation? But if Harris talked to me, I could at least relay information to

Tom. I looked straight into Harris's eyes. "How did you end up talking to the coroner's investigator?"

"Lydia came to the hospital and—"

She put a hand on his arm. "I'll do the talking." She leaned toward me, unaware that Syrah was watching every tiny movement of her tunic. "Since no one is telling me anything to help me file my reports, I went to the hospital to speak with that woman who owned the house where the crime occurred."

"But surely Harris told you Minnie can't talk to you. She's very ill." I sounded as incredulous as I felt.

"How was I supposed to know that when I went there?" she shot back. "Like I said, no one is telling me *anything*. I need information to do my job and—"

"To do what part of your job?" I asked.

"Just like you, I was at the scene of the crime—only I had a *right* to be there. It wasn't Chester's house. What was he doing there? Has Tom located the murder weapon? What does Harris's mother have to do with this? Does *Acting* Police Chief Stewart believe she could have killed Chester?" She turned to look at Harris. "Does that about sum it all up?"

"I—I . . . don't really know," he replied. "I believe I did tell you that things were off with Mama for months." He reached down to pet Dashiell, but our tabby cat took one sniff of Harris's hand and hurried off.

"Has the autopsy been done?" I asked. "That would answer questions about the cause of death so you can do the death certificates. That is what you do, and as far as I know, cause of death to this point shouldn't be discussed with Harris."

"You have no idea all that goes into me performing my duties or what I can say to whoever I want. When there is a disturbing death, all of those affected parties are included in my investigation." She leaned back and the tassels moved so much that Syrah leapt onto her lap and latched onto the tunic hem.

Lydia stood, trying to push Syrah off, but his claws were caught in the fabric.

Before I could even bridge the gap between us to protect my cat, Harris made the *huge* mistake of grabbing Syrah from behind. My boy turned and bit his hand before taking off and racing away into the kitchen.

While Lydia muttered angrily and examined her hem, Harris clutched his bleeding hand.

"Let me help you with that. And for future reference, never come at a cat from behind—especially one who doesn't know you." I took him by the elbow as he stared at his own blood in horror. It wasn't much blood, but it obviously upset him.

I led him into the kitchen and put his hand under warm water and gently rubbed a little soap into the wound. I whispered, "What are you doing with *her*?"

"I don't know." He couldn't take his eyes off his hand. "There were things at the house in boxes and she asked if they belonged to me. She said she heard the items were things a young guy might have ordered and had shipped to my mother's house. Expensive things like cell phones. I'm low on cash and I thought maybe my mother had come to her senses and—"

"Wait a minute. She told you what was in those boxes?"

"What are you two talking about?" It was Lydia, who was obviously unaware that now both Merlot and Syrah were interested in those tassels. Their eyes didn't waver from her.

I had this secret wish that Syrah would jump onto

her shoulder and hang on, maybe play with that rhine-
stone barrette holding back her hair on one side. That
would make her leave.

Harris closed his eyes and breathed a sigh of what
seemed like relief. "It's stopped bleeding. Thank God
it's stopped."

I glanced at him and saw he'd gone pale as Elmer's
Glue. "Are you bothered by the sight of blood?"

He nodded, swallowing hard. "I did pretty good this
time. I didn't faint. Used to faint when I was a kid." He
offered me a smile. All the sullenness I'd seen at the
hospital had faded. Harris Schultz had become a little
boy right before my eyes.

I said, "Is Henry like this, too?"

His left eye twitched and I saw his features tighten
at the mention of his brother. "We're way more alike
than people think. Yeah. Same thing for him."

"Do you have a Band-Aid?" Lydia said. "I mean,
come on, Jillian. We don't have all day."

I pointed behind Lydia. "You still have kitties quite
interested in what you're wearing."

She turned and stomped a foot in their direction, but
neither of my boys moved. They just sat there looking
up at her. Meanwhile, Chablis and Dashiell watched
the action from the window seat, and if a cat could
have looked amused, I'd say that was Dashiell's expression. Chablis simply seemed bored. She'd seen all this
before.

While Lydia kept trying to shoo away the cats, I
took the antibiotic ointment and a Band-Aid from my
first aid basket in the pantry and fixed Harris up.

He held up his hand and examined my work, then

smiled at me. "Thanks. It doesn't really hurt. But blood? I can't take the sight of it."

"What are you? Twelve?" Lydia, more irritated with the cats than with him, no doubt, made the mistake of taking it out on Harris, the person she'd used as an excuse to find out what I knew about the investigation.

Harris didn't like it. "At least I'm not a walking fashion disaster."

Her eyes widened and the hostility she felt for me seemed to be transferred to Harris Schultz now.

Worried that a war of words might break out, I said, "Why are you really here, Lydia?"

"I am supposed to be informed about this case so I can pass that information along to the coroner. I repeat, no one is talking to me."

"You decided I could tell you something?" I said. "I'm not a police officer."

"Lydia told me that since you were married to the police chief, you knew things. If my mother bought me and my brother gifts, they belong to us, right? Because I am getting super low on cash and—"

"Are you saying you want to sell things from your mother's home? I don't think the police will hand over evidence." As soon as the words left my mouth, I realized my mistake.

Lydia leaned on my kitchen counter and smiled, her mauve lipstick jarring against her white teeth. The shade didn't suit her tanning salon complexion. It made her look more clownish than usual. "So, this merchandise I'm hearing about, the items in all those boxes I saw? It's considered *evidence*?"

"Why don't you wait for Tom to return your call,

Lydia? He will eventually." I wanted desperately to get off the topic of what I'd seen in the house. "When is that autopsy, by the way? You do all the scheduling, if I remember right."

"It already happened earlier today. But if you think I'm telling you anything about it, you're wrong. Come on, Harris. Let's go."

She whirled and stomped toward the foyer, but Syrah got in one last swipe and came away with the tassel he'd had his eye on earlier. He marched proudly in the opposite direction toward the mud room, the purple tassel clutched between his teeth.

Twenty-five

I'd fallen asleep on the sofa again, surrounded by cats. That's where Tom found me after he came in through the back door. I'd even managed to bring Simon and Otto upstairs and the transition, though not without hissing and a little swiping at Simon on Dashiell's part, had gone better than I expected.

"Look who's the crazy cat lady *now*," Tom said as six pairs of sleepy eyes—seven if you counted mine—stared up at him.

I eased Chablis off my chest and sat up, trying hard not to disturb Otto, who had chosen a spot between my knees. "It's quite the crew. What time is it?"

"Past midnight. I hear you had visitors. I called Lydia earlier and she said she was just driving away from our house. Is that true?"

"For sure. She brought Harris Schultz with her. I will never figure that woman out, but I guess she thought his presence would make me open up about all the things we've found at Minnie's place. Apparently word leaked out about the contents of those boxes."

Tom picked Otto up and I moved my legs so he could sit next to me. He held the sleepy boy to his chest. "This town is a leaky bucket of information. The autopsy was finished today, but Lydia apparently needed to hear me ask politely for the report before she'd send it to me."

"Did you learn anything you didn't know?"

"Not really. Blunt force trauma. As for other evidence, the fingerprints on the empty litter pail we found near Chester's body came back to Mrs. Schultz. I'm guessing she saw all that blood and believed she needed to clean it up like I'd clean up an oil spill in the garage. Litter absorbs all sorts of things. Who knew a brain tumor could make her behave in ways she'd probably never done before?"

"Seeing that body and all the blood could have triggered her trip down Main Street with Otto," I said.

He nodded. "My theory is she saw a dead man and it scared her out of the house, but we can't ask her, can we? I talked to that shrink's brother when I went to the hospital to speak to Minnie's sons. Did you know he's a doctor, too?"

"I did. He's such a nice man and so concerned about Brenda."

"I agree. Anyway, I tapped his doctor brain about Minnie and asked if he thought she'd remember anything about the crime—because I'm guessing she was there when Chester was murdered."

I stroked Chablis, who was now fully awake and nudging my hand for petting. Then she spotted Otto asleep on Tom's chest and decided the kitten needed a thorough cleaning. She actually pulled him down to Tom's lap and started licking him all over. "What was Peyton's opinion about Minnie's memory returning?"

I asked this even though I'd already heard the answer. Tom needed to work through this case by talking as much as possible.

"The brain isn't his specialty, but his educated guess was that her memory wouldn't be reliable. We probably have an eyewitness to a murder who won't be able to tell us anything."

"Just seeing all that blood would have wiped my memory. And speaking of blood, Syrah bit Harris Schultz and—"

"What?" Tom stared at me as if I had two heads.

"I know. Not very Syrah-like, but he grabbed Syrah from behind and got bitten as a reward. Anyway, Harris had a small puncture wound on his hand and the guy nearly passed out at the sight of his own blood—and it was like a few drops, Tom. Not some gaping wound."

His puzzled look turned to realization almost immediately. "Oh. Not the type to go bashing a person over the head with a heavy object if he's afraid of a little blood. That's not exactly proof of his innocence, but I see your point. If Mrs. Schultz has the same problem, it could explain why she poured kitty litter on Chester's body."

I nodded. "Could be. According to Harris, Henry Schultz has the same issue. And get this. Lydia heard about what we found in the boxes at Minnie's house and generously shared that information with Harris—and maybe others. That was her excuse for bringing him with her when she came to visit. He had questions about whether his mother bought any of that stuff for him."

Tom released a sigh laden with frustration. "Why would Lydia, someone who's been trained to follow procedure at a crime scene, do something like that?"

"I don't know. It baffled me for sure. Anyway, Harris was practically salivating over the contents of those packages. He mentioned more than once that he's low on cash."

"You think? He hasn't had a job since he graduated from college with a degree in Spanish. Someone with that kind of skill could be a teacher or a translator. He could do *something*."

"Spanish? Wow. What about Henry? Does he work?" I asked.

"He's a banker, or rather a bank teller. But he does have a finance degree, so maybe this will help him climb the ladder. He and Harris live together, and from what I determined when I interviewed Henry, he's tired of his freeloading brother."

"Henry talked? He didn't lawyer up like Harris did?"

"Henry seemed to understand I was only interviewing him, not getting ready to arrest him. If Harris laid off the weed, he probably wouldn't have been so paranoid."

"Ah. He did look out of it when he was here. If he's broke, how does he afford marijuana?" I asked.

"Maybe's he broke because he can't afford it. But users always seem to find a way to get what they want. We're trying to follow a lot of money trails—and how Chester is connected. All I know is, I could smell Harris Schultz coming a mile away."

Then I remembered Dashiell sniffing at his jeans. "Oh. Is that why Dashiell was so interested in Harris's clothing? And here I thought maybe the guy had stashed catnip in his rolled-up jeans. Silly me."

Tom squeezed me closer. "You always imagine the innocent explanation first." Then I felt Tom tense and he sat up. "Wait a minute. I'm always so quick to dog on Lydia, but what if *she's* the innocent one this time?"

"What are you talking about, Tom?"

"Did you actually hear her say *she* told Harris about the stuff in Mrs. Schultz's house?"

I tried to recall what had transpired today and found the details fuzzy at best. "I'm not sure, Tom. It seemed as if Lydia thought the way to get information about the case was to bring one of Minnie's children here and somehow that would make me tell her things you supposedly told me. Ridiculous, I know, but Lydia is not known for being normal."

"I'm thinking out loud here, but what if Harris Schultz already knew what was in that house? Maybe he decided he'd use Lydia to find how he could get access to that merchandise. Drug users need money. There was plenty of stuff to sell in that place—which is why I believe Chester considered a confused woman who loved cats to be the perfect target to exploit in the first place."

"I get it. You're saying it was *Harris's* idea to come here and dig around for information? That he tricked Lydia into bringing him along?"

"Exactly." He smiled. "It's always good for a cop to be married to a good listener. You distilled that information into a few sentences after I rambled on." He stood, being careful not to disturb Otto and Chablis, who were snuggled together between us.

"Shouldn't you get a little sleep before heading back to work?" I said.

He took out his phone. "I can't. Waking up a suspect is my favorite pastime, and if Harris Schultz still wants his lawyer present, he's gonna have to wake that person up, too."

He leaned over and kissed my forehead. "Thank you."

As he walked toward the kitchen and the back door, I heard him say, "Candace. Were you asleep?"

She isn't now, I thought. I didn't have to rouse any cats to head to bed. They followed me willingly, because sleeping on a quilt in the bedroom was far better than wrangling for space on a sofa.

Twenty-six

"The question I asked myself, Jillian, was this." Kara lifted her coffee mug and stared at me over the rim.

"Go on," I said.

I sat with Simon on my lap, Merlot and Syrah at my feet, all the while watching Otto toying with Dashiell's ear, hoping he'd play. *Good luck with that, silly boy.* Chablis was purring away with her head close to Kara's ear. It had been a short night because Kara showed up early, anxious to talk.

"Okay, here's my thought. If Brenda was run off the road, she knew something that put her in danger. She heard or saw something she shouldn't have about the murder case. Isn't that a logical conclusion?"

I wanted to crawl back into bed and sleep for two more hours, but she was so passionate about getting answers, I had to be her friend as well as her stepmother. "Sure. Logical, though an assumption. Her purse and phone are missing. It could have been a crime by a stranger. The question is, when did she end up putting herself in danger if it *is* connected to Chester's murder?"

"At the hospital. She bought journals for Minnie and—"

"After picking up Minnie's personal items at the house?" I asked.

"Yes. I talked to a clerk at Dollar General who remembers her. She actually bought *three* cheap little journals. She took them to Minnie, they talked and my guess is that someone was listening to that conversation. Minnie maybe told Brenda something important related to the case, perhaps while she was doodling and scribbling in that book. The twins hadn't shown up yet, but the daughter was there, right?"

"You think *Greta* is responsible?" I shook my head trying to reconcile the notion of new mother Greta as a cold-blooded woman bold enough to run Brenda off the road.

"I know, I know. I can't see her doing that, but who else was there? What about those twins? Could one of them have been sneaking around waiting to talk to his mother? Does Tom know if the sons knew Chester? What secret did Brenda learn from Minnie that made her a target?"

"The sons might not have known Chester, but Chester's son went to school with Harris and Henry—and also with Lucinda, the daughter-in-law. But while you digest that piece of information, here's the latest on what I know. Maybe you can pull something out of what happened yesterday." I summarized Lydia's visit, how Tom smelled marijuana on Harris and how Harris possibly knew, from one source or another, about the merchandise in Minnie's house. "Harris is the brother who asked for a lawyer. Maybe *he* was involved with Chester. You could well be correct about him lurking in the hospital and hearing a conversation that put Brenda in danger."

Kara said, "All of those boxes you've mentioned are at the center of this mess. They have to be. I didn't hear this from Tom, but my police source tells me the financial documents show that Minnie was racking up credit card bills. And get this: That credit card is nowhere to be found."

"Your *police source*?" I smiled. "Candace? B.J., who has a major crush on you? Who?"

She grinned back at me. "A journalist never gives up her sources. Besides, you don't want to know, especially if your husband questions you concerning how I found this out."

I had to agree with her on that one. "I heard that Minnie had some money. Was she being bled dry?"

"Not really. See, I know about that, too. I've been busy. Her retirement money is safe because it's stashed in protected accounts. She was left with a nice nest egg when her husband died, so that money is invested—or so I am told."

I grinned. "Your source has to be B.J. What did he tell you about those journal pages we found in Minnie's dining room?"

"What journal pages? Aren't we *looking* for missing journals that Brenda bought?" Her eyes grew keen with interest.

"Oh boy. Now I'm in trouble. Don't go asking your source because this probably has nothing to do with Brenda. The pages we found yesterday were dated before Minnie even met the doctor." I went on to tell her about the ripped-out pages that had been missed in the initial search of the house.

Kara squinted at me, considering this. "Why were these particular pages ripped out and hidden? You told me there was a stack of journals in the closet and yet now there's something she'd written that seemed important enough to hide."

"Kara. Come on. The woman was walking down Main Street in her nightclothes carrying a cat. If she's the one who hid those pages, what she wrote might not mean anything."

"True enough. Do you happen to know what she wrote on those particular pages?" she asked.

"Kara, this can't have anything to do with Brenda."

Kara pointed with her mug in my direction. "That's where you're wrong. If Minnie knew something suspicious about Chester, something about him that led to his murder, then we have to follow the crumbs. It could very well be the same thing that Brenda learned and what put her in danger."

"Here's all I know. Tom's quick look at the pages indicated it didn't make much sense. Poor Minnie was so clueless and so neglected." I sighed. "You know what my main question is? Why didn't her children help her?" This thought upset me so much that I felt the burn of tears behind my eyes.

Kara set down her mug and reached across the small table for my hand. Her tone softened when she spoke. "Jillian, your heart is almost too big. What did Tolstoy say about families?"

"'All happy families are alike; each unhappy family is unhappy in its own way,'" I said quietly.

She sat back. "I believe that explains it. Be assured that our family is not unique—because we're happy."

I nodded and smiled in agreement.

Though I didn't want to leave my cats yet again, I couldn't allow Kara to visit the Schultz brothers all by herself. She was determined to pay them a visit and she refused to wait until Liam was free later today. She also wanted to get her hands on that second journal.

We took Kara's car and decided we were both fatigued enough to require more caffeine and maybe a hefty dose of sugar for the almost hour-long trip to the town where Harris and Henry Schultz lived. We stopped at Belle's Beans for pastry and coffee to take along. Kara said she would buy and went straight to the counter after we walked in.

I glanced around and saw a familiar face, but it took a few seconds to place her, maybe because she wasn't in the spot I always saw her—the county animal shelter. But it was the person she was with who made my stomach do a flip-flop. Should I talk to them? My heart was saying no, but my mind screamed yes. *You have to.*

"I see two people I'd think you be interested in talking to," I whispered to Kara. "Join me in a second."

I walked over to the table where the two women were conversing.

I addressed the young woman who manned the intake counter at the animal shelter. "Hey there, Sara Jo."

She blinked in surprise when she looked up at me. "Oh. Hi, Jillian."

"So sad about Chester." It was all I could do to keep my eyes averted from Sara Jo's companion—the woman who'd been in the shouting match at the hospital. This was Chester's daughter-in-law, Lucinda.

Though I hadn't addressed her, Lucinda spoke. "Ain't it enough your husband woke us both up and told us to come to Main Street so he can talk to us again? Leave us alone so we can drink our coffee and then get this so-called *interview* over with."

"I'm sorry," I said evenly. "I don't think we've met, but you seem to know me."

"Oh, and you want me to believe you don't know me. Cut the crap, lady." Lucinda had fire-red hair and a temper to match. But of course I already knew that. I'd witnessed it firsthand at the hospital.

"Did I see you being escorted out of the hospital the other day?" I added a smile to punctuate my sentence, but did I really want to get into a verbal sparring match with this person? So I added, "I truly am sorry for your family's loss and I hope you believe that."

Sara Jo gently punched Lucinda on the upper arm and the diamond on her engagement finger caught the light and flashed brightly. "Jillian is cool. She means it. She's not the cops."

Lucinda sullenly responded with "Maybe."

I looked at Sara Jo and said, "How are you managing without Chester? The county shelter is such a busy place as it is."

"We don't have a replacement, if that's what you're asking. I swear they don't pay me enough for what I do." She smiled at Lucinda. "But I'm making time for Lucinda and the rest of Chester's family. They need someone to lean on. It's tough times when the man is dead and folks are talking so mean about him."

Kara joined me. "What are people saying?" she asked.

"Who are *you*?" Lucinda's fading haughtiness returned full force.

"She writes our newspaper," Sara Jo said. "Don't you know anything, Lucinda?"

"Well, excuse me for livin'." Lucinda folded her arms over her large bosom and stared off to her left.

"I'm sorry, sweetie." Sara Jo rested her hand on Lucinda's forearm. "Come on, now. Don't be like that."

Lucinda didn't take her eyes off whatever she'd fixed on across the room. "If you're my friend, tell these people to leave."

"You know what, sweetie?" Sara Jo said. "If you think people are talkin' trash about Chester, these are the people you should be tellin' the truth to. These here are nice folks and Miss Kara Hart could maybe write something nice in Chester's obituary."

Lucinda turned back and I saw her eyes had filled with tears. In a quavering voice she said, "Thing is, he wasn't a nice man. But he was my husband's daddy. I've known him half my life. We loved him in spite of how he acted. We're the only ones knowin' he could be kind when he set his mind to it."

That Tolstoy quote was running through my head, truer than ever. I chose as gentle a tone as I could muster. "Can we sit down and talk to you about him? Kara presents all sides in the newspaper and I know she'd like to hear what you have to say."

Lucinda said, "We're just gonna have to repeat it all when we have to go talkin' to the police chief—to your *husband*. Why's he need to talk to me again? I told him all I know."

"I have no idea, Lucinda. But one thing I do know? He wants to find out who killed Chester and bring that person to justice. I promise you that."

Sara Jo was nodding. "See? That's what I told you. We got nothing to be scared of 'cause we didn't do anything wrong. We just go in there and tell the truth. You did tell the truth the last time, didn't you?"

Lucinda stared at her friend as if she could set Sara Jo's hair on fire if she sent enough hostility her way. "Did *you* tell the truth, girl?"

Kara pulled out a chair and sat down. I followed suit.

Kara cleared her throat. "You've both lost someone you knew well and for a long time. Grief hurts, I know. I lost my daddy when I was about as old as the two of you. I hated the world, even hated Jillian. But it was all because I was afraid of how to get along without him, afraid of missing him so much my heart would burst. Grief is a whole lot of fear. Don't turn it into anger and lose the support you get from each other."

Quiet descended like an anvil as we took in her words. Kara had proven once again what an amazing person she was.

Finally Lucinda spoke in a near whisper. "Would you write something kind about Chester? From what you just said, I'm thinkin' you could do that."

Kara smiled. "In an obituary, we write what the family wants to say about the person they loved and lost. You give me some facts that you want the world to know and I'd be happy to write it up."

What she wasn't saying is that obituaries aren't free. I wondered if Kara was willing to do an obit at no cost if she could get these two young women to speak to her about Chester. My guess was yes.

Lucinda looked at me. "Last time we talked, that top cop you married didn't want to know nothin' good about Chester. He just wanted to know why someone wanted him dead. I was thinkin' he wanted to blame me or my husband. No matter what our differences, me and Earl would never hurt Chester. He said he had money comin' in real soon and would buy us that big flat-screen Earl's been wantin'. So why would he go and kill his daddy if that was the case?"

"You're right. That doesn't make sense," I said. "Did you tell the chief that?"

"Didn't get a chance," Lucinda replied. "I heard Earl in the other room down at the station shoutin' at that girl cop and I couldn't have her gettin' him all riled right after Chester was murdered. I told the top cop I was done. I walked into that other little room where they was talkin', grabbed Earl by the arm and off we went." She lowered her voice. "Earl's got a little trouble with his blood pressure what with his weight bein' what it is. But if Chester left us that money he promised, I'm puttin' us both on one of them fancy diets where they deliver the food to your door."

Ah, I thought. Chester promised his family money. Despite the fact that I was beginning to believe Lucinda, I still had to remember how Tom probably looked at this situation. What if they wanted that payday sooner rather than later? Maybe they figured killing Chester was the best way to get it. "The chief called you back in today because you never finished your interview?"

"That's right. We thought we'd fuel up on caffeine first. But surely your top cop told you all kinda twisted stuff about us, 'specially since you was in the hospital hallway when me and Earl got into it with those silly boys pretendin' to be men. Knew those two from high school and they were always trouble."

"You mean Minnie's sons?" I said.

Lucinda pointed at me. "That's right. What the heck

is wrong with them? They was sayin' we went into their mother's house and there was valuable stuff there and who did we think we were trespassin' and all kinds of lies."

Kara cocked her head, her tone curious. "What *kind* of valuable stuff?"

"How the heck would I know?" Lucinda's tone was strident and a few others in the café turned to stare at her. She ignored them and went on. "We never set foot in that woman's house. Didn't know her from Adam."

Sara Jo had been watching our exchanges with interest and spoke to Lucinda now. "Didn't you know Chester spent a lot of time with Minnie?"

Lucinda gaped at her friend. "Are you sayin' *you* knew he spent time with Mrs. Schultz, Sara Jo? And if so, why didn't you tell us?"

At some point Kara had placed my to-go coffee and a little white paper bag with my pastry in front of me. I picked up the coffee and sipped, anxious to hear what Sara Jo had to say.

Sara Jo's fair skin pinked up. "Chester said she was a crazy woman, that's all. And finally, after he said it about five times on different days, I asked him what he was doing visiting with her."

Kara said, "What was his answer?"

"He said he only dropped by to make sure she was okay. She had a lot of cats and he said he was worried about them. But, you see . . ." She held up a hand in Lucinda's direction. "Don't you go all ballistic on me again. Promise?"

Lucinda eyed her and then her features relaxed. "Promise."

"Chester didn't much care for animals—and you know

that's true, Lucinda. He got bit by dogs and scratched by cats so many times he'd had about enough of them. Anyways, him telling me he was checking on those cats? I didn't believe it for a minute. I was thinking he found himself a sugar mama."

Maybe he did, I thought. Problem was, Minnie probably had no idea that was what she'd become.

Twenty-seven

The drive forty miles north of Mercy to find Henry and Harris Schultz took nearly an hour, and I wished after speaking with Chester's daughter-in-law that I'd brought a few cats along to cuddle with. Putting a human face on Chester Winston—though no doubt he was a flawed man—had left me feeling down. No matter what his character, his family was grieving, and that helped me understand why they had behaved so poorly in the hospital that night. Love, I'd learned long ago, was complicated.

Lucinda and Sara Jo had offered new information, and Kara gave them both her card before we left Belle's Beans. Maybe after they'd spoken with Tom, he would jog their memories even more, and then one or both of them would share this with Kara.

We'd been quiet on the ride to Fellowship Hills, and as we parked in the apartment complex lot, Kara broke the silence. "I hope I hear some pleasant details about Chester for his obit, or it will be a short column on the back page. *The man worked for animal control and didn't like animals?* That bothers me. You may be feeling sympathetic toward Lucinda and Earl, and perhaps even Chester, but I'm not."

"Shawn always knew Chester didn't like animals. That's why when Shawn ended up on a lonely road with an injured animal, those two got into it. Shawn has the restraining order to prove it," I said.

"I guess I should have figured that out, but it never crossed my mind."

We both got out of the SUV and walked side by side toward the block of apartments where Harris and Henry lived.

"Kara, let me explain why I am a little sympathetic to not so nice people. The family *is* being visited by the unpleasant ghost of Chester Winston. They have to live with his legacy, and by acting the way they have been, they're not helping themselves. Maybe if one person in Mercy can show them some kindness, well . . ." I glanced her way. "When you have to write both sides of a story to be fair, how difficult is that?" I asked.

"Oh, it's hard. This country is sliding away from that kind of reporting. I don't like that one bit. Opinion is not fact, so you can be sure that I will tell the truth about this murder. But most of all, I want to tell the truth about Brenda and Minnie."

I smiled as we made our way up a barren concrete walkway tinged with dead leaf stains and mildew. Fellowship Hills sounded like such a pleasant name for a town, and yet this complex seemed bleak and run-down. The gray ceiling of impending rain didn't help.

Kara knocked on the door to apartment 1A and it couldn't have been more than five seconds before the door swung open and Henry Schultz proclaimed, "Did you find him?" Then his anxious expression changed to disappointment. "Oh. You're not the cops."

"Kara Hart. Can you spare a few moments, Mr. Schultz?"

He glanced back and forth between me and Kara, and his gaze settled on me. "I know you, but who is this? A plainclothes officer from Mercy? Because—"

"I'm the editor of the *Mercy Messenger* and I have a few questions. Since you know Jillian, and she happens to be my stepmother, I thought—"

"You're writing a story about his disappearance?" He nodded vigorously. His anxiety had him blinking and biting his lip and rubbing his fingers and thumbs together. "That's a great idea. Come in."

Kara and I exchanged glances and she shrugged as we followed Henry into his apartment.

If the outside of this place was run-down and uninviting, the apartment was anything but. Someone who lived here liked order and cleanliness and I was guessing that person was here with us now.

"Sit down." Henry gestured at what seemed to be a brand-new charcoal-colored sofa with tufted cushions and a chaise on one end. Two matching chairs sat opposite. He went on as he paced, saying, "But I can't sit. I have to walk, to move . . . yes, keep moving."

As I settled onto the sofa, I said, "Harris is missing?"

Henry chewed on the corner of his mouth as we walked back and forth in front of us, but my question stopped him in his tracks. He dropped his hand and stared at me. "You don't know? That's not why you're here?"

"We want to know." Kara's tone was gentle. "We want to help. Tell us what happened, Henry."

"Harris disappeared. Even when he's out with his slacker friends, he always comes home. But last night, he didn't. I called the police here in town and they gave me that song and dance about adults having the right to walk off the earth if they want to and—"

"And that upset you," I said.

"So I called your *husband*." His attitude had turned cocky, the same attitude I'd seen in his brother when we'd spoken the first time we met.

Kara pulled her tablet from her leather cross-body bag. "You called Chief Stewart because . . . ?"

"This must be because of that murder. Something has happened to my brother and no one cares." He took a deep breath and smiled. "Except for your husband, Jillian. He acted like Harris's disappearance mattered. That he is important."

I smiled. Tom *would* convey that. "What did he tell you?"

Henry glanced at the chair behind him. Much to my relief—because he was making *me* nervous—he sat on the edge of the chair. "The chief asked me a lot of questions about Harris's routine, like had he been to visit Mama last night, had he even been in Mercy at all yesterday, when did he leave, when's the last time I saw him. Things like that. Important things. Harris was driving my car, so I was able to give Chief Stewart that information. He said they'd give the plate number and car description to all local law enforcement."

"It's still early enough I could get a nighttime edition out with his picture," Kara said. "Please, tell us everything you told the chief."

"You'd do that? Put out this special edition? Since I don't have my car, I can't even go to the office supply store and make up a flyer. But I have tapped into social media." He gestured toward the small kitchen eating area, where a laptop sat open. "Twitter, Facebook, Tumblr. Every site we're both on."

"Okay, then. Tell me everything you can about Harris." Kara readied herself to take notes, tablet on her knees.

He began to talk, but seemed so distraught that his narrative was disconnected and Kara had to stop him several times to clarify. She was being extra patient with him but had gotten very little useful information. Then a knock on the door interrupted them.

Henry rushed to answer and both Kara and I stood to see if Harris, perhaps without an apartment key, had returned home.

But it wasn't Harris. Candace stood alongside Captain Osborne.

My heart sank. Were they here to deliver bad news to Henry?

Candace's eyes said, *What in the heck are you two doing here?* But she solemnly refocused on Henry without speaking.

Osborne said, "We need to talk, Henry." He looked at Kara and me. "Alone."

"What is it? Where's my brother?"

Candace stepped across the threshold, apparently unconcerned about Osborne's need to take control. "We don't know where your brother is yet. We did find your car."

Osborne was right on her heels. "Hang on, *Detective* Carson. This is my county and I'll handle this."

"*Really?* Who found the car and where? And how

long did you plan to string this guy along? Can't you see how upset he is?"

Oh boy. Candace was tired and probably couldn't take much more of Osborne and his take-charge attitude. But Osborne had been around the police block a lot longer than she had.

He pointed at me. "Out of here, Jillian, please. And Miss Hart? You'll have to get your story another time. I assume that's why you're here."

"What is going on?" Henry practically screamed.

I went to his side. "It's okay, Henry. There are too many people in here and you need answers without an audience. Come on, Kara."

Kara looked downright angry, which was unusual for her. I gestured for her to come with me and she reluctantly complied. Osborne walked past us, already talking to Henry. As I passed Candace I whispered to her that I would text her in a second.

She nodded briefly and we left. Outside, we saw both a Mercy PD cruiser and a small black SUV with COUNTY SHERIFF in bright green letters on the side.

"That was a bust," Kara said.

"Maybe not. Let's park around the corner, where Osborne can't see us when he leaves. I told Candace I'd text her. I'll tell her to stay behind and grab a journal, or maybe more than one, if Henry does have them."

Kara smiled as she pressed the ignition button. "I should take you along on all my interviews. You get things done."

When I'd sent the text, I told Candace where we were parked. As we waited to hear back, I brought up the cat cam.

But what I saw scared the bejesus out of me.

Tom was home and he and Morris were in the living room. Tom had his hands on his hips and seemed troubled. What was going on? Where were my cats?

I phoned him using the FaceTime feature, my hand shaking as I touched the speed dial number. I couldn't even respond when Kara asked me what was wrong.

Once he answered and after my rather hysterical-sounding first sentence, he tried to calm me. "It's okay, Jilly. A little vandalism, is all."

"The cats. Where are they?"

"All present and accounted for. Simon was tough to find. He was hiding way in the back of our closet, facing the corner."

My racing heart slowed. As long as the kitties were okay, I could handle just about anything. "Aw. Poor baby. Simon's such a scaredy-cat. What happened?"

He explained that he'd been alerted that our security system was activated through the app on his phone while he was working in his office. I wondered then if I'd been too busy sticking my nose in other people's business to hear the alarm I'd set for the app.

He said, "Someone threw rocks at the house and dented a few gutters. They also spray-painted a message on the curb. Whoever it was probably knew they could be caught on-camera because they somehow avoided getting in any frame. I'll have to fix those blind spots when I get a chance."

"What was this message, Tom?"

"And I quote, 'this five-oh house was visited by weed-smoking dudes.'"

"What?" That seemed absolutely bizarre.

"Yeah. Not exactly a threat, aside from the rock throwing."

"What does *five-oh house* mean, Tom?"

"Gang slang for a police officer's place. They wanted to make sure I knew they had my address. On top of everything happening right now in Mercy, I don't have time for this kind of stupid stuff."

"Could the mention of weed have anything to do with Harris Schultz? I mean, you're the one who told me he smokes pot. Could he have done this? Could that be why he's gone missing?"

"So you know about that. How?"

Kara called, "She's helping me, Tom. We came to interview Harris and Henry Schultz."

"Hey there, Kara. I knew you couldn't stop doing what you do." Tom smiled. "I thought it looked as if Jilly was sitting in your fancy car. As for Harris being our vandal, I don't think it's possible. See, he went missing in the middle of the night. Since he stole his brother's car and then exchanged it for an early model Chevy from a used car lot—we did get the car theft on-camera—we believe he was long gone before what happened at our house. They picked up the stolen car on a traffic cam up by Greenville. He's fleeing. But fleeing what? I don't know yet."

"His brother will be relieved he's okay," I said. "Will you call him with that information?"

"I will. Or you can have him call me when you talk to him," Tom said.

"We kind of got kicked out of his apartment—by Captain Osborne." I went on to explain how we'd hoped to find Minnie's journal, but that Candace and Osborne had arrived before we could even learn whether Henry had it.

"Brad Osborne must have picked up on my dispatch to Candace. I told her to interview Henry." Then Tom seemed to surprise Kara by saying, "Good to follow up on that journal. Not good that Osborne is sticking his nose in our business again. He wants to solve this case in the worst way."

I heard Morris in the background. "That guy's building his reputation on what he's plannin' to do tomorrow."

Kara laughed and said, "That is so true."

Tom grew somber. "We can't alienate local police agencies, so we all need to be careful how we react to Captain Osborne. If one of my people sends out an *officer needs assistance* call, I don't want the sheriff's department taking their sweet time coming to the rescue. We can and we do work together. He's just been more . . . *present* when it comes to this case. Murder is a big deal and he can make his name off being the one to solve this."

"I never thought about how much small-town police might need help from other departments. Even the state police, right?" I said.

"That's right. For the most part, we all get along fine."

"Just to reassure you," I said, "when Captain Osborne told us to leave Henry's apartment a bit ago, we left right away."

"Good." He smiled. "I explained to him the other day that you help out anyone who needs it and he seemed to understand. Maybe once he can be in the limelight concerning all that's gone down in the last week, he won't be such a jerk."

I then filled Tom in about running into Sara Jo and

Lucinda and what we'd learned from those two. Before he disconnected he told me not to worry about the vandalism. He'd find out who did this, but maybe not right now. He was only glad I hadn't been home.

After Tom disconnected, Kara said, "Sometimes kids have nothing better to do than cause trouble. But here's the problem I have with this situation. Vandalism usually takes place at night, when no one's watching. My fear is someone *was* watching—as in watching you and waiting for you to leave."

The idea of someone watching me made that pastry I'd eaten earlier seem like a bad decision. "Kara, this *does* seem like kid's stuff. Maybe it was just a gang-initiation thing."

"Could be. With the meth problems in our more remote areas of the state, gangs *have* sprung up. But you aren't exactly someone a vandal would target. Still, that reference to weed after what we think we know about Harris can't be ignored. I'm certain it wasn't lost on Tom, even if he didn't say he thought it was connected."

"But Tom believes Harris had already left town before the vandalism occurred, right?"

Kara contemplated this. "I guess he did say that. Maybe this vandalism *was* just a random act of stupidity."

But neither of us was totally convinced if the uneasy silence that fell between us meant anything.

Twenty-eight

Candace finally answered my text and said she'd meet us in a few minutes. Worried about my spooked cats, I tapped the cat cam app again. But before I did, I saw that I had indeed missed the alert from when our home security system had been activated. That's when I realized the volume on my phone was turned down, something I probably did accidentally—though I had no idea how. It wasn't the first time. I turned the volume all the way up, determined to check for that problem more often.

Once the cat cam was running, I saw that Tom and Morris were gone. But Syrah seemed on high alert. He was on the window seat, front paws on the window frame. His ears were tilted forward, so he was paying close attention to whatever was going on outside. He probably didn't want any rocks hitting the house and taking him by surprise again. He certainly was a watch cat, if such a thing existed.

Candace's squad car pulled up next to the SUV about five minutes later. We decided we were all hungry and she knew of a place not too far from here that had food to accommodate my vegetarian stepdaughter. Since Kara and I weren't native South Carolinians, it was a good thing Candace knew where we could get good food—that is, if my stomach was settled by then.

The town nearby seemed quite different from Fellowship Hills, but that's because it was home to a small college. We ate at a place called the Cabbage Patch, and I swear Kara was as excited as one of my cats at a mouse show when she saw all the vegetarian choices on the menu.

Once we'd ordered, I finally got to ask the question that had been on my mind for the last hour. "Did you get the journal?"

"Yup. I put it in an evidence bag, but it's been handled so much, I'm not sure that will help when it comes to DNA or prints. Heck, I'm not even certain it *is* evidence."

"Did you read what she wrote?" Kara asked.

"I did. Not that it made any sense. There was a repeat of what Greta Kramer said Mrs. Schultz wrote before—the stuff about 'no uniform.'"

"Can I read it?" Kara asked.

"Nope. It's bagged up. I don't think the incoherent scrawls of a woman who had a brain tumor can lead us anywhere, Kara. And why don't you ask Liam how it would go over in court if I opened that evidence bag now? We need to preserve some semblance of a chain of evidence should we hope to convict a killer."

"Darn it, Candace. Show it to me through the plastic, then."

Candace just shook her head, her lips tight.

Our food arrived, thank goodness, and the mini-argument ceased. We must have all been hungry, because we remained silent through half the meal. I had the restaurant's specialty—cabbage soup—and though it was delicious, I should have opted for something less tough on my gut. The vandalism still bothered me. Even if Tom said he'd find out who did it, I dreaded going home to that scene.

Candace and Kara had huge salads with every kind of green known to humans. The homemade rolls were wonderful and the smell of yeast bread that filled the little place was certainly soothing—though not soothing enough.

On the way back to Mercy, Candace led the way, and for once she kept to a reasonable speed. But the roads were winding and narrow, as were many of the back roads in our area of the state. She pretty much *had* to take her time.

Candace waved good-bye out the driver's window when we hit town. She took off in the direction of the station while Kara and I went to my house. It wasn't a pretty sight. The paint the vandals or vandal used was neon yellow. Tom had failed to mention the large yellow X painted in front of the driveway.

As I slid out of the passenger seat, I muttered, "How will we ever get that off?"

"I'm sure there are ways. You can paint over it, maybe?" She was trying to make me feel better, but it wasn't working.

"It feels like such an invasion." I looked at her, my eyes welling. "I hate this, Kara."

She gave me a strong hug and then stepped back. "I think I should stay with you."

"I'm not about to argue. You have to visit with my new friends, Simon and Otto, anyway."

I wanted to erase the defacement from my mind and cats would help with that.

The two of us were soon sitting on the kitchen floor with the kitties crawling all over us. Even Dashiell and Scaredy Simon came to comfort us. Felines have a strong emotional bond with their humans. They know when something is wrong and they try to make it all better with purrs and nose bumps and staying close.

The afternoon quietly slipped into early evening and when I saw Kara checking her phone for the fourth time, then texting someone—probably Liam—and generally growing restless, I was ready to set her free from babysitting duty. Besides, I'd had plenty of time to think and I wasn't about to let some random stranger disturb my peace of mind. We both needed to find a little bit of normal amid the chaos of the last few days.

But Kara's phone rang and when she said, "Hello, Peyton," I had a feeling we were off again to our home away from home, the hospital. And so it was.

We each took our own car since I insisted Kara should go home to Liam after this visit to Brenda, who was apparently fully awake now. But there had been another development. Minnie Schultz was also awake, though as Peyton told us, she wasn't allowed visitors.

What did a no-visitors policy matter at this point anyway? One son had no car, one son had fled, which made him guilty of *something* in my book, and her daughter had a brand-new baby.

The women's two rooms on the fourth floor weren't that far from each other. Peyton was pacing in the hallway near a large food cart. A hospital dinner had apparently been served—and my guess was it had been far less than yummy from the smells that surrounded us. I was glad the memory of that delicious cabbage soup helped me ignore whatever unidentifiable food odor permeated the hall.

Peyton seemed happy to see us and took us into Brenda's room, where bouquets of flowers sat on the windowsill and filled the room with sweetness. An IV was connected to one hand and a heart monitor bleeped a steady rhythm. A tray of uneaten food sat on the over-bed wheeling table that had been pushed away from the bed. Brenda managed a sleepy smile. But her bruised face, the cast on her leg and her pained expression tugged at my heart. They'd also shaved off her lovely hair on one side, which gave her an odd punk-rock look.

She saw me staring and said, "That's the one part of me that doesn't hurt. They had to relieve the pressure from a subdural hematoma. They drilled a hole in my skull and—"

I held up my hand with a smile. "I'm just glad to hear you speaking as if nothing happened to your poor head."

She glanced Kara's way and Peyton said, "This is the newspaper woman I was telling you about. She's been so wonderful."

"Ah, Jillian's daughter. You've been such a comfort to my overprotective brother."

No one corrected her by saying *stepdaughter*. Kara had, after all, truly become as close to me as any daughter could.

Kara took a seat close to the hospital bed. "Do you recall anything about the crash?"

She started to shake her head no and winced. The heart monitor sped up when she experienced this pain.

Brenda grabbed the back of her neck and Peyton responded at once with concern.

"I'll get you a new ice pack." He hurried from the room.

"He's such a worrier, but the whiplash *is* pretty severe. To answer your question, I don't recall a blessed thing about the accident."

Her heartbeat began to slow and I felt relieved. I'd even clenched my hands but relaxed my fingers now. Being around someone so injured, so wounded, had me worried for her.

"This 'accident' was no accident," Kara said.

"Why would someone do that to me? None of my patients are violent, despite what the public believes. The mentally ill are, for the most part, harmless. I still can't believe I didn't do this to myself."

I stood back, not wanting to interrupt this conversation. Maybe something Kara asked her would jog her memory. But then I remembered that Peyton said he doubted she would recall anything.

Kara placed a hand over Brenda's free hand, the one without the IV. "You definitely didn't do this to yourself. I talked to the wrecker driver and he's seen plenty of accidents in his time. He said you were run off the road."

Brenda closed her eyes. "This is so disturbing. Why would someone do this to me?" The bleeping sped up once again.

I stepped closer to the bed. "We didn't come here to upset you. There's time to figure this out."

"What about Minnie?" Brenda asked me. "I remember she was sick and Peyton said something about her being on this floor not too far away from my room. But he didn't want me worrying about her, so I don't know anything. While he's gone, please tell me about her. It would help to know if she's recovering."

I said, "She had her surgery. I plan on visiting her—even if I have to sneak in. Maybe I'll head to her room right now and—"

"Hang on." Kara gestured at me. "Jillian has a direct line to the police chief and I want her to stay while I ask a few questions. I believe the attack on you has something to do with Chester Winston's murder. But we have no proof."

Brenda's expression betrayed her frustration. "But I can't make that connection, Kara. I don't *remember* anything."

The last thing I wanted—and I was sure this was Kara's wish as well—was to upset this broken woman. "Let's take this back to before the accident, then. And we'll just call it an accident."

I gave Kara a bit of a warning look. I felt as if she was being a little too enthusiastic about pinning what happened to Brenda on Chester's killer. Brenda was traumatized and fragile. She needed a gentler approach.

Brenda smiled. "You'd make a good shrink, Jillian."

I returned her smile. "I take that as a compliment. Were you leaving here when the accident happened? Or somewhere else?"

She squinted, but the bruising around her eyes obviously made her rethink the use of those eye muscles. "I picked up something from Minnie. Yes. I was here."

"A journal?" Kara asked. I was relieved that her tone was softer. Kara didn't fall off the stupid truck. She understood she needed to chill.

Peyton came back into the room carrying a towel that was obviously wrapped around the ice pack—a long one, probably made for exactly the kind of neck injury Brenda had.

As he helped his sister move so he could put it in place, she said, "You know, pain means I'm healing. Pain isn't a totally bad thing."

"I hate what happened to you, Brenda." I saw his eyes shine with unshed tears.

She clutched his hand. "That's why these two strong, healthy women are helping me figure out what happened. I want you to allow them to ask me the questions that need to be asked. You sent the police officer away, I know, but I need to understand. You're an internist and I'm the psychiatrist. I know better."

His shoulders slumped. "Are you *sure*?"

"Yes. Now sit down and rest. You look exhausted." She weakly waved at a reclining chair in the corner near the window.

He did as she said.

Meanwhile Kara was already asking a question. "What police officer came to talk to you?"

Maybe Tom and Candace had finally made the connection between Brenda's attempted murder and Chester's death.

"A man from the sheriff's office. I never got his name."

I closed my eyes for a second. Osborne was everywhere. But I remember what Tom said about cooperating with the sheriff's department and how important it was. I hoped Kara would remember as well.

"Oh, that makes sense," Kara wisely replied. "The sheriff's deputies responded first to your wreck."

Wanting to steer this away from an issue we had no

control over—police infighting—I said, "You mentioned
something about the journal you bought for Minnie. Do
you remember that you bought three of them? That you
took one from her that she'd written in?"

Brenda closed her eyes. "She was so happy." She
looked at me then and I could see a spark in her gaze.
"That young policewoman found that stack of journals
in the closet. Minnie has probably journaled all her
life. It gave her comfort to hold a pen, to write."

"She wrote the words *no uniform*. Did she tell you
what that meant?" Kara asked.

"Well, there was a security guard hanging around and
the police officer sitting in the room. I took it to mean
she wanted them to leave—that she wanted the uniforms
to go away."

I nodded. "That makes sense when you put it in the
context of what was going on around Minnie at the
time. And the scaredy-cat Simon? Do you recall her
writing about him?"

"Yes. Yes. The cat." Brenda's mind was working at
full speed now, but I worried this would be too tiring
for her.

"Simon, the scaredy-cat, seemed important to Minnie?" Kara said.

"Yes. She mentioned something about the tall man
frightening her cat, but then we were interrupted. The
security guard and the Mercy officer—what's her name
again?"

"Lois?" I said.

"That's it. *Lois*. Anyway, this security guard came
into the room and started up a conversation with her.
Minnie was so confused as it was, and their talking dis-
rupted her train of thought. She could never get back on

track. She just put down the journal and sat there staring into space."

"Can you remember anything else?" Kara said.

I could tell by her tone that for Kara, this conversation was a bit of a disappointment. The only revelation
was that Osborne—was it even Osborne or perhaps
one of the officers who'd found the crash site?—had
come here to see how Brenda was doing. We already
knew what Minnie had written in at least one journal.

The conversation seemed to have tired Brenda, and
when she asked Peyton to help her adjust the ice pack,
we were already up and headed for the door after telling Brenda she needed to rest.

"I didn't help you much, did I?" she said.

"Oh, you did," Kara said quickly. "I'll come back
tomorrow because you'll probably be stronger then.
I've worn you out and I'm sorry for that. But I won't
give up trying to find answers for you."

Peyton smiled. "You two are the absolute best."

Brenda smiled, too, and if she could have nodded
her agreement she would have. Instead, she offered a
quiet "Yes, you are."

Twenty-nine

The food cart was rolled away by a dietary department worker as Kara and I stood in the hall. Liam had texted her and she was late for the dinner date she'd promised him.

When I saw Lois hanging around another doorway down the hall, I knew I'd found where Minnie had been moved.

"I don't know if Minnie is even conscious enough to talk, but I want to see her. Maybe she'll know at least Lois and I are here for her. Go meet Liam and I'll call you if I learn anything."

We hugged and I watched as she left. I noticed the security guard leaning on the nurse's station counter nod at her as she passed him. Was that the same guy who'd escorted the fighting families out of the hospital the other evening? From this far away I couldn't tell, but between his presence and Lois being here, I felt safer than I had since seeing that awful paint on the curb.

Lois seemed happy to see me and I also sensed she was glad to be once again protecting Minnie. The patient might have important secrets locked away in her healing brain, ones that could help catch a killer.

"Is it okay if I visit?" I whispered.

"No visitors, I'm told. But I'm making an exception for you—if you promise not to tattle to that surgeon."

"I promise," I whispered.

"She's in and out, but when she wakes up, this little lady actually makes sense now. You know, even when she was so out of it, I felt something for her. Like we were connected somehow."

"I saw that, Lois. You were there for her—that's for sure."

Lois led me into the darkened room. She lowered her voice. "They said to keep the lights dimmed. She had a big surgery and she's sensitive to the light."

I nodded in understanding. Minnie, looking frail but comfortable, slept with the bed raised, her head bandages nearly blending with the stark whiteness of the pillow.

Lois took me to the far end of the room as far from Minnie as we could get. "I heard Minnie has her first grandchild now, but I don't think it's our place to tell her."

"If she wakes up, I won't mention it." I walked over to the bed and sat in the straight-back chair that Lois had probably been sitting in. She'd stayed close to her charge. That made me smile.

The room was devoid of machines aside from the IV and the monitor clipped to her finger that registered her blood oxygen. I placed a hand over Minnie's small, cool fingers.

Her eyes slowly opened. "Why, it's you. How's my Otto?"

She remembered. I was a little stunned.

"He's doing great, Minnie. Do you want to see him?"

"Oh, that would warm my heart. As cold as they keep it in this darn place, maybe it would warm the rest of me, too."

She was indeed making perfect sense. I pulled out my phone and tapped the cat cam app. Since I'd left all the cats together upstairs, I was hoping her two fur friends wouldn't be camera shy. "Guess who else is visiting me?"

She wanted to sit up straighter, but Lois came quickly to the other side of the bed. "You don't need to move around too much. I can raise the bed a little more."

Lois did this and, to my relief, the first cat I saw was none other than Simon, our scaredy boy. "Guess who else came to stay with me, Minnie?" I showed her the image on my phone.

"Simon? But he was hiding from the tall man and I couldn't find him. Where was he?"

"In a closet. He's fitting in with my cats just fine and Shawn is taking care of the rest of your crew." Her mention of this "tall man" wasn't lost on me and I wondered if she was referring to Chester. But Chester was by no means tall.

She said, "There's Otto, too."

I craned to see what she was looking at, and sure enough, Simon and Otto, along with Merlot and Syrah, were all on-camera. "Here. Let me do something so you can talk to them." I took the phone and activated the chat feature. "Okay, say hello to your kitties."

"Really? They can hear me?"

It was obvious they'd already heard her because Otto stretched up and began pawing at the camera. She moved her mouth closer to the phone and said, "It's your mama, my babies. I'll be home soon."

Simon opened his mouth and let out the sweetest, most plaintive meow.

"I love you," Minnie said to her cats.

Lois was grinning—actually *grinning*—and this visit was the by far the best part of a difficult day for me.

"You can keep looking, but can I ask you a few questions, Minnie?"

She closed her eyes. "I'm having trouble looking too long because it's bright, so you can put your little TV down for now."

I almost laughed, but it was like a TV. "You mentioned the tall man. Are you talking about Chester?"

"No, the man in the uniform, except then he had no uniform on the very bad day. He scared all the cats, but especially my sweetheart Simon."

No uniform. That's why she'd written those words.

"He and Chester got mad at each other. It had something to do with all those awful boxes. Why did they keep bringing in those boxes? I couldn't move in my own house. And then there were the cats. So many cats. I tried my best to care for them because Chester kept coming with a new one almost every day." She paused to take a breath because she was talking so fast.

I gripped her hand, being careful not to hurt her fragile fingers. "Slow down, Minnie. It's okay."

But I noticed that Lois had taken out her phone, touched an app and placed it on the pillow near Minnie's head. She wanted to record what was being said.

She nodded slowly. "Slow down. Yes. I got tired with so many cats and Harris coming in with that man who all of a sudden wasn't wearing his uniform and . . ." She withdrew her hand and squeezed her forehead between her thumb and her middle finger.

Harris said he hadn't seen his mother in months. Obviously that wasn't true.

Lois said, "Do you need medicine for the headache, Minnie?"

"That would be good, Lois. Yes."

Lois pressed the call bell and a voice came over the intercom seconds later. "Can I help you?"

She relayed that Minnie had a headache and the woman who'd answered said she'd be there in a few minutes.

"You mentioned your son Harris. He came to visit you with the tall man?" I said.

"Yes . . . no. I'm getting confused again." Minnie covered her eyes with one hand.

"Do you want me to leave so you can rest, Minnie?" I said.

She removed her small fingers from her face, but I could tell she was in pain. "Oh no, Jillian. But I remember something happened at my house. Something bad. It's not a good memory. I was in the closet with Simon. When it was safe, I knew I had to leave and Otto was the most vulnerable. He was the youngest, you see, so I took him with me."

"Yes. You protected him and I'll bet he's grown since you gave him to me to care for the other day." I could tell she was not only in pain. I was tiring her out with my questions.

A male voice said, "Tammy wanted me to tell you she'll be here with that pain medicine in a minute, Mrs. Schultz."

It was the security guard.

"What are you doing acting like a medical assistant, Norm?" Lois said.

"You know there isn't much going on around here, Lois. I just help out where I can." He eyed Minnie. "You feeling better, Mrs. Schultz?"

Minnie squinted his way. "Better, yes. Don't I know you?"

"We talked some before your big operation. Good to see you back in a regular hospital bed." He waved his hand and was gone.

That was definitely the guy I'd seen escort the arguing families out of the hospital. "You know him?" I asked Lois.

"Sort of. I met him doing this job. Seems like a nice guy. Former law enforcement. Lots of security guards are. He told me he wanted more time with his fiancée, so he quit the force. I sure can't blame him for that."

"I do remember him," Minnie said. "Nice young man."

Seconds later the nurse came in with a rolling medication cart. After much checking of orders, and Minnie's ID bracelet, the woman in pink scrubs helped Minnie swallow down what looked like two horse pills. Then she looked at me and admonished me for visiting a patient with a no-visitors order before hurrying off.

A lot of hurrying went on in hospitals. It was probably a stressful place to work, because it was certainly a stressful place to visit.

"There, now," Minnie said. "What were we talking about?"

I'd been caught and worried Norm would soon be escorting me out of the room. But I pressed on gently. "The tall man? Not Chester but someone else?"

"He knew my son Harris. I have twin boys—well, not really boys anymore. But I could tell the man made Harris nervous. Uniform one day, no uniform another day."

"What kind of uniform?" Lois asked. This sure piqued her interest.

"Why, I don't really know. I don't remember." Minnie squinted and again raised her hand to shield her eyes. "I think that man had something to do with the boxes. And there were so many of them and all those cats to contend with. I understood nothing about any of it. Chester told me I'd ordered the packages, but I didn't remember doing that. Plus he kept telling me the county shelter was at capacity and how could I not take in these cats he kept finding? Then he'd take one away and pretty soon, he'd arrive with another baby that needed a temporary home. How could I refuse?"

I saw a tear slip down Minnie's cheek.

I trapped Lois's gaze and shook my head.

Lois smiled at Minnie fondly. "No need to get worked up. It's not good for you. You get some rest now."

The poor woman's eyes were only half open now. I patted Minnie's arm. "I'll leave you now. But I will be back to see your progress. You are one tough lady."

She mumbled, "Promise you'll come back?"

I bent and kissed her forehead. "Promise."

As I left the hospital, I realized it was dark. I'd totally lost track of time. Plus, now Norm, the security guard, was in the lobby. And he was watching me. Something about his presence everywhere I turned was disconcerting. When Norm asked if he could walk me to my car, I declined with a smile and hurried to the van.

It wasn't until I was on the road headed for home that

I began to wonder about this uniform business. The security guard wore a uniform. Could he be the man Minnie was talking about who'd been in her house, maybe *without* a uniform? Had this confused her?

But then the bigger picture emerged like someone had punched me. Kara had been searching for a connection between Brenda's crash and Chester's murder. When Minnie, a potential witness to murder, showed up at the hospital, what happened? Dr. Ross became involved. No matter how confused Minnie was, there was always the potential she might say something to incriminate someone or even name the killer. Who had been around to hear conversations? That security guard, for one. Brenda had even confirmed this earlier this evening.

Did Chester know this Norm guy? There was one way I might be able to find out. I asked the remote digital assistant who resided in my phone to get me Sara Jo's phone number. Sara Jo, unlike Lucinda, was much more likely to answer my questions.

When she answered the phone, I could tell she was surprised that I'd called. "What's up, Jillian?"

"I'm driving and using Bluetooth, so I hope I don't break up. I have a question for you about Chester. Did he know a man named Norm? I don't know his last name, but he's a security guard at the hospital."

Silence followed and for a second I thought I'd lost the call, but finally Sara Jo spoke. "Oh, Chester knows—sorry—*knew* him. He introduced us. Norm Garrett is my fiancé."

"The one who gave you that giant diamond I saw sparkling away on your finger when we spoke at Belle's Beans?"

I could hear the smile in her voice. "One and the same. Why do you need to know about Norm and Chester?"

"I just wondered. I saw him tonight when I was visiting Minnie and he seemed like a nice guy." I so wanted to end this call and talk to Tom, but I didn't want to make Sara Jo suspicious.

"He *is* a nice guy. The best." Her tone had changed. She sounded as if she'd grown as cautious as I felt.

"Listen, tell him I said hi when you see him. Thanks, Sara Jo."

I disconnected before she even said good-bye. *Please blame that on Bluetooth for my abrupt disconnect, Sara Jo,* I thought as I gave my phone the command to call Tom.

I explained all that had gone on at the hospital, told him that Harris had probably lied and been in his mother's house recently. He was heading out of Dodge because no doubt he was part of the scheme to bleed the poor woman dry of every penny. Then I gave him my theory about the security guard—that he could be the link connecting the crimes. Maybe Sara Jo's wonderful fiancé, who'd given her that flashy engagement ring, had been in cahoots with Chester and the credit card fraud, too. "Maybe the three of them argued and it got ugly?" I said.

"What's this security guard's name again?" he asked.

"Norm Garrett."

"Great information, Jilly. I'll run a background check and maybe head over to the hospital for a little chat with the man. We sure need a break in this case before all my suspects flee in stolen cars."

"Harris *was* involved," I said.

"Oh, you know he was. If you're innocent, you don't run."

"I love you, Tom. I hope this helps you get to the truth."

"Love you, Jilly."

I rode home feeling better than I had in days. Tom would get to the bottom of everything that had happened in the last week. I was sure of it.

Thirty

Once again, I sat on the kitchen floor surrounded by my cat crew. I doled out affection first, then treats, then more affection. I needed a double dose as much as they did. Dashiell's blood sugar checked out fine and he even got an extra piece of freeze-dried chicken.

Since both Brenda and Minnie seemed to be on the road to recovery, I definitely felt a sense of relief. If they found Harris and brought him back to Mercy—and I had no doubt that would happen—I was certain he would name Norm Garrett as the third wheel in the trifecta of evil that had invaded a poor, sick woman's life. What was wrong with these people?

My lunch seemed as if it had happened yesterday, and with my stomach no longer rebelling, I opted for my favorite easy dinner—a peanut butter and jam sandwich. As I slathered the peanut butter on slices of whole wheat bread, I wondered about that beautiful engagement ring I'd seen on Sara Jo's finger. Had it come from the box of jewelry we'd found in Minnie's secret closet? Was that why the poor woman had hidden the box away?

Because someone named Norm had taken a piece of jewelry for himself and Minnie knew it was gone? I wouldn't doubt it.

After I'd eaten, I took a long bath. The cats enjoyed being *near* the tub, but all of them were careful not to get too close. Though Chablis didn't mind a bath every now and then, she shied away from the tub. Too much water, perhaps? Probably.

I donned my pajamas and decided to call Kara now that she'd had time for her dinner with Liam. I settled onto the sofa and soon found myself among all the cats. Chablis settled in my lap and even the scaredy-cat chose a spot close to me on the sofa. Poor Otto was exhausted and fell asleep almost at once. But the rest of them weren't about to let me out of their sight. Syrah was by my head, Merlot was at my feet and Dashiell was right alongside Simon, the cat he'd pretended to dislike so much. In the days to come, I would carve out plenty of time to make up for my recent absences.

After I called Kara and told her about my visit to Minnie, she said, "The security guard? *Of course.* Why didn't I think of that?"

"I mean, I could be wrong, but who else was all over that hospital? That's why Brenda was run off the road. He feared she could make sense out of what Minnie's words meant about 'no uniform.' Some days when he was at her house he might have worn his uniform and some days, maybe not."

"You said Tom planned to talk to this person? When do you think that will happen? Or maybe it already has."

"He said tonight. What if I'm wrong, Kara? I don't suppose Sara Jo will ever speak to me again if I cast suspicion on an innocent man. It could all be about Harris. He needed drug money and Chester was no doubt partnered with him. He certainly lied about not seeing his mother in ages. She clearly said that she saw him recently inside her house—with the tall man." I paused. "But the security guard isn't tall. In fact, he's below average in height."

"I'm hearing doubt creep in, Jillian. Minnie was confused. Who knows what a brain tumor can do to a person? Maybe her vision was distorted."

"Maybe. But something isn't right . . . Something seems off."

I heard the crackle of Kara's police scanner in the background. She went silent as she listened and then she came back on the line and offered an emphatic *"Yes."*

"What is it?" I asked.

"I told you they'd catch Harris. He's in custody in Virginia. Listen, I have to open the newspaper office and pull all my information together for a story. I think Tom and Candace will be able to mark this case solved tonight. Talk to you later."

She sounded thrilled and of course she'd have a great front-page story. But though Harris's capture was a good development and would certainly provide answers, doubt still niggled at my insides. Why? It was all about the tall man. That was the piece of the puzzle that didn't fit.

I doubted Tom would be home any time soon, especially now that Harris had been located. I thought about Minnie then. The truth would come out and I sure didn't want to be there when she learned that one of her kids had betrayed her so horribly.

To take my mind off all of this, I reached for the

remote and decided to catch up on a few shows I enjoyed that had been set to record. But I made the mistake of leaning my head back against the cushions.

Unfortunately, it wasn't the sound of Tom's voice that woke me minutes or hours later. The house was pitch-black, the TV wasn't on and Chablis's claws were digging into me.

I realized that the power had gone out. It wasn't raining—there hadn't been a true thunderstorm in more than a week. What the heck had happened?

But the silence helped me understand. There was a metallic scratching sound at the back door. Chablis's claws dug deeper into my thigh and then she took off. My eyes were still adjusting, so I couldn't see where the other cats were, but when I felt around on the sofa, I knew they weren't nearby.

What the heck was that noise?

But before I could think another thought, I heard my back door squeak open.

What was happening?

I heard his not-quiet-enough footsteps as he walked through my kitchen. The dark figure came around the sofa and stood above me. I recognized him even in the dark. The tall man had come here.

Captain Brad Osborne.

I drew my legs up and shrank back against the sofa cushions. He flipped on a bright flashlight and shined it in my face. I had to turn my head.

"It's all over, thanks to you." His voice was soft, almost gentle.

I felt a throbbing pulse in my throat as adrenaline and fear coursed through me.

I blinked and stared away from the light, but I could

still see him. He wore no uniform. He was dressed in black so he would blend with the night.

"If it's over," I said, "why are you here?

"I'm giving it my best shot. The brand-new police chief is arrogant. If he's taking me down, I'll make sure he pays the ultimate price. If I take your life, he'll have learned a valuable lesson."

I lifted my chin and though I was terrified, I kept my voice steady when I said, "So where's your gun?"

"Gangs like knives. You've been threatened by a gang, I hear. They commit random acts of violence and you're about to learn that firsthand. Then your husband will learn it, too."

My eyes were adjusting and I could see him pretty well now. I could also see two of my cats, Merlot and Syrah, sitting behind this terrible man. Syrah's ears were laid back. He was as angry as I was at this intrusion and these threats. "*You* did that spray-painting? Really?"

"Oh, I rarely do much for myself anymore, Jillian. It's much easier to hire one of the many thugs I've met in my days working as a sheriff. I'm owed plenty of favors by a lot of bad people."

I saw he had a hunting knife sheath attached to his belt. It was hard not to focus on it, but I had to make him believe I wasn't afraid. People like Osborne took pleasure in the fear of others. I wasn't about to give him that satisfaction.

"Since they've caught up with Harris, I'm sure you realized your gig was up. What is your game, anyway, Mr. Osborne? Conning sick people?" I refused to use his title as a police officer. He didn't deserve that much respect.

"You don't know the first thing about my *game*, as

you call it. Was it a mistake to get involved with Chester Winston? Biggest mistake of my life. What an idiot he was. But he was connected to county officials. If he decided to talk—which he threatened to do—I was done. I've spent years building my business and his little two-bit operation nearly ruined it. Then you picked up where he left off by thinking you could take me down."

I was thinking about what Tom had once told me, how sociopaths like this guy had egos the size of the moon. They loved to talk about how smart they were. Osborne had admitted to a mistake, though. I needed him to feel smart again. Only then would he make another mistake—or so I hoped. "But you said *nearly*. A smart man like you surely has a backup plan, and money stashed in offshore accounts."

"You're pretty bright yourself, Jillian. If I didn't dislike your husband so darn much, I might spare you. He had a bead on me. I could see it in his eyes every time we talked. If this hadn't happened with Chester, we would have crossed paths in the future."

"Did you kill Chester?"

"Now, don't try anything so silly as trying to get me to spill my guts to you, Jillian. You're smarter than that. I shouldn't have said as much as I have—but then, you won't be telling anyone about it once I get finished here. Gang slayings are brutal, you know. But I'll make sure to make this as easy as possible on you. See, I kind of like you, even if you did finger my guy Norm. The girlfriend called him and he called me. Your death was always in the works, but I had to step up the timeline. We deal a lot in timelines in the police business, but I'm sure you know that."

Despite his words about not spilling his guts, he sure

was talking a lot. He was probably enjoying this terrible conversation. I tried to keep my breathing steady and my voice even. "I do know about timelines. So, you're saying this is about Tom? Getting revenge for arrests he hasn't even made yet? I don't get that."

"He refused my help. His predecessor never refused my help. Who does he think he is?"

Uh-oh. I'd taken a wrong turn. I'd heard the hostility in his voice. "He's new at the job," I said. "I guess he's simply green."

"But, you see, that's what you should have told him. I'm betting you could have convinced him to bring me on board if you'd wanted to."

My mind began to race. I was running out of things to say. Stroking his ego would only go so far. He possessed a highly intelligent criminal mind. He'd probably already seen right through me and was simply toying with me right now.

How could I . . .

Simon, who must have been curled up and heavily asleep under the coffee table that sat between me and the man who was about to kill me, suddenly raised his head. I thought this scared boy would run out of the room, but then I realized he was familiar with Osborne. The man had been in Minnie's house, who knew how many times?

And Simon didn't like him. This became obvious when I watched him slink out from under the table, stand up like a prairie dog on his hind legs and hiss as loud as he could at Osborne.

It was the small distraction I needed. I grabbed the back of the sofa and hiked over, racing for the basement. I would rather have run to my craft room because some very sharp scissors and seam rippers resided there, but he would have caught me had I run in that direction. We had tools in the basement. Sharp things. *Like what? And where are these sharp things?*

The adrenaline was pumping harder now, but it was working against me, making me tremble all over. Garden shears. Where were the garden shears? Screwdrivers. Surely I could find the screwdrivers in this whole new level of blackness in my basement.

He had the benefit of a flashlight. I had the benefit of knowledge of my house.

Since I was barefoot, I managed to get down the stairs on little cat feet. I heard a thud above me. He'd probably run into side of the counter separating the kitchen from living area. I'd done it a dozen times myself in broad daylight.

His steps, the ones that had been so quiet after he'd broken in, now seemed heavy and full of rage. I heard the patter of kitty feet coming down the stairs to join me. I wanted to shoo them away, keep them safe from this knife-wielding madman. Since they'd come down, Osborne wouldn't waste time checking the pantry or mudroom or to even see if I'd run outside. Sure enough, I heard his slow steps on the stairs.

"Come on, Jillian. Don't delay the inevitable." He said this so calmly it infuriated me.

I took a deep, quiet breath from the spot I'd chosen to hide under the laundry sink. I had no makeshift weapon. There had been no time to find those precious garden shears. This was the cat area. It smelled like the litter needed changing yesterday and I now had clay granules between my toes and stuck to the soles of my feet. A standing cabinet for extra supplies like paper towels and detergent was next to me. I wondered if I had the strength to topple it onto him when he finally found me. And he *would* find me.

He was sweeping his flashlight around and walked over to the cat room. He kicked the door open. I had known that there was nowhere to hide in there. He didn't, but he soon found out.

Osborne then started in my direction, his light focused on the cabinet next to me. I moved a little bit more into the darkness provided by the side of that cabinet, trying to slide my hands behind it. There was no space for my fingers. No space at all. I willed back the tears of pure terror that threatened. Did he have that knife in his hand now? Was this his endgame?

And then I was betrayed not by any sound I made but by Otto. The kitten offered a plaintive meow and rubbed against my drawn-up knees.

The light swept down and caught me in its awful glow.

This was like a horror movie. This wasn't real.

"Come on. Get up, Jillian." He extended his free hand.

Yeah. Like I wanted to touch this freak. At least he still hadn't taken the knife out.

When I didn't move, his voice was sharp when he spoke. *"Get up. Now."*

So I used the only tool available: a tray filled with hard clumps of dirty kitty litter. I lifted it like it was nothing and tossed the contents in his face. Maybe there was something to that adrenaline thing after all. He dropped the flashlight and shouted some very unpleasant words at me. But the more he rubbed his eyes, the more it had to hurt. Clay litter is not eye friendly.

Fearing he'd recover sooner rather than later, I picked up his hefty Maglite and smashed him over the head. He fell unconscious, flat into a pile of urine-soaked litter.

I loved cats for so many reasons. Dirty litter, however, surprised me.

Thirty-one

Tom must have flown home, he arrived so fast after I called him. Soon the entire emergency response team known as the Mercy Fire Department and paramedics had arrived, too. Plus there was Candace and Morris and B.J. and one very distraught Kara.

I was busy cleaning my feet with illumination provided by Osborne's now-bloodied Maglite. There's nothing I hate more than kitty litter between my toes.

Tom knelt beside me as I sat on the kitchen floor surrounded by cats—all six of them. He gripped my shoulders, which caused his flashlight to illuminate the ceiling. "Are you okay?"

"I'm fine." I felt so devoid of emotion it seemed surreal. "I just hate it when I get litter on my feet."

"You said he's in the basement. Is he conscious?"

I simply nodded. For some reason I couldn't look at Tom. Why couldn't I look at him? "He is now."

Over his shoulder, he said, "Candace, Morris, get down there and contain that bastard."

"He's hog-tied with clothesline. Growing up on my

grandparents' farm, I learned a lot of things and some of those things you just never forget."

Marcy and Jake, the paramedics, were standing behind Tom, though it was a little too dark to see their faces.

Suddenly the lights went on.

"Ah," I said. "That's better." I glanced around at the cats. "Isn't that better, sweethearts?"

Tom sat on the floor facing me, still holding my upper arms. "Jillian, look at me."

"Who turned the lights on?" I finally focused on his face.

"Billy Cranor fixed the problem. Jilly, did he hurt you?" When I didn't answer, just kept picking litter off my feet, Tom glanced back again at Marcy and Jake. "What's wrong with her?"

"Chief?" Marcy said quietly. "Let us check her out, okay? I think she's in shock."

There is nothing like sweet tea—two big glasses of cold sweet tea—to help a woman get her bearings. Maybe I had been in shock, but I wasn't anymore. I came completely out of that strange, detached state when Morris shoved the handcuffed Osborne up our basement stairs into the kitchen and said, "Just how I like my crooked cops. Covered in cat piss." He pushed the man, who also had blood all over his face, out the back door.

I laughed—not the hysterical laugh I thought might come. It was simply relief leaking out of every pore. Tom seemed to relax then, too. Maybe he wouldn't be watching me so closely for the rest of the night.

I said, "I don't break, Tom Stewart. Got a little close to crazy there for a few minutes, but I'll be just fine."

"I can tell." He slipped off the barstool he'd been sitting on right next to me. "Come on. Let's get more comfortable and you can tell me what this guy said."

"Formal statement time?"

"No. That can wait. Just talk it out, because trust me, you may think you're fine, but you need to talk."

Candace and Kara ascended from the basement and joined us in the living room. B.J. was waiting in the squad car to help take Osborne to jail. I wondered how the other prisoners, none of them Mercy's finest citizens for sure, would appreciate their fellow cell mate smelling like a toilet. Or maybe it wouldn't bother them at all.

I related what had happened in detail as the three of them listened intently. Kara seemed the most distressed, though she probably had nothing on Tom. I knew he was beating himself up inside for me being home alone after the fake gang warning. But we'd work through all that later. I hoped I'd proven that I can take care of myself, not that I wanted to do it in such a fashion ever again.

When I was done, I said, "Okay, it's your turn. There are gaps as wide as the Grand Canyon that I'd like you to fill in."

Candace said, "Harris Schultz confessed to the Virginia cops that he first asked Chester Winston to help him buy weed and it was Chester who hooked him up with Osborne. We think Osborne was stealing evidence after drug busts and selling it. Unfortunately, compromised evidence means compromised cases. It'll be a mess for the county prosecutor going forward."

"So why did Harris take a hike? Because of Osborne?" I asked.

Tom nodded. "He was scared to death and wanted the Virginia cops to keep him in jail up there. It doesn't work that way, of course. His crimes are here. But he will make an excellent witness against Osborne should this ever get to trial. I doubt that will happen, though. Dirty cops don't do well in the general prison population. He'll want a deal that protects him from getting shanked his first week there. Probably solitary confinement."

"He's such an egomaniac, he'll enjoy spending time with himself," I said. "What about that security guard?"

"He started talking up a storm when we picked him up at the hospital," Candace said.

"I will argue for *no deal* as far as that jerk is concerned," Tom said. "Seems that before we nabbed him leaving the hospital, he called Osborne and warned him everything was about to come unraveled. That's what put you in harm's way."

I said, "This whole credit card con that Chester was playing around with at Minnie's house . . . I don't get how Osborne got involved. He admitted to me it was a mistake and obviously it was. Couldn't Osborne have been doing more lucrative things than splitting money with Chester and Norm—because Norm obviously knew Chester for quite some time, right?"

Tom squeezed my hand. "Norm probably hung around the county shelter courting his girlfriend and had known Chester for ages. He also knew Osborne."

"Let me guess," I said. "Working for him in the sheriff's department."

Tom smiled. "You really should help me out more often. Anyway, I believe the trouble began when Harris realized he had to tap into his mother for money to pay for drugs. Norm was selling drugs while Chester was already running the recovery fee scam. When Harris came to Norm, complaining about his mother and how he needed help getting money from her to finance his drug habit, he told Norm she was a confused old woman. Maybe she could be a good source of income if they could figure out a plan. Norm and Chester combined probably didn't have a big enough brain to figure out that credit card fraud. They asked for Osborne's help and he said he had an idea, but he wanted a cut. The rest is history. Osborne came up with the plan, and knowing the low-level criminal types he was dealing with, he checked up on the 'business' those two were running out of Minnie's house."

"It was all about his greed." I shook my head. "Osborne did make a mistake. Why didn't he cut his losses and just refuse to supply Norm with more drugs to sell to people like Harris Schultz?"

Candace finally spoke. "Osborne was afraid of being blackmailed by Chester, who, despite being a lowlife, did have a county position. Chester could have made waves and he wanted his income with the credit card fraud to continue. That meant Chester and Norm had to keep Harris well supplied—keep him happy so he wouldn't talk, either."

Tom nodded his agreement. "Osborne's various crimes probably go back ten years or more. Ironic that getting involved in a stupid thing like what Chester and Norm were up to would be what brought him down."

Kara had been awfully quiet. I looked at her and could tell by her tight expression that she was upset. "What's wrong, sweetie?"

"This is my fault. Pushing to connect the cases and

then going off with Liam for dinner and leaving you alone." Tears began to stream down her face.

I got up and went over to her, not caring I was still in my pajamas or that clay litter still clung to my feet. I held out my arms. "Hug. Come on."

And that was one of the best hugs we ever shared.

Kara and Candace left not long after, and it was time for Tom and me to share a moment. He took me in his arms and held me tightly—until Otto started to crawl up his leg.

We both laughed and he put Otto on his shoulder. "Come on, crime stopper. Time for bed."

"I have to take a shower first," I said.

"Oh, so do I." Tom grinned. "Let's conserve water."

Thirty-two

The next day I did have to give that formal statement, so Tom and I drove together in my van. He'd be staying at work after I was done telling my story yet again, but he promised me dinner at The Finest Catch tonight, and since I had the wheels, he'd have to keep that promise.

Grace Templeton stood up when we walked through the door and smiled. "There's our hero. We are all so proud of you, Jillian."

I paused in front of her. "Are you sticking around—because the job will slow down now that half the population is in jail."

She laughed. "I am sticking around—for now."

"Okay. It's almost midterms and Tom and I have someone we'd like you to meet when he comes home for his break from college."

"Are you talking about Finn? I've heard plenty about him from the chief."

I nodded. "I am. Unless you're opposed to being set up on a blind date by the guy's parents."

"I am not opposed in the least." She smiled at Tom.

"That picture of him in your office is kind of persuasive. Hot guy."

"He is very . . . *good-looking* inside and out," I said. "Time to talk about crime now. See you later, Grace."

Tom and I went to his office and I took one of the padded chairs across from where his swivel chair was.

He said, "You called us *parents*. That means a lot."

"I'm through with all this stepdaughter/stepson thing. Family is the most important thing in the world and I don't have time to qualify my relationships."

"I like the way you think."

Once I was done relating the events of last night again, we tossed around ideas about what happened the day Chester died. Tom believed it was manslaughter, not premeditated murder. We both decided that those fingernail pieces found in the closet probably belonged to Minnie. Chester and Osborne argued, she hid with her scaredy-cat Simon in that secret part of the closet and when Osborne couldn't find her and eliminate her, he left. Her ending up in the hospital where one of his flunkies, Norm Garrett, was a security guard, probably made him as happy as a pig in mud.

"He overheard Minnie talking to Brenda in the hospital about the tall man and no uniform and relayed that to Osborne," I said. "Did Norm run her off the road?"

Tom shook his head no. "Osborne is a control freak and a lot smarter than Norm Garrett. I'm guessing he had one of his more experienced coconspirators in the sheriff's office take care of Dr. Ross after Norm called him. We'll find out who it was, trust me. Anyway, Osborne had to get rid of anything connecting him to Chester or Brenda or Norm or anyone else. He probably stole her phone just like he probably stole the burner phones from

Mrs. Schultz's house. Chester, not the brightest bulb in the pack, bought those burner phones that he used to communicate with Mrs. Schultz using *her* credit card."

"That is pretty dumb," I said.

"No kidding. If Harris Schultz and Chester's son and daughter-in-law hadn't gone to high school together, none of this probably would have happened. Strange how the past always connects to the future."

"You know, Sara Jo was sporting an engagement ring that Norm gave her. Do you think Norm was paid, in part, by Osborne with the ring? Because the jewelry box was hidden in that closet along with Minnie's journals. She wanted to keep those things safe, maybe because something went missing weeks or even months before. Trouble was, she got so confused, she probably didn't remember why she hid that box away after a while."

"You're probably right," he said. "Maybe we need to borrow that ring from Sara Jo and show it to Mrs. Schultz. She'll probably be able to identify it now."

I smiled and thought it was about time for me to leave when Tom's phone rang. "Hang on while I catch this. I need a proper good-bye kiss."

He answered, and when his smile began to fade, I feared he was hearing bad news. I sure hoped Osborne hadn't escaped. Someone was talking a long time and Tom kept nodding and finally said, "That is so sickening. Thanks for filling me in."

He hung up, his eyes filled with sadness.

"What happened?"

"Well, it happened five years ago. As expected, Norm Garrett wants a deal almost as bad as Osborne. He knows a lot of things about the corruption in the sheriff's department. But he knows something about Minnie Schultz—or more specifically about her husband . . . something we never considered in our investigation."

"What are you talking about?"

"Apparently Osborne himself ran a man off the road five years ago—Otto Schultz."

I was too stunned to speak for a few seconds. My hand covered my lips as I said, "I don't understand. What did he have against Otto Schultz?"

"Norm Garrett says he and Osborne were shaking down businesses."

"Businesses like Otto's jewelry store?"

"Yup. Norm was an enforcer for Osborne. He collected protection money from a lot of people in the county who owned small businesses. When Otto refused to pay, Osborne decided to take the poor guy out—and Norm knew it. Osborne then told Norm it was no longer safe for him to work for the department. He got him the hospital job—and they kept their criminal relationship going. It was safer for Osborne that way, not really so much for Norm."

I sat back, the pieces falling into place. "When Minnie ended up in the hospital, he already had his enforcer in place."

"Yup."

"Do you think Sara Jo knew she was engaged to a criminal?" I asked.

"I'm not sure. But I intend to find out." Tom tented his hands and smiled.

I nodded, lips tight. Big crimes in small towns can bring a lot of people down, even the ones who seem nice.

Epilogue

Kara brought flowers in through the back door of Minnie's house and set them on the dining room table. Belle had made the most beautiful cake for Minnie's homecoming and it sat on her sideboard. With all the boxes long gone, the house was as beautiful as it probably had been before the poor woman had fallen so ill.

Otto and Simon were busy exploring each room as if it was the first time they'd been here. They would be so happy to see Minnie. The living room was once again crowded, but not with boxes this time. Until Minnie finished with her rehab, her son Henry and daughter, Greta, decided a hospital bed would be easiest for her to get in and out of. For now, this bed would help keep her visits to the bedrooms to a minimum. That was a room she had once shared with her husband, who had been murdered because he stood up to Osborne and Norm. The guest bedroom certainly wasn't a good idea since Chester had been murdered there by the tall man who at times wore a uniform and then did not—Brad Osborne. In his plea deal, the dirtiest of cops had to admit his crimes, including running Brenda Ross off the road, just as he done to Otto Schultz five years before.

Brenda, though hobbled by her injuries, would arrive soon. It had been *her* idea that Minnie stay away from those bedrooms until she was fully recovered. Both Kara and I thought it was an excellent idea. When Minnie had been told that her husband hadn't died in an accident but had been murdered, Brenda Ross said it had been a setback. For a week afterward, Minnie's confusion returned. But now she was well enough to come home and Brenda would be helping her deal with the revived grief of losing a man she had loved very much.

"This cake is amazing," Kara said as she stood by the sideboard. "All these little cat decorations are wonderful."

I heard someone coming in through the back door and Tom called, "Where do you want the drinks?"

I went to the kitchen to help him and saw that Liam was helping to carry a big cooler. I suggested a corner near the entrance to the dining room.

The doorbell rang and I left the kitchen. The first guests to arrive were a surprise—Lucinda Winston and Chester's son, Earl. I felt awkward in their presence, but they had suffered a loss, blamed the wrong people for murder and now, I hoped, were ready to make peace with the past. Chester had not been a decent man, but even he hadn't deserved a violent death.

Since Tom knew them and sensed my discomfort— what could I say to them?—he took over. Earl wanted to see where his father had died and Tom took him to that little bedroom down the hall.

It got quite busy after that. Shawn arrived, but without Minnie's cats. She was still too frail to care for them and he had already promised her he would keep them safe and healthy until they could return home. Simon and Otto would be her companions for now.

Candace, B.J., Lois and Morris came in through the back door next, with Morris immediately complaining about the fact that there were only soft drinks and no beer.

"You're in uniform," I said. "Doesn't that mean you're on duty?" I sipped sweet tea from a big red cup and offered a smile with my eyes.

Morris looked down at himself. "Oh. I wondered what these strange clothes they make me wear meant all these years. No beer."

As we awaited the arrival of the guest of honor released just today from rehab, we all talked about how many people now sat in jail and how satisfying it was that every one of us had helped put them there.

Brenda and her brother entered the home next, but her wheelchair wouldn't fit through the door, so Peyton carried her in and set his sister lovingly down on the sofa. B.J. folded up the wheelchair, brought it in and set it near her. A chair was brought from the dining room so she could prop up her casted leg.

She glanced at all the happy faces greeting her and smiled with her heart as well as with her mouth. She had a crocheted hat on and wisps of her blond hair escaped the edges of the multicolored cap. The scars left by the hole that had to be drilled in her skull were covered until her hair grew in.

She said, "Small towns are the best. Look what all of you have accomplished. I'm used to dealing with tears and unhappiness, but this room is filled with the joy of a job well done."

Peyton beamed at his sister, her hand clutched in his. Their small family had an attachment as strong as if there had been a hundred members rather than just two. Kara's instant bond with this man had started so many things in motion and helped lead to Osborne's downfall.

A minute later, supported on either side by Henry and Greta, Minnie walked into her home. It had been a month since she'd been found wandering in the street with a kitten in tow. One son was missing from the gathering, but Minnie did not seem to have this on her mind now. She had mentioned how sad his arrest had made her and how disappointed his father would have been—but she hadn't mentioned Harris since that brief conversation.

The look of wonder on her face as she took in all the smiling faces brought tears to my eyes. The shadow of confusion that had once clouded her face was completely gone now. This was the real Minnie, a sweetheart of a woman who had suffered so much.

She saw the bed, but chose to sit on the sofa next to Brenda. Two more guests followed—Aaron Kramer came in with Minnie's new grandson. The tiny boy was fast asleep in his father's arms. Lots of oohing and aahing ensued, but Aaron Junior slept right through it.

Minnie's eyes shimmered with tears and Brenda put her arm around her. Then she gave Minnie a hat that matched her own. We laughed as Greta helped her mother put it on to cover the scars on her head.

Brenda said, "We are connected, you and I."

Tom cleared his throat. "The first thing I want to do is thank all of you for coming here today. We all worked together and—"

Suddenly Otto raced into the room with Simon hot on his tail. He ran straight to Minnie and leapt onto her lap. The smile on her face as Simon joined his friend made my heart swell. Cats don't forget. Cats know when they are needed and loved. These two would be better medicine for Minnie than anything that came out of a pill bottle.

Tom didn't bother finishing what he had been about to say. Kara played hostess with Liam at her side. Soon everyone had a delicious slice of cake, a drink and friends to talk to.

Tom put an arm around me and pulled me to him. "There's a lot of good in this room."

I nodded. "You got that right."

Minnie touched Otto's nose with a bit of frosting, and he jumped down on the floor in front of her and began to clean it off. He must have decided he liked it, because he was back on Minnie's lap looking for more.

"Getting back to normal has been nice, but you have a decision to make," I said.

"Well," Tom said. "I know what you're talking about. I've consulted with Dashiell, Syrah, Merlot and Chablis. They told me I should ask you."

"Our cats talk to you, do they?" I said with a smile.

"All the time."

"You don't have to ask me anything, Tom Stewart. You are doing the job you were meant to do, Mr. Police Chief."

"You're on board with my decision to make the job permanent?"

"I'm on board with you for the rest of our lives."

We kissed. He might not have known that he'd *never* been an "acting" police chief. But I did.

Turn the page for a sneak peek
at the next book in Leann Sweeney's
Cats in Trouble Mystery series,

The Cat, the Boy
and the Bones

Available in October 2017.

The sound of a mewling newborn kitten could slash at my heart like nothing else. A whole chorus of kittens was even worse. I was on the top step of a ladder at Mercy Middle School in South Carolina—and I was worried. August was not usually a month for a new litter, and if we didn't rescue these babies from the ceiling, they would melt.

Why was I in a school on a ladder in August? Good question. A call had come from an unlikely person. His name was Jack West, and he was twelve years old. I'd met Jack several years ago when his mother's cow had gone missing. Yes, you heard that right. That story was for another day.

My friend Allison—the newly minted veterinarian Dr. Cuddahee—was having a hard time finding a safe place in the rafters to keep steady so she could hand me each kitten and then the mama cat—if Allison got lucky and could catch her, that was. I would then hand each kitten to Jack's mother, Robin, who would place the kittens in the special incubator-type box Allison had brought with her.

"Keeping my balance is tough, Jillian," Allison said to me. "Point your Maglite more in my direction so I can see that my knees are on a wide-enough beam."

While I tried to help her out, the kittens ratchetted up their noise. Their mother had raced away into the depths of the attic the minute we'd removed the correct ceiling tile to gain access to the brood. I glanced back down at Jack, as well as at the principal of the school and the custodian, Mr. Johnson. He had been told in no uncertain terms by Principal Florence McNeal that workmans' comp might not cover injuries sustained during a cat recovery. That was why we were here after school hours and only after we'd signed waivers promising not to sue the school should we fall through the ceiling. Considering how old the building was and how flimsy the ancient ceiling tiles were, that was a real possibility.

"Do you feel safe over there?" I asked Allison.

She gave me a thumbs-up before reaching toward what looked like a tattered plastic bag. Soon I was holding a squealing, fat gray kitten whose newly opened eyes blinked when it was brought into the full light of the school hallway. *Boy or girl?* I wondered. It was often impossible to determine gender with kittens as young as this. My guess was they were about three weeks old.

Two creamy white kittens followed—they were about the same size—and the last one had what seemed to be Siamese markings: charcoal-tipped ears, dark feet and a dark smudge on its nose. But this one seemed thinner than the rest. It might need more help than its wailing siblings. They wanted their mama—and right now.

"Jillian, bring another flashlight and get up here with me. We need that queen, even if she's freaked-out. Of course if she's feral, we might never find her."

"Let me put my gloves on." Both of us had brought heavy leather gloves for the possibility of handling an angry mama cat.

Soon I joined Allison in the stuffy area, which wasn't as stifling hot as I thought it would be. Warm enough that sweat now dripped from my hairline down my neck, but not unbearable. This wasn't, I realized, actually an attic, but merely the crawl space between the roof and the drop-down ceiling. The blown-in insulation wasn't good for those babies, and I wondered how in heaven that mama had gotten up here to have her litter. Maybe she'd crawled into a cupboard, found a hole in the wall and gotten up that way. Cats were resourceful—that was for certain.

Just as I joined Allison by creeping carefully along metal beams that made my fortysomething knees scream in protest, I heard Jack's voice behind me.

"Let me help. I have a pillowcase. Maybe you can carry the mother cat down inside it."

I heard the panicked Robin West below us announcing her protest to this idea. "Jack, no. You'll get hurt. You'll fall. You could suffer a serious injury and—"

"Mom, I'm twelve. Not to mention you are supposed to be allowing me more freedom. Our therapist said so."

I had to smile. Jack, with his genius IQ, was learning to manage his mother better and better as he got older.

Then Principal McNeal piped in. "Jack, I cannot allow this. We have no signed waiver for you. If you should tumble—"

"Too late," Jack said as he crawled toward us. He certainly was Jack Be Nimble getting up here, compared to Allison and me. "Will this pillowcase help to bring her down? Because kittens this age will require their mother's milk to survive. I understand there are substitutes for mammals who—"

"It will help, Jack," Allison interrupted. "Plus, you might be the best person for the job. Mama is over in that corner where the roof slopes. It would be a tight fit for Jillian or me."

I glanced in that direction, and sure enough I caught the glint of lovely cat eyes.

With my Maglite then turned on Jack, I saw him absolutely beam. Ever since he'd called me at lunchtime, this had probably been his most fervent wish—to be a hero and not just the weird boy who knew a hundred times more information than the other kids in this school.

Robin's head appeared in the opening created by the ceiling tile we'd removed. "Jack. Please."

"Robin," I said evenly, "I won't let anything happen to him. I can hear those kittens we saved, and they could sure use some comfort. We'll be down in a sec."

"Are you sure? Because—"

"She's sure, Mom. Remember how she helped us before? She is a most trustworthy person."

Robin disappeared, and I heard her groan a little as she descended the ladder. This was truly more of a job for superkids like Jack.

Allison had pieces of kibble with her, and when the mother cat made a few tentative steps toward her outstretched hand, we all knew what Jack whispered to be true. "Not a feral. That's a good thing—right, Dr. Cuddahee?"

"Very good," she whispered back.

The mama was a mixed shorthair who looked very much like the runt of the litter we'd rescued. We took our time talking to her, reassuring her, feeding her—and, wow, was she hungry. Finally, Jack was right next to her and petting the sweetheart. I heard her begin to purr, and that's when Allison told Jack to put her in his pillowcase.

He did this so gently that I thought my heart might dissolve. The cat did not protest. My guess was, if a cat could be relieved and grateful, this girl was. She'd gotten herself and her babies into quite a fine mess.

Allison led the way out with the flashlight I'd brought for her. I told Jack to go next. He could actually walk on the beams and not crawl like we had to do. I went last, and as I edged past the shredded bag where the queen had nested, I caught a terrible whiff of something. *Oh no*, I thought. *Had a kitten died in that bag?*

As Allison and Jack made their way out, I said, "I'll be right behind you." *I have to check. I have to make sure.* Perhaps the mama had been feeding on rodents and that was what I smelled, but I would not leave a dead animal behind—not even if it was a rat. Good thing I had my gloves.

I made my way to the bag and shined the light directly on it. I couldn't see anything but tufts of milky cat hair. Then I noticed another bag resting between beams behind the area the mama cat had used as her nesting spot. The black bag was tied up, but was beginning to fall apart in the heat and humidity of this space.

Why would someone leave a bag of garbage up here? But it explained why our mama might have been drawn to this spot. She might have thought she would have food. Even garbage would work for a cat in need.

Holding the Maglite above the bag, I carefully peeled back one of the plastic shreds.

I blinked, not sure what I was seeing. Being careful

to begin from the top of the bag, I pulled away at another tear to make a wider opening.

"Oh no," I cried. "Oh no, oh no."

I heard footsteps on the ladder ascending rapidly while I remained frozen, unable to move or even breathe.

It was Allison. "Jillian, are you all right?"

"Y-yes," I rasped. "But someone isn't."

"What are you talking about?" She was now crawling toward me.

I help up a hand. "Don't come any closer. There are bones in this bag. Human bones."

I shined the light on the skull I'd uncovered.